Praise for *Those Other Women*

"I devoured it, loved it, and totally escaped into it. . . . Fun and topical."　　　　　—Marian Keyes, internationally bestselling author

Praise for *The Fifth Letter*

"Lifelong friendships, secrets, and pages I couldn't turn fast enough. *The Fifth Letter* is one of my favorite books this year, and Nicola Moriarty is now on my short list of favorite women's fiction authors."

—Susan Elizabeth Phillips, #1 *New York Times* bestselling author

"The meandering stories of these women are held together with the powerful question of who wrote the last letter, which reveals just how precarious childhood friendships are. . . . The book . . . adeptly exposes the striking differences among the four friends and the five letters."　　　　　—*Publishers Weekly*

"Readers . . . will race to the end as a credit to Nicola's fine sense of pacing and suspense. An author to watch."　　　　　—*Booklist*

"The brilliant unraveling of this sisterhood of secrets will leave you wondering how well you really know the best friends you've known forever. A must-read before your next girls' night."

—Mary Hogan, author of *The Woman in the Photo* and *Two Sisters*

"A delightful, heartwarming exploration of the twists and turns of true friendship, *The Fifth Letter* was simply delicious from the very first page to the last. . . . Relatable characters, a fast-moving plot, and just the right amount of mystery. I was hooked!"

—Rachael Johns, internationally bestselling author

PAPER CHAINS

PAPER CHAINS

A NOVEL

NICOLA MORIARTY

wm

WILLIAM MORROW
An Imprint of HarperCollins*Publishers*

PAPER CHAINS. Copyright © 2013 by Nicola Moriarty. All rights reserved. Printed in the United States of America. No part of this book may be used or reproduced in any manner whatsoever without written permission except in the case of brief quotations embodied in critical articles and reviews. For information, address HarperCollins Publishers, 195 Broadway, New York, NY 10007.

HarperCollins books may be purchased for educational, business, or sales promotional use. For information, please email the Special Markets Department at SPsales@harpercollins.com.

Originally published as *Paper Chains* in Australia in 2013 by Bantam.

FIRST U.S. EDITION

Library of Congress Cataloging-in-Publication Data has been applied for.

ISBN 978-0-06-241354-3 (paperback)
ISBN 978-0-06-295216-5 (hardcover library edition)

19 20 21 22 23 LSC 10 9 8 7 6 5 4 3 2 1

For Diane and Bernie
(better known as Mum and Dad)

PAPER CHAINS

The elderly couple were a little apprehensive when she approached them at the train station. Gina generally didn't trust anyone with piercings in their nose and George couldn't really understand how her hair could be so blue. But her gigantic smile put them at ease. They listened as she explained what she wanted them to do and at first Gina was apologetic.

"Oh, love, we would if we could, but I'm afraid we're not going that way."

But she reassured them that it didn't matter, that it could be passed on to someone else and eventually it would find its way there—if it was meant to.

Gina was struck by the romance of it all, while George puzzled over how ridiculous it was. Either way, they accepted the envelope and promised to do their best. There was a moment after she left where Gina found herself wondering if she might be able to convince George to change their travel plans . . . but she knew that there was no chance of it; she would just have to find the right person, maybe someone on the train, or later, on their flight.

PART ONE

London in
the Spring

CHAPTER 1

When Hannah first met India, she thought she was the most wonderfully extraordinary person she had ever encountered. Hannah was working behind the jewelry counter in the gift shop of the Victoria and Albert Museum in London. This section of the store was her favorite, because most of the precious little stones had stories accompanying them, explaining their mystical powers or their "deeper meaning." She had quickly learned these stories by heart and loved to discuss them with the customers. A brief chance for some human connection. This meant she was a fantastic salesperson, as most people ended up buying the item just to shut her up.

She was carefully placing a silver necklace with a blue topaz stone into a paper bag when she heard a small child scream out in agonized tones, "But I *need* it!" She handed the bag over to the customer and then moved down the counter to take a closer look at what was going on.

A toddler was tugging on his mother's arm, leaning back with all his body weight and pointing at a beautifully carved wooden train set in the children's section of the store. Hannah had seen other children demand that their parent buy them this very same item. But as the train set cost in excess of one hundred pounds, she didn't often see many children granted their wish. This particular mother was looking slightly panicky as she attempted to subdue the toddler.

"Oh, sweetheart, no, I'm sorry but Mummy can't afford that. Come on, time to go."

The child did not look as though he was willing to give in that easily. He continued to scream and pull at his mother's arm, and more and more customers stopped to watch the scene unfold. As the child's screams rose and the mother's demeanor became increasingly flustered, Hannah felt her own nerves start to build. Glancing down, she noticed that her hands were becoming sweaty, that her chest was beginning to rise and fall in quick succession. Just as Hannah was wondering if she should try and leave her counter and hide out in the staff room before anyone noticed her somewhat odd reaction to the unfolding drama, she saw another woman step purposefully toward the mother. Hannah paused to see what was about to happen.

The woman looked to be perhaps Hannah's age or younger, mid

to late twenties she guessed. She had short, spiky, platinum blond hair, a huge, wide smile and ridiculously long eyelashes. She was wearing a silk wraparound skirt over the top of army green cords, and a purple T-shirt with a faded peace sign on the front. Over one shoulder was slung a brown leather satchel with rainbow-colored tassels. She was one of those people that Hannah had always envied for being able to pull off any outfit while still looking unselfconsciously cool. This was India.

India gave the upset-looking mother a quick wink and then grinned down at the screaming boy. "Hey, that's a fabulous tantrum you've got under way. Can I give you some tips though?"

The boy dropped his mother's hand and continued to scream, "I WANT THAT TRAIN!"

"Yep, that's great. Now I always like to stamp my feet, so can you do that with me? Just like this." And India began to join in on the yelling, so the two of them were chorusing together, *I want that train!*" Several customers were now gathering to watch; the mother was standing slightly back from the two of them, her eyes wide with alarm.

"Okay, next let's say 'It's not fair!' Come on, really let it out!"

As India continued to stamp her feet and yell, the small boy started to look unsure. "It's not fair," he said, his voice beginning to falter.

"Now we sit down on the floor and we stick our legs out like this and we bang our fists and we yell, 'I'm not moving till I get my train!'"

Customers watched, stunned, as this grown woman plonked herself down on the ground and began to pummel the floor. The small boy stood and watched too.

India stopped and looked up at him. "Oh, are we all finished with our tantrum?" she asked. He nodded silently. "And do you feel much better?" she asked as she began to get up from the floor. He nodded again.

"Wonderful! Let's take Mum for a coffee then, shall we?" And India led the bewildered-looking mother and her subdued toddler from the shop.

As they passed the jewelry counter, Hannah tried desperately to compose her face and give the mother a supportive smile, reminding herself that it was not her but the mother who had just been involved in a highly stressful situation. But the mother didn't notice her. India did though; she shrugged her shoulders at Hannah and gave her a "what are you gonna do?" kind of a look from behind the mother and Hannah attempted to give her a knowing look in return.

Later that night, when Hannah was back in her tiny flat, heating up a frozen pizza for dinner, she thought again about how impressive that girl had been today. All afternoon she had been running different scenarios, trying to figure out how *she* might have been the one to have helped that mother, rather than freezing up for no good reason. Well okay, so she knew why she had been affected by the situation, but still—it was silly, and melodramatic.

That had always been Hannah's problem. She obsessed too much about things, playing scenes over and over in her mind, trying to figure out how she might have dealt with a situation better. Once in high school, she was telling a friend on the bus that Ben from her drama class had asked her out. She couldn't believe she was going to have her first-ever boyfriend.

A boy from the year above her overheard the conversation and leaned forward from the seat behind them to whisper in her ear, "How could someone ask *you* out? You're too ugly to have a boyfriend."

The skin on the back of her neck had turned cold, the chill spreading itself down her arms and up across her face. Of course he was right. What was she thinking? And she had fought to keep the tears from spilling over until she was off the bus, when she then sobbed all the way down her driveway. The next day she had arrived at school to see Ben standing by the front gates, a hopeful expression on his face as he awaited her answer. She had taken a shaky breath and told him four simple words: "I'm sorry, but no."

It wasn't until much, much later that she realized what a fool she had been. How could she have let that nasty, fourteen-year-old boy take away her first-ever chance to have a boyfriend? Imagine the first kiss she might have had. Perhaps it would have been in the back row of a movie theater, with popcorn crunching under their feet. Maybe they would have just watched a romantic comedy together, probably something with Julia Roberts or Sandra Bullock in it, and he might have held her hand through the film, leaning in to kiss her just as the credits rolled up. And when the lights came on, they would have pulled apart, embarrassed, and laughed.

But instead her first kiss had been a very different experience. It had been at a seedy nightclub in the Western Sydney suburb of Penrith. She was sixteen and she and another friend had snuck in with fake IDs. After too many Vodka Cruisers, she had let a much older guy with three-day-old stubble growth and a mouth that tasted of Cheezels and cigarettes pull her off the dance floor and out a back door into a dirty alleyway. This was where she experienced her first-ever kiss—with one stiletto in a puddle of something that smelled suspiciously of urine.

So, consequently, she often obsessed about what she could have done to change those circumstances. If only she had ignored the taunts from the boy on that school bus. If only she had turned around and responded with confidence, "Well I think I'm pretty, so who cares what you think?" Anything would have been better than convincing herself that that boy was right, that of course she was too ugly to have a boyfriend. That Ben had been crazy to have asked her out and most likely he would soon realize his mistake. Perhaps he hadn't even meant to ask? Maybe she had misunderstood him and he was already panicking, wondering how he was going to get out of it. She often misunderstood people, misread situations, forgot to concentrate on conversations. She decided she would save him the trouble.

As it turned out, Ben didn't think she had done him a favor and he spent the next two years making her school life hell—until she moved to a fancy North Shore school when her parents divorced. But that was fair enough, she supposed.

Now, as she pulled open the clunky oven door and checked on her ham and pineapple pizza she thought to herself, *I bet that girl from today wouldn't have let some pimple-faced high school kid ruin her chance at a magical first kiss. I bet she would have punched him in the nose—or something equally cool like that.* And she sighed as she thought about how different her life might have been if she'd been that type of person, or even if she'd had a friend like that.

Maybe she wouldn't be where she was right now. Here in this tiny flat in London, working in a museum gift shop—her law degree wasted, and of course not to mention . . . best not to think about that. But still, a friend like that, maybe she would have stopped her, before it was too late.

Stop it! Stop obsessing about things you can't do anything about. You can't go back and you can't change what you've done. It's too late and it can't be fixed and if you start thinking about it, it will hurt too much and you'll start crying and you know how sick you are of crying all the time. It's self-indulgent and it's pointless. Remember, it's better for everyone this way.

So she took her pizza out of the oven, slid it onto the green plastic plate she had waiting and then sat on the floor in front of the television and watched reruns of *Charmed* on Channel 4. For some strange reason, watching American television shows made her feel more at home than watching Australian programs; whenever *Neighbours* or *Home and Away* came on, she felt slightly sick and had to change the channel. The pizza turned out to be still frozen in the middle, but she ate it anyway. Sometimes she liked to do small things like that, to punish herself. *You deserve to eat frozen pizza*, she thought as she crunched through the icy pieces of ham. And then she laughed. "As if that comes even close to making up for what you've done," she said out loud. She threw the remaining pizza against the wall instead. "You don't deserve to eat at all," she whispered.

But at 3:00 A.M., she woke up hungry and ate her way through three Snickers bars anyway. So tomorrow, she would have to find a new way of punishing herself. She supposed cleaning up the pizza might be a good start.

The next day was Thursday—her one day off a week. Annoyingly, she didn't realize this until she was halfway through her shower. *Dammit, I could still be in bed, sleeping in. I could have been drinking wine last night.* But then she reminded herself that she didn't deserve a sleep-in, so it didn't matter anyway. When she had started her job at the museum, just under a month ago, she had offered to take on all the shifts available; she was prepared to work seven days a week if possible. But her boss Helen had insisted that she have at least one day off and she had had to begrudgingly accept. "Go and see the sights. Isn't that why you're here?" Helen had exclaimed. "Hardly," Hannah had murmured to herself.

She turned off the shower and stepped carefully out of the bathtub and immediately thought, *Why are you being so careful?*

You deserve to slip and fall. If you were to crack your skull open on the edge of the tub, you could watch your blood seep down the drain as you take your last breath.

Oh, stop being so mean.

She dried herself off and wondered what she would do today. But there was no point asking herself that question, because inevitably she would do what she always did on her one day off. She would run. She would punish her body with a grueling jog through the park. And she wouldn't stop for lunch.

She was on her third trip through the center of Hyde Park when she saw her. The girl from yesterday—her hair was different today, but it was her. She was sitting on a picnic blanket, eating a giant piece of watermelon. And was she . . . *waving* at Hannah?

This is fate, isn't it? Maybe she's supposed to become my friend.

You don't deserve to have friends.

At first the young man assumed that they must have been lost. He was already opening his mouth to tell them that he wasn't a local when they spoke and it took him a moment to realize that they weren't asking for directions.

Tom took in the instructions and then laughed. "Is this a joke?" he checked.

The woman looked affronted. "Never mind, we'll find someone else," she said coldy.

"No, wait. I can do it. I was just making sure," he said. "I'm heading south though, but I'll see if I can find someone on the train who's going in the right direction."

The woman still looked reluctant to hand over the envelope, but her husband snatched it out of her hand and thrust it at Tom. "For goodness' sake, Gina, the boy has said he'll do it, so I'm sure he will."

After they had walked away, Tom ran the envelope between his fingers; this could make for an awesome opener to pick up chicks. He couldn't wait to try it out.

CHAPTER 2

I ndia could be extremely persuasive when she wanted to be. Generally, her charms worked on anyone and everyone, but in particular she was quite good at manipulating the opposite sex to get what she needed. Today she had a mission. It was all because of that obnoxious little boy that she had seen throwing a tantrum in the museum gift shop yesterday. It took seconds to look around and see that all the tourists in the store were gearing up to watch a great show, oblivious to the poor mother's panic.

Helping the mum out had been easy. India was good with people, and that extended to kids as well. And besides, it was what she liked to do—help people—even before everything had been changed for her. Her grandmother had always said she would have made a perfect counselor. But what had surprised India was the girl she happened to make eye contact with on the way out of the store. Man, the look on that chick's face—she was seriously freaking out. Her face was as white as a scoop of vanilla ice cream. This piqued India's curiosity. Kid throws massive tantrum, mother freaks out—that's normal. But kid throws massive tantrum and girl-behind-counter has a meltdown? Now that was odd. India's first thought was that this girl was an opportunity, a new project—someone to fix, someone to save.

Tracking down *girl-behind-counter* was easy. India visited the museum again, scoped out the jewelry counter, picked out a guy that she knew would have no problems telling India anything she needed to know and . . . voilà. Here she was in Hyde Park, sitting on a picnic blanket, waiting for girl-behind-counter (now known as Hannah thanks to guy-behind-counter) to go running past. The boy's name was Joe, and at first it looked like the only useful info he could give her was Hannah's shift schedule. But eager to please he had suddenly exclaimed, "Oh wait, Hannah usually goes running on her day off. Takes one of the tracks through Hyde Park—the one that goes right the way around the Serpentine. Only know because she mentioned it the other day in the staff room."

Now her information gathering had paid off. She had spotted Hannah. She was easy to spot, in a "mousey brown hair, innocent pretty face, would usually blend into the crowd if it weren't for the sign on her forehead that said HELP ME" kind of way. India subtly caught her attention—by madly waving her arms above her head until Hannah looked her way—and Hannah hesitantly headed over. When she reached India, she stood there, blocking the sun and throwing a shadow over the rug. India squinted up at her, shading her eyes. She then extended a sticky, watermelon juice covered hand; Hannah took it and shook.

"I'm India. You work at the museum, right? Sit."

She watched as Hannah hesitated briefly and then obediently followed her instructions. "I'm Hannah," she mumbled.

"Well, Hannah, have some watermelon. I've got too much. I'll make myself sick if I eat all of this on my own."

When Hannah didn't move to pick up a piece of watermelon, India sighed at her in an exasperated sort of way and prodded her in the side. "*Eat*, please. I can tell you're hungry. How long have you been jogging for anyway?"

Hannah shrugged. "Since I got up I guess. About seven I suppose."

India gasped. "Hannah!" she exclaimed, using her name naturally, as though they were old friends. "It's three o'clock! Did you even realize that? You haven't stopped all this time?"

"Well, I slow down sometimes. Just before you saw me I'd been walking for about half an hour. I mean, I haven't been running flat out the entire time; I think that would be impossible anyway."

Hannah took a bite of watermelon and wiped her chin self-consciously. India laughed at her and then asked, "Why?"

"Excuse me?"

"Why do you do it? Why are you running like a maniac all day? Training for a marathon or something?"

Hannah took another bite of watermelon and India sensed that she had done so in order to avoid answering the question for a few more seconds. Eventually she swallowed the lump of fruit and nodded, keeping her eyes low.

India smiled as she asked casually, "Which one?"

"The New York marathon." Then she choked on a seed and India, a bemused expression on her face, had to thump her on the back.

"You're Aussie, right?"

"Mmmm."

"And you're training for the New York marathon here in London?"

"Mmm."

Liar.

"How far is that anyway?" India was thoroughly enjoying watching Hannah squirm.

"Umm, I'm pretty sure it's something like forty-two kilometers," Hannah responded, her voice rising slightly as though she was nervous.

"And when is it on?"

"Oh, a few months," said Hannah.

"Fair enough." India leaned back on her elbows and sighed. "How gorgeous is this weather, Hannah? The sky is all, like, 'Enid Blyton cornflower blue,' am I right? I've literally been soaking up this English sunshine for half the day. It's a myth that England is always dreary, by the way; it's not, it's freaking beautiful."

Hannah nodded without responding. They sat in silence for a little while, watching people walking or jogging past until Hannah blurted out, "Why did you invite me to join you?" And then she drew her knees up to her chest and hugged them to her as though she had frightened herself by asking the question.

"Why not?" India shot back.

"But you don't even know me. How are you this outgoing? I saw you help that woman in the gift shop yesterday and you didn't even care what people thought of you when you joined in on the tantrum with that kid. And didn't you have blond hair yesterday?"

India grinned at her. "I change the color of my hair every couple of weeks or so. Today I felt like being a redhead. Next time . . . maybe blue. And I like meeting people. It's why I decided to travel. As for not caring what those people thought of me—I just don't. In fact, every morning, without fail, I wake up, look in the mirror and say this: 'You are beautiful. You are strong. You deserve to live. You deserve life. You can do whatever you want and fuck what everyone else thinks.' It's like my mantra. You should try it some time."

"But how can you be so confident?!" Hannah was gazing at India with astonished admiration in her eyes and India almost flushed with uncharacteristic embarrassment. *Jeez, it's not that amazing. For goodness' sake, girl, you're looking at me like an adoring puppy.*

She paused before responding evenly, "Well, a little while back,

I found out I had cancer. I fought it and I won. The confidence is kind of a side effect I guess. If you'd kicked arse against a terminal illness, you'd feel pretty damn good about yourself too."

"Wow, I'm so sorry," Hannah said.

"Don't be—I told you, I beat it and I've never felt better. For a while there, I thought I was helpless, you know? At the beginning, before I took control. But now—bam, this is me, baby—take me or leave me."

Hannah nodded. "I see," she said, looking for all the world as if she didn't see at all. India opened her mouth to speak, about to ask Hannah some more questions about herself, when Hannah stood up so abruptly that she almost tripped over her feet. "Well, it was nice meeting you. Thanks for the watermelon," she said.

She turned to leave, but India called out to her, "So dinner tonight then? What time suits you? I know this great little restaurant in Piccadilly Circus; food's yum and it's cheap. You're free, right?"

Hannah swung back around. "Why are you being so nice to me?" she asked, her voice rising a little hysterically.

India laughed. "God, I don't know, Hannah." She shrugged as she searched for a reason. "Look, how about this—shouldn't us Aussies stick together?"

"You're from Australia too?" Hannah asked.

"You didn't pick the accent already?"

"I guess not," Hannah said, sounding embarrassed.

"I'm from Western Australia. I'm guessing you're east coast?"

"New South Wales."

"Ah, a Sydney girl?"

Hannah nodded.

"So, is that enough of a reason for you? I'll meet you on the steps by the fountain, the one with the little cupid statue on the top. Eight o'clock, okay?"

Not a cupid, an archer, thought Hannah, *an angel archer*. But she didn't bother to correct India before walking away from the rug in a slight daze. As she headed back through the park she chanced a glance behind her in India's direction. She was still sitting on the rug, her face tipped back, enjoying the sun. *Look at that girl*, she thought to herself. *Look at what she's been through. She's incredible. You are nothing by comparison to her.* Partial lyrics to an old playground song jumped into her head: "*Nobody likes me, everybody hates me, think I'll go eat worms, big, fat, slimy ones . . .*" She shook her head as she attempted to dislodge the tune from her mind.

Was she really going to go and meet India again tonight? she wondered as she headed toward the road, turned right and started jogging again. What would they talk about? What if she asked her more questions about the marathon that she was supposedly training for? She didn't even know why she had blurted out that lie. But then again, a marathon seemed like a perfectly reasonable explanation—what other reason was there for spending an entire day running? She hadn't even realized she'd been out so long. And a marathon sounded much more normal than saying, "I'm running all day to punish myself for this awful thing that I've done. I deserve nothing less than constant physical pain, but as hacking away at my skin with razor blades seems a little excessive, a grueling run looks to be the best option."

It seemed, though, that lies or no lies, she was probably going to accept India's invitation. The girl was too intoxicating; she wanted to spend more time with her. Wanted to see if maybe they could become friends.

Later that night, standing in front of the bathroom mirror, combing her hair after a hot shower, Hannah couldn't believe how her day had changed. Yesterday, she had witnessed this amazing, confident woman rescuing a mother from public embarrassment and been slightly in awe of her. Today she had spent an afternoon sharing watermelon with her and had just now had dinner with her and a few of her friends. Of course, could you consider it to be a true friendship if you spent the entire evening lying about every part of your life?

She thought back over the questions India had asked her that evening that she had responded to with lies. When they had walked into the restaurant, India had leaned over to whisper to her, "The Brazilian guy is single by the way, and he's been checking you out since we met up with you at the fountain."

"Oh really?" Hannah had asked, but on the last syllable her voice rose to an odd pitch and then she had to cough to clear her throat. The thought of flirting with another man seemed sort of horrific to her—she wasn't a cheater. But then was it really cheating considering the circumstances?

India had scrutinized her face. "You are single, aren't you?" she'd asked.

Hannah had paused; she honestly didn't know the answer to that question. But she could hardly explain it all to India. "Uh, yes . . . I am," she had responded.

The confusion and lies had continued from there. She soon recognized that she really ought to have prepared a better cover story before coming out tonight. Several times she caught India staring at her, seeming to be searching her face, eyebrows raised, as Hannah stumbled over a response to a question that most people would find perfectly easy to answer. She was certain at times that she had managed to contradict herself and India wanted to know more details about the New York marathon—details that Hannah didn't have a clue about.

Worse still was avoiding the advances of Carlos the Brazilian. He was amazingly good-looking, charming, tall, tanned, like an oversized Ken-doll on steroids—but these facts were irrelevant. Even if Hannah was for all intents and purposes single, what would be the point? It was not as though it could lead anywhere. What would happen if they ended up in a relationship? Would they eventually get engaged? Get married? And then what? Kids? That was out of the question. So why even start anything at all? Unless of course it was all about sex—but then, could she really do that? Have sex with another man? And wouldn't she be thinking of *him* the whole time? It would feel wrong and she didn't deserve to have sex anyway. Sex was too much fun and she wasn't here to have fun.

But still, despite all of this—and despite the fact that she wasn't supposed to be enjoying herself—she had still managed to have a good time. She'd had a few glasses of wine and the food was fantastic. She had forgotten what it was like to socialize. Even though she couldn't quite be herself, there were still moments when she had started to relax. Like when Alex (backpacker from New Zealand) had announced that he could read palms and had gone around the table predicting their futures. Or when Liv (student from Scotland) had challenged a waiter to a drinking competition and he had sat down and downed five shots in a row before returning to his job clearing the tables looking perfectly sober while Liv looked ready to pass out.

Now as Hannah put on her pajamas and climbed into bed she found herself wishing for the first time that she did have another day off tomorrow. India had asked her if she wanted to come and watch "the boat race"—a rowing competition on the Thames between Cambridge and Oxford universities—with her the next day. But still, she supposed it was for the best that she was working and unable to make it—it wouldn't be right to go along to something that was that much fun. She set the alarm on her phone and then rolled over and closed her eyes. She was thinking of India as she drifted off to sleep and wondering whether or not they really could become friends.

A couple of hours later she woke to the sound of her phone ringing. There was only one person who could be phoning her at this time—it must have been about three in the morning. Her heart quickened as she picked it up and looked at the screen. She recognized the number immediately. Her eyes clouded over and her head swirled. She squeezed the phone tight as she fought against the desire to answer. It didn't ring for long.

After it had stopped she lay sobbing in her bed for an hour. It had been about three days since the last time he had rung. At first he used to ring every day, sometimes five or six times a day.

He's already starting to give up, she thought.

And she cried even harder.

The two girls were falling about giggling when a cute-looking guy knocked on the door of their compartment. It was a little after two in the morning and they had decided against using the overnight train journey as a chance to catch up on some sleep. Consuming vast quantities of vodka seemed like a much more sensible use of their time.

He held out an envelope and announced that he had an important mission for them. Christine caught her friend's eye and they both collapsed into further fits of hysterics.

"He. Has. A. Mission. For. Us?" gasped Michelle through wheezing bursts of laughter.

"Maybe he's CIA, or I don't know, what would the secret service be called in this country?" Christine cackled at her own wit.

The boy was looking a bit upset then, and they realized that they must have hurt his feelings.

"Oh, we're sorry, sweetie," said Christine and she patted the seat next to her. "Tell us what the mission is then."

After it had been explained both girls gave the obligatory chorusing Awww sound that he had been hoping for.

An hour later when the envelope had been safely stashed in Michelle's bag, she carefully squeezed past the tangled legs and out of the compartment in order to give Christine and the boy whose name they didn't even know yet a little privacy, rolling her eyes at the wet sound of their vodka-ry kisses.

CHAPTER 3

ndia was making friends again. She was sitting at the long wooden table in the common room of the hostel, playing a card game called Up The River, Down The River with a group of American backpackers. It was late, and her opponents were all incredibly drunk, so India was winning with ease, which was especially good because they were playing for money. Not that India particularly *wanted* to relieve them of all their cash, but they were the ones who had suggested getting money involved, and a bit of extra traveling coinage could always come in handy. She tried not to feel guilty about the large amount of money she had tucked away in her savings account—she preferred to keep those funds untouched for a rainy day if possible.

The other good thing about the game was that it was taking

her mind off Hannah. At dinner that night India had been acutely aware of the fact that pretty much everything that had come out of that girl's mouth had been complete and utter bullshit. India had actually quite enjoyed hammering the poor girl with questions and watching her attempt to come up with realistic responses. She was quite certain that Hannah was hiding something fairly significant and while she knew she should have been wary of her (because she supposed it was possible that the girl was a serial killer on the run), she got the feeling that she was harmless, and more importantly, that she needed help. Besides, India understood what it was like to be hiding something and have it scrabbling at your insides, desperate to be let out.

The only thing that India was confident Hannah *had* told the truth about was her name. It wasn't easy to leave something as significant as your name behind. Even when you're running away from something, you have to really mean it to let go of your name.

"Fuuuuuckkkkk!!!" said one of the guys to her right suddenly. "She's done it again, hasn't she?" He shook his head somewhat admiringly as he pushed the pile of coins and notes across the table to India. "That's it, I'm out—going to bed," he announced. He turned around to a pretty dark-haired girl who was lounging on the couch, watching the game. "Care to join me?" he asked, winking suggestively at her.

The girl looked up in surprise and India half expected her to flirtatiously respond, "Who, me?" But instead she said quietly,

"Umm, maybe," and then dropped her eyes to her lap. The guy shrugged. "Down the hall, first door on the right," he said before sauntering off toward his shared room.

"Think I'm done too," said India, smiling at the remaining players around the table. "Taken enough of your cash for one night," she added. India pushed back her chair so that it scraped noisily on the floorboards and wandered over to the couch, sitting down next to the young girl.

"How's it going?" she asked her gently.

Once again the girl looked startled at having been addressed. "Oh, I'm okay," she replied. She had a sweet southern accent and her fingers picked at a hole in the knee of her jeans as she spoke.

India glanced at her watch; it was after 3:00 A.M. She couldn't be bothered making small talk this far past midnight. "You going to have sex with that guy?" she asked.

The girl stared back at India in shock. "I don't know," she replied quickly.

"Okay, talk me through it. What's your thought process here? I'll help you make up your mind."

"Really? Umm, isn't this sort of . . . weird? I don't actually know who you are."

"So? My name's India. Feel better? I can tell you're stuck. Talk to me."

The girl relented. "All right, fine—I *am* confused. That guy's part of my tour group. We've been flirting over the past couple of weeks. But, I kind of thought we'd, you know, have some kind of romantic moment, maybe kiss by the Eiffel Tower when we get to Paris or something—not just hook up in the middle of the night like this."

"You're disappointed."

"I guess."

"And do you want to sleep with him?"

"Ye-e-s," she replied slowly. "But you know, eventually, after a couple of proper 'dates.' But I'm worried if I turn him down he'll move on to someone else."

"Ahh, well then, the answer is simple. You don't do something just because you're trying to keep someone else happy. You do things for yourself. You do what *you* want to do. Me? If I feel like sleeping with a guy, I sleep with him. If I don't want to, then I don't do it. Hang on, actually. Let me fix this for you. What's your name, hon?"

"Monique."

"Hold up one second." India stood up and walked briskly out of the common room, stopping at the first door on the right. She knocked and then swung the door inward. There were three sleeping figures on bunk beds and the American guy from the card game was sitting on the edge of a fourth bed, taking his shoes off.

"Oh, hey," he said in surprise, looking up at India.

"Dude, Monique's into you, right. And I know you're trying to be all cool and New Age with your 'take me or leave me' shit. But don't be that guy; take her out to dinner, maybe a picnic in front of the Sacré-Coeur when you hit France. Got it?"

She turned and left the room without waiting for a response.

Back in the common room, she smiled at Monique. "It's up to you, babe, but I'd wait until I knew for a fact it's what I wanted to do. And don't forget, you can always ask *him* out on a date, okay?"

She headed to her own room wondering if interfering was the right thing to do—but then again, she didn't really care if it was right or wrong, because it *felt* right. Besides, she liked to meddle, it was fun; it made her feel like a puppet-master—a benevolent puppet-master, though, not an evil one. It was something she had always enjoyed doing when she was younger, although perhaps not with as much confidence as she displayed now. In primary school, she could recall writing a love letter to her friend Jen and signing it from Michael Green—a boy she could tell had a crush on her friend, but who probably would have never told Jen, had India not given them that little prod. Michael and Jen held hands in the playground at little lunch and big lunch every day from that day onward. India remembered how her chest had swelled with pride the first time she had seen Jen reach over and take Michael's hand as they sat side by side eating their Vegemite sandwiches.

As India reached her room and climbed quietly into her bed in the dark, without bothering to change, she realized that playing matchmaker yet again and seeing those two contemplating the beginning of a holiday romance had made her start thinking of Simon and, more specifically, about sex with Simon.

The first time with Simon had been, to say the least, quite mind-blowing actually. India was by no means inexperienced; she was very open about her sexuality, more than capable of separating sex and emotions when she needed. But with Simon . . . God, he'd made her see stars, he'd made her want to fall asleep curled up in his arms afterward. He'd made her forget—for just a little while—everything that had happened to her over the past couple of years.

No! Naughty India, you're not supposed to think about him, she chided herself. Perhaps it was time she had some one-night stands of her own.

Hannah made the mistake of mentioning the invite she'd received to watch the boat race to her boss, Helen.

"Take the day off," she said immediately.

"What? No, that's not what I meant. I wasn't asking to go; I was just making conversation!"

"I know you weren't asking, but for God's sake, woman, give yourself a break. You deserve a weekend. There are enough staff here to cover all the counters. Go."

She headed back to her flat to change and found herself putting on shorts, T-shirt and sneakers.

You shouldn't be going out and having fun. If you've got the day off then you're going to run instead.

As soon as this thought entered Hannah's mind, she knew that it was the right thing to do. Still, she couldn't help feeling disappointed as she left her flat and jogged down the several flights of stairs. She'd love to stretch out in the sunshine, maybe drink a

beer or a Pimm's and lemonade while she watched the boats glid-
ing swiftly past.

As she headed out the front door of her building and started
off with a light jog, she found herself absentmindedly heading toward the Thames. She tried to convince herself that she wasn't
heading this way to try and watch the race, just that a run along
the river might make for a good track. When she reached the
Thames, she hesitated. The race started later that afternoon at
Putney. India would be at a pub that overlooked the river in Hammersmith, halfway along the course, watching the boats pass with
a few friends. It couldn't hurt to head in that direction, could it?
After all, running all the way to Hammersmith along the river
would be hard work; it had to be ten to fifteen kilometers at least,
didn't it? And then double it for the run back. That was practically
a marathon in itself, wasn't it?

She turned left and started running along the pathway, following the wide, winding river. As she ran, she wondered if
she would actually go and find India and her friends when she
reached Hammersmith. She still wasn't sure that she deserved
to join them. But then, maybe she would have earned the break
after this run?

About two hours later, Hannah began to suspect that something was wrong. She thought by now she should have reached
the starting point of the race. In fact, she had expected to begin to
see crowds of people a good half an hour ago. But the surrounding streets seemed quieter than ever. *You just haven't run far*

enough, she scolded herself. *It's further than you first thought. Stop complaining.*

She picked up her pace and continued on for another forty minutes. She checked her watch; the race would be starting soon—how could she not be there yet? Spotting a café up ahead, she slowed down to a brisk walk, reaching the doors of the café just as a woman stepped outside, flipping over a closed sign as she went and pulling the door shut behind her.

"Excuse me," Hannah began.

"Sorry, love, we're closed until dinner time." The woman gave her a brief smile and turned away.

"Actually, I was hoping you could help me with some directions?"

"Sure, where're you headed to?"

"I've been jogging along the river and I was hoping I might catch the boat race . . . but I thought I would have reached Putney by now—I feel as if I've been running for ages."

"Putney?" the woman exclaimed. "Goodness, love, that's nowhere near here. Which direction are you coming from?"

Hannah pointed. "That way, from the very center of London. So it's further than I thought then?"

The woman widened her eyes. "Oh, I'm sorry to tell you this, love, but you've come the wrong way. Should have been following the river in the other direction. I've got some more bad news for you too—even if you hop on a train you'll never make it in time. Race will be over within half an hour."

"Ah."

Hannah thanked the woman for her help and turned away, back toward the river. She could feel the woman's sympathetic gaze on her back as she started to jog again.

Karma, she thought bitterly as she watched the water flash by and felt her heels start to burn against the back of her shoes. *This is karma for what you've done. You should never have tried to go and watch that race. It's bad enough that you went out last night, that you had fun.*

She was going to have to give up on the friendship with India. It wasn't right—this was proof of that fact.

A vibration against her leg told her that her phone was ringing. She slowed down to a walk and pulled it out. It was him again. Simultaneous emotions welled up inside her. First, elation—*he hasn't given up.* Then, fear—*why is he calling me now? It's the middle of the night right now for him.*

What if something was wrong? After all, that was the reason she had let him know her phone number—for emergencies— although deep down she'd known he wouldn't stick to that.

Her hands trembled; maybe she should answer . . . just this once. She took a gusty breath and pressed the green button to take the call.

"Hello," she said in a small voice.

"Hannah!" His voice sounded tinny, far away. But hearing the warm familiar tones was making her knees weak. She should never have answered; this was a mistake.

"Oh my God, I thought I'd never get to speak to you again. Are you okay?"

Hannah hesitated. It didn't sound as though anything was wrong; he sounded excited that she had actually picked up. She clenched her teeth and then said quickly, "Is everything all right, Liam? Why are you calling so late? Nothing's happened, has it?"

"Are you joking, Hannah? Where the hell do I even begin? No nothing's happened, not since you bloody left. Hannah, please, *where are you?*"

"I can't, Liam. I just can't, okay. But if there's not some emergency, then I'm going to have to hang up. I'm sorry." The last two words were left hanging in the air for a moment, and Hannah immediately wished she hadn't said them. *I'm sorry* didn't even begin to make up for what she had done. Nothing could.

"Hannah, this is insane. DON'T hang up! We need to talk, and don't you even want to—"

What he thought she wanted to do, Hannah didn't wait to find out. She whipped the phone away from her ear and jabbed the Call End button before she could change her mind. She could guess though—in fact she was more than positive she knew what the end of that sentence would be—and yes of course she wanted to, but that didn't mean that she should. She had to stay strong; it was better for everyone this way. There was no going back from what she had done and she needed to find a way to move on, no matter how painful it was.

She sat down on a low brick wall nearby and rested her head in her hands. She wondered if he would call back again straightaway, but after waiting fifteen minutes she decided he wasn't going to.

"Do you hate me right now?" she said out loud, without really meaning to.

"Excuse me?" asked a voice.

Hannah lifted her head to see who had spoken. A man stood in front of her, a quizzical expression on his face.

"Oh, sorry, I thought I was alone, didn't really mean to speak out loud," she explained.

"No need to apologize. But maybe you need someone to talk to?" He motioned to the wall next to her and Hannah realized how miserable she must have looked.

"That's okay, you don't need to," she began, but he was already sitting down beside her.

"Sometimes it feels good to get it all out, especially to a complete stranger. Why don't you tell me what's going on?" He gave her an encouraging smile. Something about the smile was a little bit creepy, though, as if he was sort of leering at her. Hannah became aware of just how close he was sitting to her and then— even more startling—of just how quiet it was around here, deserted in fact.

"Umm, you know what, I'm actually fine, thanks." She made to stand up and the man placed a heavy hand on her thigh to stop her. "Don't be afraid, I just want to talk," he said quietly and his fingers briefly squeezed her leg.

Panic started to flutter in Hannah's chest. How had she ended up in this situation? Suddenly her phone rang in her pocket. The noise startled the man and he loosened his grip. Seizing the opportunity, Hannah elbowed his arm away, leapt up and started sprinting up the river. She could hear footsteps following after her and his voice calling out, "Don't run away, sweetheart, I just want to help you to feel better." And then rolls of hideous laughter. But she didn't turn back. Evidently he couldn't run as fast as she could and eventually his footsteps started to die away while Hannah continued to pelt down the pathway. She didn't slow down until she absolutely had to—not until her chest felt so tight she thought it might burst and tiny lights were darting in front of her eyes— and even then she kept up a brisk jog. Finally she felt safe enough to turn around and check behind her. He was gone.

Thank God.

She turned back and continued to jog, pulling her phone out of her pocket as she ran so that she could check on the call that had rescued her. It must have been Liam, *had to be*. He had saved her, even after everything she had done. Oh God, she so desper- ately wanted to be with him right now, wanted to curl up in his arms and hide from the world and tell him how sorry she was. She wanted him to take away the sick, acidic, burning taste at the back of her throat, to make the aching pain in her gut evaporate. But when she looked at the number, she saw she was wrong. It wasn't Liam at all. It was India. India had saved her.

Maybe she shouldn't end that friendship after all.

She jogged for another half an hour and waited until she was surrounded by people before she felt comfortable enough to stop and return the call.

"Hannah! Where are you, babe?" India's voice sounded bright and animated when she answered.

Hannah felt instantly comforted. "Umm, I've just been for a jog, I'm by the river—not sure where exactly."

"Well, come and join us for a drink, woman! You missed the race but celebrations will continue, and this is the best part anyway. We're at the Old Ship. Jump on the tube; we'll see you here in shall we say, twenty? I'll have a cold beer waiting for you."

"I don't really know how long it'll take me," Hannah began.

"You better get moving then, see you soon!"

India hung up and Hannah couldn't help feeling relief that she hadn't been given a choice in the matter. She needed company, couldn't bear the thought of going back to her flat alone right now—not with her flesh still tingling from where that man had touched her. She shivered and started jogging again, keeping an eye out for a tube station. She hoped people weren't going to be too dressed up at this pub because there wasn't time to go home and change; her shorts and T-shirt were going to have to do.

India was squeezing her way through the crowds, back toward her table and her newly adopted group of friends. She hoped Hannah was okay; she'd looked slightly alarmed when India had stood up to head to the bathroom. India was all for helping people, but she didn't particularly want Hannah to become *too* needy. For goodness' sake, if the girl couldn't cope on her own for five minutes with a group of friendly strangers then perhaps she was socially inept? India was enjoying the mix of people filling the pub; it reminded her of the crowd you might find in a beer garden back home in Oz. Everyone was dressed in shorts and tank tops, all with that slightly too rosy appearance that came from a day out in the sun combined with a little too much alcohol.

Finally she reached their outdoor table and sighed, exasperated at the sight of Hannah, sitting on a bench, her shoulders pressed against people on both sides, a giant beer clutched in her hands, her eyes lowered, avoiding conversation. As India circled the table to stand beside her, Hannah looked up at her and visibly relaxed, her tensed shoulders dropping at least five centimeters.

"Who are all these people, more backpackers from your hostel?" Hannah hissed.

India shrugged. "Umm, I think that guy's name is Aiden, or Adrian maybe. But that one is definitely his sister, Sammy. Or cousin . . ." India paused to think. "No, cousin, yes that's it. And that's Brendan and Clare, I think they're an item—or if not they ought to be, don't you think so? Check out the way he keeps touching her arm, right? Anyway, I'm not sure about the rest. None of them are from my hostel; I met them all today, watched the race with them."

Hannah was looking up at India with eyes filled with awe. India felt like snapping her fingers in front of her face. *Stop it, it's not that amazing.*

"Come on, let's go for a walk," said India, beckoning to Hannah. Hannah managed to extricate herself from the bench seat while holding her beer up in the air as she tried not to lose her balance. They paused for a moment, watching as the space where

Hannah had been sitting instantly vanished as the people either side of her automatically swelled and fused themselves together and India found herself wondering how there was ever room for her shy new friend there at all.

India linked an arm through Hannah's and led her through the crowds and down some steps to a paved area overlooking the river.

"Got the feeling you were getting a bit claustrophobic in there," India said, hoping she didn't sound too accusatory, because what she really wanted to say was "Lighten up!" Instead, she continued, "Thought you could use a bit of fresh air."

"Thanks. Sorry, your new friends are lovely. I'm just not so good at meeting people and making conversation with strangers."

"You met me. Became my friend. I like you." India listed these things off matter-of-factly despite the niggling voice at the back of her head that was whispering, *At least I think I like you, but I tell you what, you're making it difficult, girl.*

"Yeah and I still don't get that," Hannah responded immediately. "You're not the sort of person I'm usually friends with. Not in a bad way," she added in a rush. "I just mean . . . well to be honest, I don't generally have friends at all, haven't for a long time anyway."

"Why not?"

"Not sure really. I guess I just forgot how to make friends. I moved halfway through high school, and when I changed schools, I lost all my old friends. The girls at the new school didn't like me, and from then I was just never any good at **meeting** new people, apart from guys. For some reason dating I could do—just not making friends."

Ahh, so this explains her social awkwardness, to an extent anyway. "Why, Hannah, I do believe we're getting somewhere." India smiled mysteriously at her.

"What do you mean?"

"I mean, you're starting to give me some honest answers, my girl. It's very exciting. Progress!" She shot her fist up in the air in a triumphant gesture.

Hannah gave her a startled look. "Umm, honest answers?" she croaked nervously. "What makes you think I haven't been truthful with you before now?"

India laughed. "Oh, sweetheart, don't fret. I could just tell that most of the things you've been telling me have been bullshit so far. Like the marathon that you're supposedly training for. Ha. Call me perceptive. It's okay, I don't mind. You have your reasons. I mean, we all have secrets, don't we? It's just that I've made it my goal to find out yours, because I get the feeling yours need telling. Don't worry, I don't expect you to spill everything here and now. I get that it's going to take time."

Hannah gave her a slightly strangulated smile. "Ahh, you know what, I think I might get going back home. Got to work in the morning and it's been a long day. You don't mind, do you?"

"Crap, scared you away, haven't I? Will you stay if I promise I won't talk secrets any more tonight?"

"Thanks, but it's fine. It's nothing you've said—I just really should get to bed." Hannah pushed her still full beer into India's hands. "Here, you finish this."

She turned to walk away and India called after her, "All right, fine, you win for tonight. I'll see you tomorrow, though. I'll come and have lunch with you on your break."

India shook her head as she watched Hannah nod her head in assent without turning and continue briskly toward Hammer-smith tube station. For a moment she wondered why she was even bothering, but then she scolded herself. Hannah needed help; that was obvious. And she felt like there was someone else, hidden inside that insecure, slightly irritating outer shell. Someone who could possibly be quite a lot of fun. India glanced down at the beer that Hannah had handed her. Apart from a glass of wine here and there, she normally didn't drink, but she was feeling frustrated. She wanted to save Hannah, but she also wanted to keep traveling; she didn't usually like to stay in one place for too long. The fact that Hannah was holding out on her, that she knew she was going to have to be patient, coax the truth out of her, was making her feel fidgety.

After staring at the frothy golden liquid swirling around the glass in her hands for several seconds, she shrugged, murmured, "Fuck it," and lifted the glass to her lips to drink.

It was dark and the air was thick with smoke and heat. A low red light illuminated the walls—walls that seemed to be danger-ously swaying. Or was it her that was swaying? A bass rumbled through the floor and India tried to focus her thoughts, to remember where she was and how she had got here.

"Fucking Hannah!" She hadn't been drunk in years. But one beer pressed into her hands and next thing she was absolutely toasted, leaning against the wall in some labyrinth of a nightclub, feeling decidedly seedy. She remembered moving on to spirits. Maybe champagne at one point? And then shots. Ahh. She remembered piling into a cab with a few people at the Old Ship and now she was . . . where?

"There she is! Thought you'd run off on us, darling!"

India squinted her eyes to peer through the darkness. A dark shape materialized in front of her. Hot breath on her neck as he leaned in close. Too close!

"Wait," she murmured as hands began to slither up and down her waist. *Who are you again?* Lips pressed against her earlobe and India racked her brain as she tried to remember who this was and why he would think it was okay to grope her in the back hallway of a nightclub. A name was teasing the edges of her mind. *Nick? Nate? Tate?!*

"Tate?" she tried hopefully.

"It's Jase, baby," he replied, unperturbed.

If you say so . . . But at the sound of his name an image popped in her head, and she remembered dancing, remembered a cute guy eyeing her from across the dance floor. Blue eyes, cute curls, and one of those indents in a strong chin, Matthew McConaughey style. She hit fast forward on the instant replay in her mind and saw them moving closer and closer together on the dance floor, an invisible cord drawing them toward one another. And then . . . oh God, she'd already kissed him, hadn't she? Rather passionately if she recalled correctly. That's right; she escaped back here to give her tongue a much-needed break.

Right, so he was cute, there was definitely an attraction there. And now she knew his name. *Oh well, may as well go with it.*

But as she succumbed to Jase's wandering hands and lifted her face to kiss him again, her thoughts began to turn. She was remembering the last guy she'd slept with. Simon. And she was thinking about how different Simon's hands had felt on her body. How when they kissed it felt as though they had been kissing one another for years. How his fingers would glide over her back and how the stubble on his cheek would gently tickle her skin.

Dammit! Without another thought India raised her hands, placed them square on Jase's chest and then firmly pushed him away. "Sorry, babe," she said a little sadly and turned and walked unsteadily down the hall. A shame, she had really been missing sex these last few weeks, but apparently she was going to have to make a phone call. She made her way through the sweaty, gyrating bodies in the nightclub and then finally emerged outside, the cool night air hitting her face and sobering her up—just a fraction.

She briefly wondered what the time was as she headed up the street, looking for a pay phone—her mobile wouldn't have enough credit for an international call. Whatever time it was, she didn't care though; she needed to have this conversation. If she woke him up, he'd get over it.

When she finally found a phone that worked, searched through her pockets for the right change, slotted it in and dialed the number, she paused for a moment to take in a deep breath. What exactly was it that she wanted to say here? But there was no time to consider—a click at the other end told her someone had answered.

"Hello?" came the sleepy sounding voice. The familiar tone caught her off guard and she leaned back against the glassed wall of the phone booth.

"Simon," she breathed contentedly.

"India?" came back the voice uncertainly. "Is that you?"

"Yup."

There was a pause and the muffled sound of movement, as though Simon was perhaps pushing back the covers, sitting up in bed. Then he spoke again, "It's 4:00 A.M.! Where are you? Is everything okay?"

"Yup."

"No, seriously . . . are you okay? I thought I wasn't going to hear from you ever again. You realize you broke my fuckin' heart when you left, right?"

"Yup."

"Jesus, are you going to say anything other than 'yup'?"

India giggled. "Yup."

"That's not funny, India."

"Sorry," she said. "Did I wake you? I didn't mean to. I'll go if you like."

"No! Don't hang up. Where are you?"

"London at the moment." She curled her fingers around the receiver cord. "Tell me, Simon. Why is it that you've been on my mind lately?"

"Guilt," he replied immediately. "You knew I fell hard for you. Three weeks together, day and night. And you just take off one day. Then . . . nothing. Six weeks and I don't hear a thing from you—until now. What's that all about anyway?"

"Told you I was a free spirit, Simon." As soon as she said it India felt like a douche. "Sorry, can we pretend I didn't say that? I just don't like to stay in one place for too long. Never meant to stay in the Greek Islands for as long as I did with you." *I have to keep moving, Simon, because if I don't, then everything might start catching up with me . . .*

"So what made you phone?"

"Was kissing some random guy in the back of a nightclub. Planned on sleeping with him. But then you jumped into my head. Why is that, Simon? How did you get there? What's *that* all about?" Her voice was sing-song as she threw the question back at Simon.

"Christ. You have to tell me that stuff? You really think I want to hear about you getting it on with another guy?"

Simon's voice was agitated but India shrugged it off. "Why not? We're not a couple, are we? I'm single; I can do whatever I like."

"Fine. You're single, go sleep with whoever. But could you maybe not call in the middle of the night to tell me about it?

Where are you? Hiding out in the guy's bathroom or something?"

"Yup," she replied, unsure why she was purposely provoking him further.

"Well, that's really great, good for you." There was another pause, as though Simon was thinking it through, considering what to say next. Apparently, though, she had pushed him too far. "For FUCK's sake!" he suddenly shouted. And then there was a click as the phone hung up.

India held the phone against her head, listening to the sound of the disconnected line, a long insistent beep, until her ear began to ache.

"I've been sending you letters," she whispered to the dead air. "But I guess none of them have made it yet." And then slowly, gently, she hung up the receiver and stepped out of the phone booth. A strange uneasy feeling was stirring in her stomach as she walked on up the street toward the tube station, but although she wanted to cry, she didn't seem to be able to.

He was lighting up his cigarette when the two girls sidled up to him. He recognized their faces; they were on his tour bus. They were the ones who were always giggling, usually at something inane. He also recognized the looks on their faces.

Jeez, one of them is about to hit on me. Maybe both.

They couldn't seem to keep the bubbling hysteria out of their voices as they explained what it was that they wanted him to do. Fuck me, calm down, *thought Blake as they gushed on about the pure romance of the story they were telling him.*

They held out a slightly crumpled looking envelope and looked up at him with wide, puppy dog eyes, which he assumed must usually work for them. He wouldn't have been surprised if they had been licking ice-cream cones, seductively circling their tongues around the chocolate peaks, just to complete the image.

In the end Blake snatched the envelope out of the blonde's pink-tipped fingers and said, "Sure, whatever," just to get rid of them. When they continued to stand in front of him, bouncing up and down on their toes and waving their perky tits in his face, he sighed and gave them a smile.

"Girls," he said.

"Yes," they chorused hopefully.

"Fuck off."

CHAPTER 4

D o you remember when the last time was that you cried?"
Hannah looked up from her menu, startled. Did India know? Was it that obvious? She had cried just that
morning, in the shower. And before that, in bed last night. If she
thought about it actually, she wasn't sure when the last time was
that she had made it through an entire day *without* any tears.

"Umm, I'm not sure really. Probably the last time I chopped up
an onion," Hannah attempted to joke.

They were sitting at an outdoor table at a café around the corner from the museum. True to her word, India had turned up
at the gift shop right on 12:45 P.M. and announced that she was
taking Hannah to lunch. At first Hannah almost hadn't recognized her—her hair was bright blue today. When asked how she

knew what time her lunch break was, India had smiled mysteriously and responded, "Ahh, India knows all, my child." And then laughed hysterically at herself. Later she explained that she had just called the gift shop and asked Helen, her boss, what time her break was. Not so mystifying really.

Now India frowned. "No, cutting up *vegetables* doesn't count, Hannah. When was the last time you actually cried? Like really sobbed?"

"I can't remember," Hannah said, a little too quickly.

"Liar," India replied casually. "I'll have the chicken and avocado panini, thanks, but can you add mushrooms too, please?" she addressed the waitress who had materialized by their table.

Hannah ordered the same because she hadn't been able to concentrate on the menu with India probing her, and when the waitress left she asked India, "Why did you want to know anyway, especially if you're not going to believe my answer?"

"No reason, just something that's been on my mind."

India leaned back in her chair and stretched her arms out above her. This resulted in her knocking a tray being carried past their table by a waiter. The glass on the tray rocked back and forth as the waiter tried to steady it and then toppled and smashed onto the ground.

"Oh God, sorry!" India exclaimed as she turned to survey the damage.

"It's okay," said the waiter as he bent to start picking up the shards of glass.

"AGAIN?" came an angry bellow from the counter inside the café.

India gasped. "Have I got you into trouble?" she asked. She swiveled in her chair and squinted inside the café, then called out, "No, no, it wasn't him. It was my fault, I knocked it, when I was stretching—like this, see?" And she demonstrated with an overexaggerated stretch.

The manager inside ignored her and grumbled something that sounded very much like, "The last straw, honestly, *last* straw."

India scrambled from her chair to help pick up the glass. "Now," she asked the waiter, "when he says 'last straw,' does he mean you just dropped the last straw with that glass of lemonade and he's upset because now you've run out of straws? Or does he mean it in a metaphorical kind of way? As in you're about to get fired? Cause if it's the latter, I'll go in and sort it out. Do you know how much guilt I'll be weighed under if I find out I've got someone fired? I'll be staggering around under it all day."

The waiter laughed. "He means the latter, but don't worry, he won't actually fire me—today's my last day anyway, I'm leaving London tomorrow."

"Really? Where are you going?" India asked as she collected the last pieces of glass and piled them onto his tray.

"Greek Islands. Been saving up for the past six months and now I'm going to take a proper holiday—as opposed to a working one."

Hannah had been sitting awkwardly in her chair as the exchange had taken place between India and the waiter, unsure as to whether she should offer to help or just stay out of the way, but now she frowned as she watched an inscrutable expression cross India's face. There was a pause before India responded, and when she spoke her voice didn't have the normal bright and bubbly tone of confidence that spelled India. "The Greek Islands? Great. That's great," she said, her voice subdued. "You'll have a blast there."

The waiter smiled appreciatively and then headed inside with the tray of broken glass. Hannah's brow creased, as she tried to follow what had just happened. She hesitated, and then asked casually, "You've been to the Greek Islands?"

Hannah watched as India allowed a ghost of a smile to pass across her lips before she replied. "Yeah, I spent a few weeks there. Beautiful."

"Are you okay?" Hannah asked. It was clear that something was up.

India shrugged. "I guess. I mean yep, sure. I haven't told you about Simon though, have I?"

"Nope."

"I met him a couple months ago, traveling through the Greek Islands. He works on a boat that takes tourists between the islands. It was one of the rare occasions when I decided to stay in the one place for a little while. Usually I move on after a few days. But when I met Simon—Aussie guy, from Sydney actually—I kind of got stuck for a little while. Stayed much longer than I intended. Didn't help that he was gorgeous: dark hair, great shoulders, cheeky green eyes—you know, all the nice trimmings. About three weeks I spent with him. Then I came to my senses, remembered why I'm doing this. I left him in the middle of the night. Put a note on the pillow, kissed him on the lips as he slept, never looked back.

"In hindsight, I suppose it was just a tad melodramatic, wasn't it? Like I was a CIA agent on a secret mission or something. But anyway, I guess I missed him. So I've been writing to him ever since. But he has no idea, and none of my letters have ever made it to him. Oh, I don't post them," she added when Hannah gave her a confused look. "I just give them to other travelers, usually backpackers like me. Doesn't matter where they're headed; if it's not toward Greece, then I ask them to pass them on to someone who is. On the front of the envelope, I just write 'Simon' and the name of his boat—*The Aella*. It's more fun like this. That way, if he ever gets one of my letters, then it's fate, right? Otherwise, it's not meant to be. I suppose most of them might have ended up pasted into the inside cover of some backpacker's journal as a sweet memento of their travels. It's surprising how many people that I give them to think it's the most romantic thing they've ever heard of— they're always comparing it to a message in a bottle scenario, but it's not really, is it?"

Hannah stared at India, taking in all of the information. She had so many questions. But one was particularly bothering her. "Why *are* you doing this?" she asked.

"Huh?"

"You said you came to your senses, remembered why you're doing this—what do you mean?"

India smiled. "How about this—I'll tell you mine if you tell me yours." There was a pause as Hannah looked back at India, confused, and then India laughed and added, "What, you think you're the only one with secrets? Anyway, we're not here to talk about me, I want to know more about you, my dear. More real stuff please." Hannah was pleased to see that India seemed to be returning to her old self, looking relaxed and laid back once more.

India paused and then said decisively, "I know, you could tell me about your last Christmas. What was it like? Where were you? Who were you with? What did you get?"

Hannah didn't have time to be surprised by the random question. An image flew into her mind. She saw a beautiful Christmas tree, a live one—it had been the first time she'd ever had a real Christmas tree in her home. She could almost smell the pine needles, feel them crunching under her feet, hear them being sucked up by the vacuum cleaner—*ping, ping, ping!* She saw Liam, laughing as he sifted through their box of dismal decorations that she refused to throw out. And then she heard another voice, joining in on the laughter, jolting her senses. Her throat closed up and pinpricks speared the back of her eyes. Her words tumbled. "Do you mind if I don't . . . please?"

India leaned across the table to grab at her hands before she could escape as she had the previous night. "Okay, forget it," she said in a rush. "Take a deep breath. Here's what we're going to do: I'm going to tell you about *my* last Christmas. And you're going to picture it with me, and it's going to make you laugh and you're going to stop thinking about whatever it is that's so painful for you, okay?"

Hannah nodded and India launched into her story. Apparently she had made the decision last year to skip Christmas, she wasn't in the mood for it (for reasons she didn't divulge) and she spent the day on the beach in Ibiza, resolutely ignoring the fact that it was the middle of winter and attempting to tan anyway. Just under two weeks later she had moved on to Moscow, glad that Christmas was all over. Apparently she was wrong. It turned out that in Russia, Christmas was celebrated on the seventh of January and she had inadvertently arrived in the city on their Christmas Eve. She gave in to fate and decided to join in the celebrations. Somehow she befriended a large welcoming family at a church service and was invited to spend the night with them sharing their twelve-course feast, eating vegetarian porridge and having honey crosses drawn on her forehead. She said it came close to the best Christmas she had ever experienced and had completely renewed her faith in the holiday.

Hannah didn't press her for the details as to why she had first been put off Christmas, nor did she bring up India's revelation that she had a secret in her past; she was too busy recovering from her own moment of anxiety as she had thought about home. But India's story had managed to calm her and the rest of the lunch break continued somewhat uneventfully.

•

"You think a person can just be vanilla?"

"What do you mean?"

India had befriended a florist. Or perhaps he had befriended her, she wasn't really certain. Either way, she had been taking an early morning walk through Notting Hill and had stopped to admire some beautiful daisies, and ended up chatting with the young guy as he tended to his displays. Now they were having a coffee together at a café around the corner from the flower shop.

"So there's this girl. And all this time I've been certain that there's more to her, that she's hiding something massive. But what if I'm wrong? Or what if I finally find out the big secret—and it's not the amazing revelation that I want it to be. Or what if I'm inventing all of this, because I want there to be something there to find—when there's actually nothing at all?"

Sebastian the florist frowned back at her as he stirred his coffee, giving India the impression that he was playing for time as he attempted to come up with an intelligent sounding response. "Uhh," he said eventually. "Well, I think everyone has their own story, don't they? I mean, I would have said my year eight teacher was nothing more than gray checks and horn-rimmed glasses . . . all I ever thought of her was that she was a teacher. Like, that was her whole world; when the classes were done for the day, she just folded herself up into a box and waited quietly until the bell rang again the next morning. But that was just my thirteen-year-old perspective. Obviously she was more than that. For all I know, she could have been writing erotica in her spare time. She might have done rally car driving on the weekends. *Or* she might have just liked to collect postage stamps—but regardless of what it was, it would have been something to her, wouldn't it? Everyone holds the spotlight in their own story and no matter how bland their plot might be, to them—it's still everything. Know what I mean?"

Sebastian sat back and watched India nervously. India smiled at him. "You worked hard on that response, huh?"

"A little," he replied shyly.

"Ah, you're a sweetheart, Sebastian. You're right, it doesn't matter what it is—but as long as there's something there, it means everything to her. I'll keep digging."

Later that day, India met up with Hannah as she finished her shift at the gift shop. Sebastian's advice had made her resolve to persevere with Hannah. She stood waiting outside the museum, her back leaning against a sandstone pillar. But when Hannah stepped out through the front door, India immediately felt guilty about her *vanilla* comment. Hannah's eyes swept the ground; her shoulders were hunched and her hands fidgeted at her sides. Hannah wasn't vanilla, she was just plain scared.

What are you running from?

Why won't you let me in?

"Hannah!" India watched as Hannah's head snapped up.

"Oh hey," said Hannah, a nervous smile twitching the corners of her mouth as she approached India. "What are you doing here?"

"Waiting for you, obviously."

"Right," said Hannah. "Of course," and she looked irritatingly unsure of herself. India couldn't help it—she reached out a hand and gripped Hannah's upper arm. "Hannah! Lighten up, woman!"

she said as she shook Hannah, possibly more violently than she had intended.

"What do you mean?" Hannah sounded alarmed.

"I mean stop being so nervous around me. I'm not THAT GREAT! Just, you know . . . be yourself for once."

"Oh." Hannah paused. "What if I don't know how?"

India felt like screaming. Instead she spoke evenly, "Well the obvious thing would be for you to tell me the truth. But since it's clear you're not going to do that, we'll have to figure out something else."

She stood still, thinking, and was taken aback when Hannah suddenly spoke up. "Do you want to come back to my flat? We could have sort of a girls' night. Pizza, wine, maybe watch a movie? Or is that lame?" Hannah looked visibly frightened as she waited for India's response.

"YES!" India exclaimed. "I mean, yes to the girls' night, not yes it's lame," she clarified. She immediately linked her arm through Hannah's and they set off walking. As they passed a collection of cardboard boxes, haphazardly stacked to create a small shelter for a homeless man tucked inside, Hannah pulled away from India. "Hang on one sec," she said. Reaching into her pocket, she pulled out a packaged oat and raisin bar and walked over to the boxes. Kneeling down, she pressed the bar into the man's hand.

"Thanks, love," croaked the voice from inside the shelter. "Liked those crisps you brought me yesterday, though," the voice added.

"I'll get another packet for you tomorrow," Hannah promised. Then she stood and rejoined India.

"What was that all about?" India asked as they continued on down the road.

"That's Fred," Hannah replied. "Offered him my muesli bar once on the way home from the museum and I've just sort of been dropping something off to him every day since. I like him, he's always so friendly. I remember once back home I tried to buy a homeless woman a sandwich for her lunch and she spat on me and told me to piss off unless I had any money or cigarettes for her."

"Seriously?" India exclaimed. Then she grinned. "Ahh, Hannah, you're a good kid, aren't you? Sorry about shaking you before; you're just a bit infuriating, that's all."

They picked up a bottle of wine and a large margarita pizza on the way back to Hannah's flat. "I don't have a DVD player," Hannah apologized as they headed up the creaking stairs, "but there's usually an old movie on Channel 4 or 5 every night."

Once inside, Hannah rushed to tidy up the few items of clothing that were strewn around the single-room flat, bundling everything up and tossing it onto the bed. Then they set themselves down on the floor with the pizza box open between them and a couple of plastic wine goblets, filled with generous amounts of the red wine they had just bought. After flicking through the channels, they settled on a nineties romantic comedy. They chatted through the ad breaks and India felt pleased as she watched Hannah begin to relax and ease into her own skin. *Maybe it was time to ask her some more probing questions?*

Hannah was beginning to enjoy herself. She didn't know how she had come to invite India back to her place for a girls' night. A *girls' night!* As if she even knew what one of those involved. It had been far too long since she'd had girlfriends.

But she'd had the feeling that India was getting fed up. Their friendship was completely one-sided, with India pretty much carrying her.

Take, take, take. She needed to put some effort in. She needed to give a little.

Hannah hadn't had any close friends since she had left her first high school at the end of year nine when her parents had split up. Her mum had immediately pulled her out of Plumpton High and moved them to a small apartment in Neutral Bay and enrolled her at North Sydney Girls' High.

None of the girls at her new school were keen to accept a girl from out west into any of their cliquey little groups and mostly seemed to look down on her and her Doc Martens boots. She tried to remain friends with her old group from Plumpton, even sneaking out one night to visit that nightclub in Penrith with them, despite the fact that they were only sixteen at the time— but she soon drifted apart from them as well. While the North Shore girls looked down on her, her old friends began to think that she was most probably beginning to look down on them, and so Hannah remained stuck in the middle, friendless and lonely.

Hannah wasn't particularly close to her family, either. She and her father got along okay—they just didn't have much to talk about. Perhaps an unspoken blame still hung in the air between them from when her father had first left her mother. And although his new wife had always been perfectly nice, Hannah had never really known how to build any sort of relationship with her. Her dad was quick to remarry and Hannah had always suspected that he must have been having an affair with this new woman, because otherwise their relationship had moved awfully fast from meeting to marrying.

His new wife, Carol, had three children already, one older than Hannah, one younger than her, and then there was Amy. Amy was the exact same age as Hannah—down to the month even. And for years Hannah had felt certain that Amy had replaced her in her dad's eyes. She was beautiful—in that typical blond hair and blue eyes kind of way—and funny and talented. Hannah would spend hours at a time imagining a world where she and Amy swapped places. She fantasized about what it would be like to have a big sister who would lend her funky clothes and jewelry, who would give her advice about boys and maybe even buy her alcohol for parties. And of course, a younger brother who would look up to her and adore her.

She imagined that the three of them would share secrets, would be best friends, and one day, when they were all in their twenties, they would go backpacking around Europe together!

She would move into their gorgeous two-story house by Coogee Beach, with its hardwood floors and fresh white paint and she would become the clever, talented one. She would learn to surf and be tanned golden brown and she would have both a mum *and* a dad. And Amy could move in with Anne, into the cold, unfeeling apartment in Neutral Bay with its gray tiles and its snobby furniture. The fantasy would always fill her with simultaneous feelings of guilt and longing.

Hannah was often told off in school for daydreaming too much.

The pizza box was empty and they'd worked their way through a block of white raspberry Dove chocolate now as well.

"So why all the running?" India asked, pressing her thumb against the last crumbs of chocolate left on the silver foil packaging by their feet. She had a new purple stud in her nose and it sparkled when it caught the light. Hannah still found herself in awe of how India could constantly reinvent herself with each simple change to her appearance. Hannah would never be brave enough to just go out one day and get her nose pierced. "I mean, we've established that you're not really training for the New York marathon, right? Is it because you eat too much of this?" India asked, indicating the chocolate wrappers.

Hannah felt slightly alarmed for a moment and then she relented. *Give a little, Hannah, tell the truth for once.* "Sort of I guess . . . yes. Thing is, I don't really eat properly. Most days I starve myself, then I wake in the middle of the night famished and I gorge on chocolate. Next day I punish myself by running.

It's not about looking good," she added hastily. "It's not a body image thing, more of a self-mutilation, I guess you could say."

India peered at her. "Oh, okay, it's *just* self-mutilation, yeah, that's much better," she said. "So is that the big secret? You have an eating disorder?"

"Umm, no."

"But you hate yourself. Why?"

Hannah paused, trying to figure out how best to respond. Finally she shook her head. There was no way she could tell India the truth, no matter how much she wanted to open up to her. "I don't want you to hate me too," she said quietly.

India shrugged. "Whatever. I think I know what it is anyway. I've been thinking and it all adds up."

Hannah froze. "You do?"

"Yep. Let's see, you've a mark on your ring finger, you're clearly running away from something and you're torturing yourself for having done something awful."

Hannah waited, holding her breath.

"You left someone at the altar, right?"

Hannah almost began to laugh, as she imagined herself as a runaway bride, fleeing to the airport with her lace veil flying behind her, but then the laughter twisted in her throat. "I wish it was that simple," she said, her voice bitter.

India looked disappointed. "Dammit, I thought I was on to you. Never mind, I'll keep swinging and eventually I'll come up with a hit."

Hannah picked up the empty wine bottle, keen to change the

subject. "We're out," she announced. "Screw the girls' night in. Let's go out to a pub."

"Why, Hannah, I do believe you're becoming a bad influence on me." India looked pleased though as she leapt to her feet and Hannah wondered how long she would be able to keep up this confident façade. More importantly, she wondered how much of it actually was the real her and not just the part of her that was so desperate to impress India.

As they wandered down the road toward the closest pub, Hannah glanced sideways at India. "You know what we never do?" she asked.

"What's that?"

"Talk about you."

"Ahh." India paused. "Well that's not what we're here for though, is it?"

"Says who?" Hannah smiled nervously and looked down at the ground, her hands tucked tightly into her jacket pockets. "Tell me more about Simon," she suggested hopefully.

"What do you want to know?"

"Are you still writing to him?"

"Yes. It's stupid though, hey? None of my letters are ever going to get to him."

"So why don't you actually post them? You know, like a normal person."

India jabbed her in the ribs as they turned right to step off the footpath and head in through a vine-covered archway at the entrance to the Elephant Whistle pub's front beer garden. "Hannah! Are you *mocking* me?"

"Looks that way, doesn't it?" Hannah tried to suppress the flutter of nerves in her stomach. Was she being too confident now?

"I'm liking the new Hannah," India announced as they made their way through the tables and then inside to the bar. "It's nice to see you've got a bit of spark to you, girl."

"Half a bottle of red wine helped," Hannah admitted.

"Agh, don't tell me you're the kind of girl who can only loosen up when she has a few drinks," said India crossly.

"Oh shut up. You drank the other half," Hannah replied, getting into the swing of it now. "What do you want by the way?" she added as the bartender approached them.

"Lemonade. *I*, unlike some people, don't need alcohol to socialize," said India haughtily.

Hannah ordered their drinks—a Bacardi for herself—and then they made their way to a couple of barstools set up along a bench that skirted the wall nearby a pool table.

"So you don't normally drink much?" Hannah asked as they sat down and India picked up a cardboard coaster and began to twirl it between her fingers.

"I try not to. I prefer to always stay in control. Although . . ." she hesitated and Hannah raised her eyebrows as she waited. It wasn't like India to be stuck for words.

"What?" she prompted.

"The other night, when you left the Old Ship, I sort of got

trashed. Like, really drunk. I ended up phoning Simon in the middle of the night."

"Yeah?" Hannah asked, smiling. "How did it go?"

"Bad," said India and Hannah's smile vanished.

"Oh no, I'm sorry. What happened?"

"So it went like this. I was kissing this guy—some random in the back of a nightclub. It was nice and I was definitely thinking about fucking him. And I found myself thinking about Simon, and realizing that . . . well, I was sort of missing him. For some reason I thought if I called him and told him what had happened then it would help me to sort things out in my head. But I don't know what I was expecting him to say really."

Hannah frowned. "Explain it to me again," she said firmly. "Why is it that you can't just *be* with Simon?"

"It's simple, I like to keep moving."

"Does that mean you'll be leaving London soon?"

"Eventually, yes. But not until I sort you out."

"And what if I can't be sorted out?"

"Everything is fixable, Hannah."

"By that logic you should be able to make things right with Simon."

"Touché."

"Right. Let's start with-why you have this need to keep moving. What's that all about?"

"It's just what I do."

"Why?"

"All right, fine. Here's the 'India story.' My parents were junkies. My mum was still shooting up when she was in labor with me. She died just after I was born, and my dad was a drop-kick, took off when he found out my mum died, never even laid eyes on me. But you don't need to feel sorry for me; I was raised by my grandmother in a tiny town in Perth called Gingin. She was a beautiful woman who loved me like nothing else. The day she found out I had cancer, it absolutely broke her heart. I almost didn't even tell her. She was getting so old, and she wasn't well herself; I was afraid the shock would kill her. But in the end it did the opposite. She was so damned determined to get me better. She passed away just days after I gave her the good news that I'd beaten the cancer."

Hannah interrupted to reach a hand out and touch India. "I'm so sorry," she said quietly.

"That's okay. To be honest, it was as though she was waiting, just long enough to make sure I was going to be okay, before she could let go herself. Once she was gone, I had no family, no reason to stay in Perth any longer. But what I did have was money. Turns out my grandmother had been putting aside money for me since the day I came to live with her. She'd made some decent investments as well. She never even told me about it, though—I found out when the lawyer came to see me with her will. At first I wasn't sure what I should do with it, you know, should I be sensible? Invest in real estate? Donate it to charity? But then I realized that I deserved to do something for me. That's when I started traveling. As it turns out, I haven't needed to touch much of the money anyway—traveling on a budget is more fun. But it's nice to know that it's there . . . if I need it."

"Wow, that's one hell of a story," said Hannah. India nodded, as though that was the end of it. But then Hannah spoke. "But it doesn't answer my question. Okay, so you've had some difficult times, and maybe you want to see the world, experience life because you get how precious it is—after everything you've been through. But why does that mean you have to keep moving, and why does that stop you from forming a lasting relationship with someone you're clearly hung up on?"

"Long story. And like I've told you before, you're not the only one with secrets. So unless you'd like to open up about your sordid past, you're gonna want to lay off, girl."

"Fine. Game of pool?"

The conversation returned to lighter topics as India racked up the balls and Hannah chalked a cue and prepared to break. When they started to play, Hannah forgot all about the slight tension that had arisen between them when she had perhaps pushed India a bit too hard in her attempts to figure out exactly what it was that she was hiding from. Instead she relaxed into the game and the comforting sounds of the balls rolling and clinking and the feel of the solid, cool pool cue beneath her hands. Before her parents had divorced and she and her mother had moved into a small apartment, they had lived in a large house with a separate games room off the garage, which housed her father's pride and joy—his billiards table.

When she was small, Hannah had learned to play standing on a small white stool, which she would carry around the table and place wherever she needed to set up her shot. Throughout her life, her billiard skills had often led to guys approaching her in bars and pubs, attempting to pick up the "cute little pool shark." It was funny how certain talents always seemed to turn men on—girls who could surf, girls who could skol a beer or win a game of poker. Although in Hannah's experience, they usually started to get annoyed when they realized that they were never actually going to beat her.

India, however, seemed delighted to discover Hannah's hidden talent. "Awesome," she whispered when a pair of guys headed over to challenge them for the table. "We're going to kick their arses and I probably won't even have to sink a single ball."

It was at the end of the second game that things started to go wrong. At first, India had been enjoying the playful banter between herself and one of the guys—the tall blond one—as Hannah had continued to confidently pocket one ball after another. But then she began to notice a change in his demeanor. He wasn't enjoying losing. And the more irritated he became with the game, the more aggressively he flirted with her.

"Okay," she said lightly as they watched Hannah sink the black yet again. "That's it, we gave you best of three and you still lost. Time to take a hike." She moved pointedly around the other side of the table and Hannah looked up at her, seeming to suddenly become aware of India's tone.

"Or we could just go if you like?" Hannah suggested.

"Best of five," said the tall blond, while his friend shrugged and looked bored. He circled the table and positioned himself in between Hannah and India. "Your friend here can keep carrying the game for you and we can get to know each other a bit better." He stepped in close and placed his hands on her hips. India tried to pull back, but his fingers tightened. "I'm not going to lose with you as well," he whispered in her ear.

India was holding still, trying to decide what the best course of action was going to be—knee him in the balls, maybe?—when she felt another hand close around her arm and she was yanked sideways. Before she realized what was happening, there was a set of soft lips on hers. Her brain took a moment to register. Wait a second, was Hannah *kissing* her? They pulled apart and then Hannah turned away from her to face the ape of a guy who had moments ago had his hands creeping toward India's backside. "Sorry, buddy, but she's not your type," Hannah said firmly. With that, she swung back around, grabbed India by the hand and strode out of the pub.

Outside on their way back through the beer garden India stopped to stare in amazement at Hannah. "What is it?" Hannah asked, turning back to look at her. "Am I a bad kisser?"

India burst out laughing. "Hannah!" she exclaimed. "What the hell was that?"

"I thought you needed help. I couldn't think what else to do. Sorry—should I not have done that?" she asked.

"No, it's fine—you just, took me by surprise, that's all. You realize you've been like a completely different person tonight, right?"

"Well, you were the one who told me to loosen up. Oh, and I know what you're going to say next and the answer is *no*."

"No what?"

"No you haven't just figured out my secret—I'm not gay, so you don't need to help me come out, okay?"

They both dissolved into laughter then and as they made their way down the road, India thought, *I think I just made a new best friend.*

He had been watching the guy for a little over half an hour, just observing—fairly sure he was doing so unnoticed.

Definitely gay, he decided. But in the closet still. Shame. He was cute in an "I'm fit and I fucking know it" kind of way. James knew there was no point trying to chat him up though; the guy would probably run a mile. Man, he wished more guys would just get their shit together and come out already. He was getting sick of being single.

As James watched, the guy pulled an envelope out of his inside jacket pocket and tapped the edge of the table top with it. He seemed to be weighing something up in his mind. Suddenly he gave a derisive snort, shook his head and crumpled the envelope up in his fist. He tossed it onto the table next to his empty coffee mug and stood up, causing his chair to scrape noisily across the tiles as he did. He strode out of the café and James smiled to himself as he noticed the guy's eyes flick toward him on the way past.

Totally gay.

Intrigued about the envelope, James waited until the guy had vanished around the corner and then leapt up from his chair and walked briskly over to his table to snatch up the letter before it could be cleared away by a waitress.

On the front of the envelope were the following three words:

Simon,

The Aella

Huh, maybe he's not in the closet then. Guess I should have given it a go after all. Who's Simon? An ex-lover maybe? And what the hell does The Aella *mean?*

James couldn't help himself. He tore open the envelope to find out what was inside. At the top of the letter he saw the following words: "Dear Simon . . ." He continued to read.

CHAPTER 5

It was Thursday again, Hannah's day off. She was awakened early by the sound of the front door buzzer being pressed insistently, over and over. She sat up in bed feeling bleary and confused. What time was it? What day was it? And who was at the bloody door? She climbed out from under the covers and stumbled over to the intercom with the heels of her hands pressed hard against her eyes.

"Hello?" she said croakily when she pressed the button to respond.

"Hannah!" came back India's unmistakably bright and bubbly voice. "Get dressed and come down, babe. I'll wait out front."

Hannah glanced down at her watch then leaned heavily against the intercom. "India! It's *five* in the morning!"

"Yep. Hurry up."

Hannah pulled away from the speaker and stood still for a moment, staring stupidly at the wall. Last night she and India had been out drinking—again. Although now that she thought about it, India's drinks had pretty much all been of the non-alcoholic variety. Hannah's, on the other hand, had not. The top of her mouth had that furry carpet feel and her stomach was turning as she remembered that her drink of choice last night had been vodka. Ugh, evil, evil vodka.

She took one longing look back at her bed and then dragged herself into the shower, reminding herself to make sure she took a couple of acetaminophen on the way downstairs.

India tried not to laugh when she saw Hannah finally emerge from the apartment block. Her face had a slight tinge of green to it and she was hiding her eyes behind giant, dark sunglasses.

"Did I wake you, sweetie?" she asked in a mock cutesy voice.

"Yes," Hannah replied.

"Told you not to drink so much last night."

"You did not! You were the one doing the ordering."

"Hmm. Good point. Ah well, never mind. It's your day off, let's do something."

"What did you have in mind?"

India shrugged. "I don't know, let's just get on a train and *go* somewhere." *Because you're so close, Hannah, you're so close to opening up.* She grabbed Hannah's arm and pulled her down the last few steps to the footpath. "Come on. Fresh air will do you good."

"Coffee would do me better," India heard Hannah mumble in response, but India started striding down the road in the direction of the tube station, forcing Hannah to follow her.

They ended up traveling down to Brighton Beach for the day. It took over two hours and two trains to get there and Hannah complained most of the way. *The sun's too bright. The train's rocking too much, I'm going to be sick.* India spent the trip entertaining herself by making fun of Hannah. *Nothing better than feeling fit and healthy when someone else is hung over,* she thought, as she waved her sausage roll in front of Hannah's face, making her clap her hands to her mouth.

Although by the time they arrived, India herself was actually starting to feel a little ill. Hmm, maybe she shouldn't have grabbed that sausage roll from the food cart at Blackfriars station when they had changed trains. She didn't admit this to Hannah, though; it was too much fun being all superior about the fact that she had remained sober the previous evening.

They spent the day using India's camera to take artistic photos of the Helter Skelter at the end of the pier, the merry-go-round with the sea in the background and the keen Londoners who were braving the ocean despite the fact that the water temperature was still less than ten degrees. They both agreed that while Brighton was beautiful, it didn't compare to Australian beaches—and India found herself feeling quite loyal toward her old local beaches back home.

India and her grandmother used to spend Christmas every year at the beach. They would pack prawns and salads into a cooler, take fresh buttered bread rolls, one bottle of lemonade and one bottle of champagne, then catch the one and only bus that ran on Christmas Day to the nearest beach. To India, it was the perfect way to spend Christmas—just the two of them, sitting on the picnic blanket that they spread out across the white sand. Usually in the afternoon, her grandmother would take a nap in the shade of a tree while India swam in the ocean. It was why India had been drawn to the beach last Christmas in Ibiza—her first Christmas without her grandmother—but it hadn't been the same.

"Seriously, what's with all the pebbles?" asked India, as they stood on the beach, watching yet another swimmer emerge from the surf with their arms wrapped around themselves, shivering.

"Did you know that there are apparently over six hundred million rocks on this beach?" asked Hannah in response.

"Really? And where did you get this very useful piece of information?"

"Something my dad told me when I was a kid. He'd been on a business trip to England. Must have decided to visit Brighton while he was here, because he brought me back one of those snow globes with a little model of Brighton Pier inside. It's sort of weird looking at the life-size version of it actually. Like I keep expecting to see snowflakes swirling down around it. Anyway, it's just one of those facts that stuck with me."

India watched as Hannah's eyes remained fixed on the pier and she thought for a moment that Hannah was about to cry. But then she brightened and suggested they find somewhere for lunch, and India decided that just for today, she would leave Hannah be.

They stayed in Brighton until late in the afternoon, exploring the town, taking more photos—of the pavilion, of art sculptures, of pretty buildings and of interesting people if they thought they could do it without getting caught. On the train on their way home, India fell asleep with her head resting on Hannah's shoulder and she woke to the sound of Hannah's voice as she gently eased her upright. "Sorry—our stop," Hannah whispered.

"You're much nicer than me," India said as she sat up and stretched. "I would have elbowed me in the ribs after what I did to you this morning."

"Ha. Couldn't do it to you—you looked so peaceful."

They headed out to the platform and India gave Hannah a hug as they said good-bye. "Thanks," she said, "today was fun. Been nice lately, hanging out with you instead of always meeting new people, making new friends every bloody day."

"You should stick in one place more often then," Hannah replied.

"Maybe . . ." said India.

A couple of days later Hannah convinced India to—reluctantly—join her for an early morning jog before her shift at the museum.

"How's things?" Hannah asked as they wound their way along the track.

"Are you joking?" gasped India. "You want to have a *chat* while we're doing this?" Her face was bright red and her chest was heaving. Hannah on the other hand had barely a pink spot on her cheekbones. She would jog lightly in place to keep moving each time India stopped to catch her breath.

"Sorry, I'll slow the pace down a bit . . . better?"

"Oh yeah, that's much better," responded India sarcastically.

Hannah relented and slowed right down to a walk, realizing as she did just how much more you noticed when the world wasn't whipping past in a blur. They were following a runners' track that wound its way through the outer suburbs of London. In a park on their right, a couple were kissing passionately on a picnic blanket. A dog was prancing around them, every now and then dropping a saliva-covered ball by their feet and waiting hopefully before picking it up again and resuming its prancing.

Hannah waited until India's breathing had returned to normal before she tried to restart a conversation.

"What's been happening?" she asked.

"Not a lot."

"Ready to tell me the truth about why you won't be with Simon?"

"Ready to tell me the truth about why you're in London?" India retorted.

"I asked you first."

"Child," said India companionably.

"All right," said Hannah, "I've got something to tell you. Something *real*, as you would say. After you told me all about your parents the other week, it made me want to tell you about mine too."

She paused to take a breath, to find the right words. "My mum's dead too. She killed herself . . . almost four years ago now. I know it's not the same as your circumstances—you didn't even get to meet your mum. I just felt like I should tell you."

India put her arm out to stop Hannah. "Let's sit," she suggested and they stepped off the path and wandered through the grass to a large tree where they both flopped down, Hannah resting against the trunk, India lying flat on her back, eyes on the sky.

"Tell me about her," said India.

"My mum?"

India nodded.

"Which one?" she replied with a dry laugh.

"What do you mean?"

"Sorry, I'm being confusing. It's just that I've always sort of thought of my mum as being two different people. There's the mum I had before my parents divorced, and the one that I had afterward, the one she turned into."

"Ahh."

"For the first fifteen years of my life, Mum was just . . . Mum. You know, your average run-of-the-mill mother. She wore pale blue denim jeans and nice blouses. She kept her hair long but never wore it out. She could be fun, she could get mad, she drove me to netball practice, she forgot to pick me up from swimming once and I remember burning my tongue on the hot chocolate from the vending machine while I waited. There was one time when we went to Dreamworld on a holiday to Queensland. I was eight; I climbed all the way up thirteen flights of stairs to the top of a waterslide, only to be told I wasn't big enough to go down the slide. I had to walk all the way back down those stairs and I was sobbing my heart out the whole way. When I got to the bottom, Mum hugged me and called them fuckers and bought me an ice-cream cone with five scoops and I can remember thinking she was the most amazing mum in the world.

"And then I found out Mum and Dad were getting a divorce and it took me completely by surprise and it seemed like it took Mum by surprise as well. Anyway, from that day when Dad left, she started changing and kept changing. Withdrew from the world I guess. In the early years I kept trying to snap her out of it, to bring her back. But eventually I started to resent her. I missed the old her and I was angry with her for changing. I moved out of home when I was nineteen, shared a house with three complete strangers. I still saw her, but not often; by then she wasn't even leaving home any more.

"Then one day I got the phone call. She had finally left her apartment. For a second I thought it was good news—maybe she was getting better. Maybe she was coming back. But I was wrong. She had walked straight to Milsons Point train station, waited on the platform for the next train and then stepped out in front of it. Ever since that day I can't look at that giant smiling face at the entrance to Luna Park without almost vomiting on the spot."

India reached an arm out and squeezed Hannah's hand. "Horrible," was all she could say.

Afterward Hannah kicked herself for thinking that telling In-

dia about her mum would help her to open up. All she had suc-
ceeded in doing was bringing the focus of the conversation back
to herself—as usual. *Idiot.*

When they parted at the end of the track, India was feeling
slightly sick. She put it down to the exercise taking its toll on her
unfit body—or maybe the awful story of how Hannah had lost
her mum. But she couldn't seem to shake the distinctly yuck feeling, deep in her stomach, as she made her way back to the hostel.
When she arrived there, she headed into the common room and
was disappointed to find it empty and surprised to discover that
she was actually feeling quite lonely. She wasn't used to having
no one to talk to.

Dammit, Hannah, why do you have to work? she thought
crossly. And more importantly, why was she still holding out on
her? Was India relaxing a bit too much into this friendship—
dropping her guard, allowing Hannah to search for India's own
secrets instead of continuing to put the pressure on to find out
what it was that Hannah was hiding? She really ought to put a
stop to this. After all, there would be no point in Hannah finding out the truth about her. As much as she liked to say that
everything was fixable, she knew that she was the exception to
the rule.

As India paced the room, trying to figure out what she should
do, where she should go, who she could talk with, her thoughts
returned—as they always seemed to lately—to Simon. Frustrated,

she headed to her room to find pen and paper. She would write another letter. Surely one would have to get to him eventually, wouldn't it? Sitting cross-legged on her bunk bed, she rested the paper on a phone book for stability, and began to write.

Dear Simon,

All right, so here it is: the truth. I have a secret. A secret that lately has been making me feel edgy. Nervous. And that's not like me. I keep scratching at this one spot on my elbow. It's sort of awkward, like I have to twist my arm around to get at it. And when I scratch it, it's bliss. But then I need more. I feel as though I need to scratch until I've torn my skin into strips. I feel as though I need to keep going until all I'm scratching is bone, until I'm scraping away flecks of my skeleton. You ever feel like that?

And so I'm starting to wonder if maybe it's because the secret is scratching to get out. Like it wants to be told. And the thing is, if I am going to tell my secret, you're the one I want to tell. Isn't that funny? I mean, it's not as though I really know you that well. Intimately, yes. But well? Not so much. Like for instance, I don't know what your favorite movie is. I don't know if you had blond curls as a baby or dark spiky hair. I don't know if you're allergic to anything or if your favorite smell is cut grass or fresh rain or burnt chocolate. (Hopefully it's not the first two, cause they're a little clichéd, don't you think?) I don't know when the last time was that you cried, or the last time you laughed so hard that your stomach hurt, or the last time you stubbed your big toe.

You say that I broke your heart, but I don't know if you truly are in love with me or if you're just in love with the idea of me. Because, Simon, if you think about it, you don't really know me either, do you?

I am going to tell you my secret, though. Not right now, but in the next letter I send. It needs breathing space, this secret. It needs a piece of paper all of its own. It needs its own envelope and its own ink. It needs to be whispered, because it's really quite hard to say out loud. But it's burning a hole in my gut so it does need to be told.

Tomorrow. I'll write this new letter tomorrow. Truth is, I don't even know if I want it to reach you, but I think I have to give it a chance, don't I?

P.S. I'll sleep with whoever I bloody well want. But just by the way, that guy I told you about—I didn't sleep with him.

India folded up the paper with trembling hands. That wasn't what she had been intending on writing. She was just going to write the normal stuff—pen-pal style chitchat. She was going to tell him about Hannah and her theories about what Hannah was hiding. She was going to mention what she ate for breakfast this morning and where she planned on traveling next. But somehow her pen had run away with her hand.

Once the letter was tucked safely inside the envelope, she considered it carefully. She was thinking about Hannah's advice:

Why don't you just post it like a normal person? Maybe she was right—maybe it was time she made sure Simon knew she was thinking of him. Perhaps she could post just this one letter. But the next one—the one where she planned to write her secret—that one was going to have to be left to fate. She unfolded her legs and stood up from her bed. She needed to go and find someone to chat with, someone to keep her company. Later tonight she would head over to Hannah's place—it was time to start pushing her to open up, to tell her the truth. She would post the letter on the way.

Back in her flat that night as she heated up a packet mix of instant macaroni for her dinner, Hannah began to wonder if perhaps *she* was the problem. Maybe India didn't like her enough to share her secret with her. What if she had somehow figured out the truth about Hannah's past? What if she actually *hated* her now? But then, why would she agree to come out running with her today, especially considering she'd previously told Hannah that she was allergic to exercise. She had told her this in a matter-of-fact way, as though she was explaining her allergy to peanuts or shellfish. When Hannah had begun to laugh, India had glared back at her.

The microwave beeped and Hannah pulled out the bowl of pasta. She followed the instructions on the box and added the sachet of powder, stirring it in as she went. She stared at the contents of her bowl for a few seconds; the mixture had turned a glowing, fluorescent orange color.

I absolutely cannot eat that.

She was mere moments away from scraping it into the bin, intending to cook herself a *proper* dinner for a change, maybe a stir-fry, when she caught herself at the last second.

What the hell are you doing? Have you forgotten what you've done? Forgotten what you deserve? Let's hope the pasta's turned that color because it's gone bad. Then maybe you'll get food poisoning. Severe food poisoning. And you'll become critically dehydrated as you heave up the lining of your stomach.

Then maybe you'll end up dead.

Hannah caught her breath. She hadn't had these thoughts for a few days now. Spending all that time with India had begun to change her, had breathed new life into her. She hadn't realized it, but she had stopped hating herself, hadn't thought about dying for the last couple of weeks at least.

She sat down in front of the television and began to shovel the revoltingly gluggy pasta into her mouth. Then she waited. No stomach pains, no nausea. No food poisoning then.

A beeping noise interrupted her thoughts and she glanced over at her phone. A text message, from India maybe? She leaned across, picked up the phone and looked at the number. It wasn't India, it was him. Maybe he would be begging her to come back again. Maybe he would say he'd found a way to fix everything. To make it right again. She opened the message.

I'm done, Hannah. Done. Not going to phone any more, no point. I'll never be able to forgive you for what you've done.

Hannah stared at the words, felt their sting. She was infected—infected with blackness and mud and mold. She was rotting from the inside out and it was contaminating everything she touched. Slowly she put the phone down, got up and walked to the window, then unclasped the latch and tugged at the stiff wooden frame until the window eventually slid upward. She leaned out of the window and looked over the rooftops of London. The sky was a purple and pink swirl of colors as the sun set off in the distance, despite the fact that it was already almost 9:00 P.M. It seemed like a different world up here, a world where she could lose herself, reinvent herself, absolve herself of what she had done. She imagined dancing across the rooftops like Mary Poppins. Imagined vanishing into the spires, the chimney tops, the blackness.

Without thinking, she began to ease herself out of the window. She felt along the outside wall with her hand for something to grip onto as she lifted her knees up onto the sill, then swung her legs out in front, so they dangled out of the window. She leaned forward to look straight down and involuntarily sucked in her breath. Her head snapped back up and the sudden movement sent a wave of dizziness over her. The moment of severe vertigo took her back to another place and she closed her eyes and tried to imagine that she truly was there.

"Liam," she whispered in a sad, small voice.

She was on a roller coaster. It was the clunky, rickety, wooden type they used to have at Luna Park, and she was there with a boy. A boy she didn't particularly like. He was bossy and rude and had made her pay for all the rides because *he* was saving for a new car and seeing as later *she* would be getting driven around in this car, it was only fair. As they sped over the bumpy hills of the track, the boy clasped her hand in his sweaty palm. He looked terrified.

When the ride finished and they climbed out of the carriage, he stumbled away from her and vomited in a nearby plant. Hannah made a face. She had a feeling he would want to kiss her later and she had already had no intention of allowing him to do this—and that was before it looked as though his mouth would taste like regurgitated milkshake. She snuck away and disappeared into the crowds. She didn't care what kind of car he was planning on buying; *she* wasn't planning on being driven around in it. Fingers crossed he would take the hint and not search for her.

As she wandered through Luna Park, she found herself people-watching. It seemed that everyone she looked at had *somebody*. Groups of teenage girls, giggling as they sipped from poorly concealed bottles of premixed Midori and lemonade, arms slung around one another's shoulders in that casual, unself-conscious way that only best friends could effect. Couples holding hands, eating cotton candy, their eyes sickeningly shiny with love, or lust. A trio of young guys, pushing and shoving one another in that affectionate, boyish way.

No one else is here on their own, thought Hannah and she felt like a loser as she wished for the millionth time that she had friends. But she was wrong. Someone else was there on their own. A someone who was walking directly toward her, with a shy smile on his face and deep dimples in his cheeks. With dark brown wavy hair and olive skin; hands tucked firmly into the pockets of his dark jeans and leather boots that kicked a paper cup aside as he stepped right up to her. He was older than her, maybe five years or so, but he dressed as though he were younger. It was as if they were old friends although she had never seen this guy before in her life.

"You should pick that up you know. Recycle it," Hannah said, indicating her head toward the cup he had kicked aside.

"Not mine," he shrugged.

"So." She paused and then said as though she was mentally creating a list, "Doesn't care about the environment. That's a cross already."

"What do I get ticks for then?"

"Dimples, tick. Cool boots, tick. Nice hair without looking like you've tried too hard—for instance I don't see any hair gel in it—tick."

"Sounds like I'm doing okay then."

"Wait a second, I haven't finished. Overly confident, almost cocky, that's a cross. Creed T-shirt, definite cross."

"So I'm at a draw then?"

"Looks like it."

He smiled. "So all I have to do to tip the scales is pick up the paper cup and toss it in the bin, right?"

"I guess."

"And then I'll get to kiss you?"

She shrugged indifferently, but inside she was fizzing. She had always been good at meeting guys—but never like this before. She had never been so forward, so bold—and she had never met anyone who acted like that, either. It was invigorating, skipping all that boring small talk that usually came first. *Hi there, you come here often? You want to get dinner some time, maybe follow it up with breakfast? What's your name, what's your favorite band, favorite color, favorite song, blah, blah, blah, like you really give a shit.* He bent down and picked up the cup. There was a bin just behind her.

He placed his other hand on her waist and stepped in. Up close she saw that his eyes were coffee colored and he held her gaze as he pulled his arm back to throw. As the cup sailed through the air over her shoulder, he moved his hand to her chin, tipped her face up toward his, leaned in close and began to kiss her, first gently, then harder. Sparks exploded in her chest.

So this is what it feels like when you really *kiss a guy.*

When they finally stopped kissing, she turned around to see that the paper cup had bounced off the edge of the bin and landed on its side next to it. They both laughed and didn't stop laughing for several minutes.

This was how Hannah met Liam.

This was how she met her husband to be.

This was how Hannah met the father of her children.

And now she was standing on a window ledge, eight stories up above the streets of London, sobbing uncontrollably as she lifted one foot into the air and loosened her grip on the wall, preparing to step out into the void and make the torture end.

PART TWO

Sydney in the Summer

CHAPTER 6

On the way home from the hospital, Hannah sat in the back seat next to the baby, strapped firmly into its car seat. Sunlight streamed in through the car window; Hannah shaded the baby's face and cried quietly to herself. *A baby.* How could they be driving home with their own baby? What was she going to *do* with a baby? How could she possibly be ready for this?

Three years later, they made the same trip. This time she sat in the front seat and said amicably to her husband, Liam, "Let's stop at the shops, we probably need milk and bread and things like that, don't we?" Their three-year-old daughter sat in her new toddler-sized chair and kicked the back of the driver's side seat. Her dark-brown curls bounced around her heart-shaped face.

"Does Ethan want to eat my crusts?" she asked, holding out a fistful of squished Vegemite-covered pieces of bread.

"No, sweetheart, Ethan is too young to eat bread yet, he's just a tiny baby, see?"

Hannah felt confident, almost smug. *I've done all this before,* she thought to herself. *I know what you do with a baby now. Look at me, stopping at the shops on the way home from the hospital! When we came home with Gracie I didn't even leave the house for two weeks straight. I went into hibernation mode and cried all day long. I'm going to do so much better this time round, I can feel it!*

Liam returned to work within a week of her arriving home from the hospital. She kissed him good-bye at the front door on his first day back at work and wondered whether or not she was going to get the chance to take a shower today. All this week Hannah had done her best to maintain her confident demeanor. She refused to let Liam help out during the night; even when he offered to deal with Gracie's nightmares while she fed Ethan, she ushered him back to bed. "No, no, I'll have to manage it all when you're back at work; you'll be getting up at six, so you'll need a full night's sleep. I can take a nap during the day some time."

Why had she said that? Gracie didn't sleep during the day any more, and they had only put her into preschool one day a week, so regardless of how well Ethan slept, she wasn't going to get a chance to rest. Why was she trying so hard to be this perfect wife, when she should have just accepted his help? Liam was a great guy; he wouldn't care if she told him she was struggling.

She pulled back the blind a little and watched his car reverse out of the driveway. For some reason, despite the fact that there were two tiny children, fast asleep in the bedrooms down the hall, she felt immediately overcome by an overwhelming feeling of loneliness. It was a warm summer day, but the house seemed cold and empty. *Run after him*, she thought. *Run out there and tell him you're not ready for him to go back to work. Tell him you need a couple more weeks. Tell him you're afraid. Tell him you don't think you know how you're going to cope, how anyone copes.*

"Oh don't be silly," she muttered crossly. How ridiculous would she look? Flying out to the car in her nightie.

Five minutes after Liam left, she undressed, ready to hop straight into the shower. Her hand was on the tap when she heard Ethan cry out from his bassinet. She hesitated; if he had only waited a few more seconds, she would have been cocooned in the gushing water, unable to hear his cries, able to enjoy the shower, blissfully unaware that he was awake. Maybe she should just take a quick shower anyway? Pretend she hadn't actually heard him? *Hannah! I can't believe you just thought that. He's a nine-day-old baby; he needs to be picked up when he cries!* She slipped her nightie back on and hurried guiltily down the hall to scoop him up.

By five o'clock that evening, Hannah still hadn't found an opportunity to take a shower. Dishes were piling up in the sink. She hadn't got Gracie out of her pajamas. She hadn't even thought about dinner. Ethan fed every three hours. Each feed took an hour and he wouldn't sleep for more than half an hour in between. The remainder of the time he simply screamed, constantly. Every time she attempted to get Gracie out of her pajamas and into some clothes, she squealed and ran away from her. Hannah couldn't seem to figure out how other mothers did it. And some of them had *more* children than her. To them, two children must seem like a breeze. Bloody hell!

Liam would be home around seven. The next two hours stretched out in front of her, lonely and achingly long. So much for her plan to have everything under control by the time he got home.

A knock at the door shook her out of her thoughts and she panicked as she looked down at herself. Her crumpled nightie had sticky honey stains down the front. Her hair was a frizzy mess. Who on earth was at the door? She sprinted down the hall and pulled off the nightie, throwing a summer dress over her head. Then she tried to smooth her hair a little, before making it back to the front door in time to open it as the visitor knocked again.

An old friend of her mother's stood on the front porch, beaming at her. She wore Dunlop sneakers, neat slacks and a floral patterned blouse. "Hello, love, not a bad time I hope?"

Hannah shook her head. "No, of course not, Rita!"

"Look at you, all dressed and everything! Goodness, when I came home from the hospital with my second, I didn't make it out of my dressing gown for weeks! You must be doing so well! You always were a strong young thing, though, weren't you!" Rita said brightly as she stepped into the house. "Anyway, I won't keep you," she continued. "Just wanted to drop this off for you. Although by the look of you I bet you've already got dinner all sorted, haven't you?" And Rita held out two Tupperware containers. "The big one is chicken cacciatore and the smaller one is a salad to have with it. I thought you could always freeze the chicken and use it another time if you don't need it tonight."

Hannah took the two containers, one still warm from its freshly cooked contents, and felt a wave of relief and a rush of gratitude for her mum's old tennis friend Rita. Her mother had stopped bothering to call Rita or make any effort toward maintaining their friendship when their tennis club had disbanded some fifteen years previously, but Rita didn't seem to mind, still continuing to phone and visit, right up until the day her mother had died. Hannah didn't speak to Rita often these days, but she had kindly looked after Gracie for them on the night that Ethan was born, so it was good to see her again so soon.

Ethan began to cry from down the hall and Hannah tried not to groan out loud. He had been asleep for just twenty minutes this time. Surely the kid was tired by now?! "Oh, let me get out of your way," said Rita immediately, backing hurriedly out of the door. "Don't want to interrupt your schedule. Sounds hungry, poor little mite!" she said with a chuckle.

"You don't need to . . ." began Hannah, a touch of desperation in her voice.

"No, no, I mustn't impose."

Gracie appeared from the hallway and announced happily, "Ethan's crying, Mummy." Hannah cringed at the sight of her still in her pajamas, but Rita exclaimed, "And look at this one, already bathed and ready for bed! My, you are doing well, Hannah! Anne would have been so proud of you. All right, I'll get going, leave you to it."

Hannah barely had the chance to call out a thank-you for the food before Rita had pulled the door shut behind her. "I guess I'll never know what Anne would have thought of how well I'm doing—or not doing as is the case," she muttered to herself, thinking of her mother and how much she was senselessly missing out on by not being a part of their lives any longer.

Right, not the time to think about that just now. Rita had given her a chance to turn this whole day around. Resisting the urge to chase Rita down and ask her to stay and keep her company until Liam came home, she hurried into the kitchen and put down the containers on the bench. Ignoring Ethan's screams for a few minutes, she pulled a casserole dish out of the cupboard and stood considering the food. Would it be weird to pretend that she had been the one to cook this meal? No, of course not. If she had found the time, she might just have cooked this exact dish. And she didn't want Liam to think she wasn't coping. She ignored the feeling of guilt at taking credit for someone else's cooking and instead felt proud of herself. *Look at this, dinner all ready and waiting for him! Oops, forgot about Ethan!* And she rushed out of the kitchen to pick him up and feed him, even though he'd fed just two hours earlier.

When Ethan was finally content and back in his bassinet, she checked the time. *Crap, Liam will be home in forty minutes.* A strange nervous feeling was building in her body from the toes up, like blocks being stacked, one on top of another. Why on earth was she feeling like this? She should be desperate to see him! But instead she was anxious. Dinner was sorted now, but she still didn't have enough done. She sat down on the couch and tried to breathe deeply, tried to calm herself down. *Stop this! You're being silly. You know what Liam would want you to do right now? He'd want you to put your feet up and get some rest. He'd want you to relax and look forward to seeing him. He wouldn't care if the entire house was trashed; he just wants to see you and your two beautiful children.*

But the feeling wouldn't go away. She found herself breathing faster and faster as she looked around at the house. *There's too much*, she thought. *Too much to do. Can't possibly do it all before he gets home.* Her breath quickened further. *Look at the clothes on the couch, they need sorting. I still haven't showered, I haven't brushed my hair. There's all those dishes in the sink, I need to empty the dishwasher so I can pack it.* Her chest heaved up and down. She began to gasp for air. Gracie appeared in front of her. "Mummy, I'm hungry," she said, seemingly unaware of the fact that her mother was hyperventilating on the couch before her.

Hannah tried to slow her breathing. *Calm down, you're being ridiculous!*

"Of course, you need dinner, don't you, sweetheart! You poor thing, it's almost your bed time and I haven't even fed you yet!" she exclaimed between gusty breaths.

As she stood up from the couch she realized her legs and arms felt weak and tingly. *Come on, pull yourself together!*

"No, Mummy, I need lunch first!" She had her dad's mocha-colored eyes and right now they were wide with indignation.

"Lunch?" Hannah asked sharply. "But, but, you've had lunch . . . haven't you?"

"Umm, no, I had breakfast and then . . . now it's lunch time."

"Oh, God! Gracie! I never gave you lunch? Why didn't you tell me?"

"I want a sandwich for my lunch," Gracie replied, oblivious to her mother's panic.

Hannah checked the time again. Twenty minutes until her husband would be home. "Gracie," she said, her voice pleading, "you won't tell your daddy, will you? You won't tell him that we forgot to have lunch? Please, please—it's our secret, right? I promise we won't forget again."

"I want ham on my sandwich," said Gracie.

"Sure, of course, whatever you want." She raced to the kitchen and opened the fridge. She scanned the contents and her heart sank . . . no ham. Fucking brilliant.

"Umm, Gracie, what about this yummy chicken Mummy has in the oven? Why don't you have some of that? It's what Mummy and Daddy are going to be eating tonight. Don't you want to eat the same thing as us?"

"But I wanted ham, I said!" Gracie stood with her hands on her hips. "Ham, ham, ham!" she yelled.

"Gracie, please. No tantrums for Mummy. You can have anything you want for dinner, as long as we've got it. Noodles? Chicken? Avocado on toast? Please, there must be something you want?"

"HAM!"

Ethan began to cry again.

Liam was worried as he pulled into the driveway. Hannah's first day at home on her own with the two kids and he was late. That had *not* been his intention. He had felt a bit unsure when he'd said good-bye to Hannah that morning; her words told him she was fine—but her eyes spoke differently. He was hoping he was just imagining things though. He had picked up takeout Thai on the way home, but he left it sitting on the front seat as he had a box of samples from work to carry inside. Liam had started up his own online boutique beer and wine business over five years ago. He never would have dreamed that it would be doing so well now—a staff of twenty, a couple of trucks, an office in the city. But it did mean long hours, which he felt guilty about.

When he let himself in the front door, his eyes widened in surprise. The place was immaculate, a garlicky smell was emanating from the kitchen, and as he walked through to the eating area off the kitchen, he was greeted by the sight of Hannah, turning from the counter with two steaming plates in hand.

"You cooked!" he exclaimed, mentally congratulating himself

on leaving the Thai food in the car. Obviously he should have called and checked rather than assuming she wouldn't have had a chance to even think about dinner.

"Of course I did," she responded, and he thought her voice sounded a tad edgy. Uh oh, was she annoyed that he was home so late? He changed tack. "You look beautiful," he said, taking in her summer dress and tousled hair.

"Thank you," she replied, placing the plates on the table and running her fingers through her hair self-consciously. She did look good, but she also looked tired. Dark circles ringed her eyes.

Liam was kicking his shoes off, when Hannah said suddenly, "Listen, do you mind if I actually eat my dinner a bit later? I sort of snacked a bit when Gracie ate tea and I'm not that hungry just now."

"Oh. Sure, we don't have to eat right now. Why don't you take a bath or something? Relax. We can both eat later."

"No, no. You eat. What I really feel like doing is taking a walk. It's still so warm outside and I haven't had the chance to get any fresh air today." She paused and then added, "You'll be alright then? Ethan shouldn't need another feed for a little while yet, I'll be back in plenty of time."

"Course, enjoy yourself," Liam replied quickly, watching as Hannah scooped her plate back off the table and placed it in the fridge. She disappeared down the hall to change and Liam shrugged and began to eat. He was getting the feeling there was something she wanted to say—but maybe the walk would help clear her mind. Perhaps she'd be more relaxed with him when she returned.

As she was leaving Liam called out from the table, "Wow, babe, dinner tastes great. What did you put in this sauce?"

"Just some different herbs and things. See you in a bit." And then the door slammed shut. Liam ate quietly, and then eventually migrated to the couch where he turned on the television and flicked through the channels until he found the tennis. He was watching a close match between Federer and Nadal when he heard a high-pitched wail from down the hall.

Ahh, there's my little man, he thought, secretly pleased that Ethan was awake. He'd been asleep when Liam had left this morning, so it felt like it had been forever since he'd held him in his arms.

Ten minutes later though, Liam was beginning to wish that Ethan had waited until his mum was back before waking for his feed. "Come on, mate," he said, as he danced back and forth across the living room, jiggling Ethan up and down in his arms while he continued to scream and scream. "Your mum says you don't need a feed just yet. Come on, settle down, settle down." He watched as Ethan's gummy mouth continued to open and close like a fish; his head kept turning inward toward Liam's chest, searching. "Not going to find any milk there, buddy."

After another fifteen minutes of constant screaming, Liam was now of the mind that Ethan was in fact hungry. *Maybe Hannah had got the time mixed up?* he wondered. He was slowly feeling more and more useless as he failed to placate his tiny son. "Come on, Han," he murmured. "Where are you?"

When he finally heard the key in the lock, he breathed a sigh of relief. "Here she is, mate, mum to the rescue," he whispered to the red-faced bundle in his arms. As Hannah stepped inside, he practically launched their son into her arms. "Thank God you're back," he exclaimed. "Could *not* get him to stop crying. Think he needs to feed," he said in a rush. Hannah stared back at him, seemingly taken by surprise, but then she nodded and turned away, heading down the hall to their bedroom.

Liam hesitated. Should he follow? Keep her company while she fed? Offer to hold him while she took off her sneakers? He probably shouldn't have thrust the baby straight into her arms as soon as she arrived home. But he had been feeling his stress levels increase in time with the pitch of Ethan's cries. He didn't like to feel helpless. He decided to leave her to feed in peace and turned his attention back to the tennis match instead, just in time to see Nadal drop to his knees and punch the air in triumph.

CHAPTER 7

It was 3:00 A.M., and Hannah was having trouble sleeping. "You should always sleep while the baby is sleeping," she chanted quietly to herself as she tossed and turned. As she lay there, her eyes attempting to focus on the darkened ceiling, she thought with interest, *Tonight is the first time that you have ever lied to your husband.* She was referring to the great chicken dinner deception. But then she realized that this wasn't true and the moment didn't seem quite so poignant any more. She had in fact lied to him on the first night that they had had sex. It was eight years previously, their second date, and she had promised herself that she was going to take it slow with this guy. She thought she might actually really like him and so the grown-up thing (because of course she was a grown-up now, at twenty years old) would be to wait, *at least* until the fifth date—that seemed appropriate.

But he had invited her back to his place after the movie and she had agreed, trying to convince herself that she really was going there for a cup of coffee and also attempting not to show how excited she was to be dating an older guy who actually had his *own* place. They had been breathlessly kissing on the couch for an entire thirty minutes and every now and then his hand would creep deliciously along her thigh or down the side of her top, just tracing the rounded edge of her breasts. He had suddenly whispered in her ear, "Shall I grab a condom then?"

And she had frozen, unsure of how to respond. She had been enjoying herself tremendously for the past half an hour. But she had been looking forward to leaving him that night, filled with anticipation for their next date, both of them going to their own beds, flushed with desperate longing for one another and lingering over the perfect ending to a *somewhat* respectable second date.

As she had wondered how to respond without hurting his feelings, a thought struck her. If she said no to his question, would he take that as a no to having sex, or a no to using a condom? Imagine if she had unprotected sex, just because he misinterpreted her response! Feeling flustered and deciding she had no other option, she whispered back a nervous yes.

Later that night, as they lay on his bed, her head resting on his chest with his arm curled around her, he had told her how glad he was that she, like him, hadn't wanted to wait any longer and she had nodded her agreement and kept the secret buried inside. *The first time I had sex with my husband was due to my fear of a misunderstanding.*

Still, that had all worked out in the end, hadn't it? They'd been together now eight years, married for four and had two children together. So what did it matter that she'd slept with him on the second date instead of the fifth? Silly, really.

And she almost laughed at herself as she thought of her twenty-year-old self, lying in that messy bedroom in that apartment in the middle of Leichhardt, earnestly promising herself that *next time*, she would wait. Obviously there hadn't been another next time. The laughter dried up as it touched the air, though, as she thought about how much she had changed since that day. What had happened to that crazy, quirky girl who had sex with boys because she didn't want them to misunderstand what she said and had dinner at a different Italian restaurant almost every second night on Norton Street with her new, older boyfriend?

Why are you even thinking about this stuff? You're happy with Liam. You love him fiercely and you love your new life with your two children even more, right?

Okay, so why doesn't it feel better?

Because you're having the three-day baby blues a bit late, that's all.

And what if it's more than that?

And she forced herself to think about the one thing that had been worrying her since the day she had brought Ethan home from the hospital and everything that had at first seemed so perfect so quickly fell to pieces. Why aren't I feeling anything for Ethan like I did for Gracie when she was born? It wasn't that everything had been easy with Gracie—far from it. She had been terrified at the prospect of looking after a tiny human being—but she had definitely felt this strange sense of instant love for Gracie. And that's what got her through the difficult times, when she was struggling with this new thing called motherhood.

So what's wrong with me this time around?

Sick of lying there next to Liam's solid, sleeping form, thinking these confusing thoughts, she threw back the covers and crept out of bed. Her stomach had that empty, hungry feeling. She never had got around to eating dinner after her walk. *What have I actually eaten today?* she wondered with vague interest as she wandered down the hall to the kitchen.

I'll just grab something to keep me going, she decided, *maybe it will help me sleep?* Searching through the pantry she found a block of fruit and nut chocolate. Then she sat down at the kitchen table in the darkness, and steadily ate her way through the entire block without pausing.

When she finally climbed back into bed, she felt a sick sort of satisfaction; she had never eaten that much chocolate in one sitting in her entire life. Looking across at Liam, fast asleep and snoring lightly, she had a sudden desire to reach across and wrench the pillow out from under his sleeping head. She shuddered—where had *that* come from? Weird reaction to the sugar rush, she decided. And she lay down guiltily and fell asleep, her fingers lightly tracing Liam's arm.

•

"Latte, two sugars—am I right?" The pretty girl smiled shyly at Liam from under a straight-cut blond fringe.

"You got it," he responded cheerfully, not wanting to deflate her by admitting he actually normally ordered cappuccinos.

"How's your day?" she added as she stepped over to the coffee machine to fill his order. Liam glanced up at the clock behind the counter. It was just on 6:30 A.M., not really far enough into the day to comment. He shrugged. "Not bad, if you don't count the fact that I was up before five."

"Totally. I'm like, what am I doing out of bed? Torture. Don't know why we have to be open so early." She hesitated and then added slowly, "Although then we wouldn't be able to get you your early morning fix, would we?" and she gave him a rather cheeky sideways look as she turned to froth the milk.

Ahh, she's flirting with me, Liam realized, and then he wondered just how long that had actually been going on and whether he'd been missing the signals for weeks. Still, he wore a wedding band; he assumed she wasn't expecting any sort of reciprocation—probably just playing for tips.

Liam couldn't help but feel flattered, though, as he headed out of the café and around the corner to his office with the warm paper cup in hand. Nothing wrong with a bit of harmless flirting.

Once he was at his desk, he took a moment to stretch his arms, massage his temples, and then he rolled his chair forward and began clicking through his emails. Busy day today; he might have to head back down for another coffee in a couple of hours.

•

Hannah was having trouble figuring out how she could leave the house. She couldn't go out if Ethan was due for a feed, because the prospect of trying to breastfeed him in public seemed too daunting. It took forever to get him to latch on and when he finally did, she usually had to keep her arms in an awkward position, one elbow stuck out to the side and her hand clutching her breast, shaping the nipple for him. If she let go and tried to cradle him—and give herself a bit of privacy by placing her arm all the way around his body—then he just seemed to slide off. She also couldn't go out if he was due for a sleep—she was determined to get him into a routine and she didn't want to mess it up. That left a very small window to leave the house.

And then there were all the things she would need to do to get herself out. Pack the diaper bag. Snacks and a drink bottle for Gracie. Spare change of clothes in case Gracie wet her pants—oh toilet training was such fun. Get Gracie dressed. Get Ethan dressed. Get herself dressed: shower, brush hair, brush teeth. *Nope. Impossible task.*

Looking out the lounge room window at the cars rushing past, Hannah began to feel a claustrophobic constriction in her chest. *Trapped. I'm completely trapped in here.*

But no, that wasn't true. Gracie had to go to preschool tomorrow. So regardless of how hard it seemed, she was going to have to get herself out of the house. *That's a good thing*, she reminded herself as she sat down cross-legged at the coffee table to help Gracie open the lid on the play-dough container.

Thirty minutes later Hannah noticed there was something strange about the way she was behaving. She was feeling robotic, unnatural, as she tried to interact with Gracie. She tried to think back to what she was like before she had headed off to the hospital to give birth to Ethan. She was sure she used to be able to play naturally enough with Gracie. But right now she was feeling self-conscious, acutely aware of how her voice sounded, of how her back was stiff and straight as she molded shapes out of the dough. "Well done, Gracie, what a clever shape you have created," she found herself saying in an overly formal tone. She was aware of how odd she sounded, but she couldn't seem to shake it from her shoulders.

She switched on *Sesame Street* and stood up to leave Gracie to it. Maybe a ten-minute break, perhaps taking a look at Facebook on her laptop, might help her to feel reconnected to the world. As she scanned through her news feed, though, she slowly began to feel grossly inadequate. There was Josie, a girl she had worked with a few years back, who had three children now and was posting gorgeous pictures of her children along with adoring captions. There was Tiana, an old university friend, posting a gushing status update about how her little boy Jordan had just given her his first toothless smile. Not only that, but so many other mums seemed to be actually *doing* things with their children. They were at the park, feeding the ducks; they were out at coffee shops, playgrounds, Wiggles concerts. They checked themselves into all of these exciting locations along with bright, smiling photographs of themselves and their children. How did they do all of that?

She stared at the computer screen, feeling insecure, incompetent as a mother. And then without really meaning to, her hand moved to the mouse and she slid it over the Create-Post button. She hesitated, and then she clicked and began to type:

Hanging out at Taronga Zoo with my two gorgeous kids, Gracie is in seventh heaven!

This was insane, why was she even considering posting this? But her body seemed to be moving without her approval. She clicked the Submit button and then leaned back in her chair.

Well, that was an odd thing to do.

Liam had a ten-minute break between client meetings. He slid a frozen instant meal into the microwave and then stood back to wait as it rotated slowly. He pulled his iPhone out of his pocket to check out Facebook while he waited. Skimming the posts, one from Hannah caught his eye. "Out at the zoo?" he exclaimed. They had never taken Gracie to the zoo before; he kind of thought that was something they would do together for the first time.

Ah well, at least she's getting out, having fun. That'll be good for her.

Still, he was surprised that she hadn't mentioned her plans to him that morning.

The rest of his day was packed. Staff meeting including cake for someone's birthday. A visit to the warehouse. Going through the finances with their external accountant. It was after five by the time Liam thought he could really do with another coffee. He still had more work to do, approvals of some new marketing emails and revising last quarter's sales figures.

He headed for the door and then paused to call out to his sales manager who was working late tonight too. "You need a coffee, Mick?"

"You going downstairs, mate?" Mick called back.

"Yeah, just quickly."

"What's wrong with the new coffee machine Laurie ordered in?"

"What's with the fucking inquisition? You want a coffee or not?"

"Nah I'm good." Mick turned back to his computer, nonplussed by his boss's outburst.

Liam walked briskly around the corner to the coffee shop. When he stepped inside his eyes briefly swept across the counter. It was staffed by two young guys; the blond girl must have finished her shift already. He was surprised to note a slight feeling of disappointment that she wasn't there. But he shook it off—obviously he was just looking for a friendly face.

It was Friday afternoon and Hannah had run late to pick Gracie up from preschool. The teacher had been unimpressed to say the least, and Hannah had the feeling she hadn't bought her made-up excuse that she was late due to a doctor's appointment for Ethan that had run over time. As Hannah negotiated her way back home through the peak-hour traffic, she thought back to their life before they had had Ethan. They used to live in Liam's tiny apartment in Leichhardt together. It was a tight squeeze when Gracie was born, but it was cozy and it worked. Liam made it home from the city each night within twenty-five minutes. When Gracie was a cute, gurgling baby, Hannah would take her for walks in her stroller to Norton Street. She made friends with a sweet old Turkish woman who ran a coffee shop there and the woman would scoop Gracie out of the stroller if she cried and walk her around the café singing lullabies while Hannah finished her cappuccino. They had dinner out at one of the many restaurants there almost every weekend and got to know most of the wait staff. Hannah had felt at home on that street.

And then they found out she was pregnant. Liam was ecstatic—he had been trying to convince Hannah that it was time to start trying for a second baby for months. Hannah had been more apprehensive; she had only just returned to work, two days a week as an assistant at a small but friendly law firm in Rozelle— nice and close to their apartment. She had been enjoying using her brain again, didn't want to have to quit so soon.

Liam immediately began talking about moving. It would make more sense to move further out west, he suggested, where they could afford a bigger place, with a backyard for the kids. Sure, his travel time would triple—but he didn't mind; they simply couldn't fit in that apartment as a family of four. Hannah hadn't been prepared for how different her life would become. The house was lovely: spacious and bright. But she felt cut off from the world. The nearest shops were just a grocery store and a milk bar; no coffee shops with sweet old ladies to chat to. No restaurants to walk to on a summer's night. She felt as though she'd left her family behind in Leichhardt and Liam left for work in the morning at the crack of dawn and returned home each night after seven—if not later. Although she was used to his late arrival home now, she needed that extra time to get the house under control, to show him that she was coping—even if she knew deep down that something really wrong was going on with her . . .

"Mummy, Mummy, Mummy, MUMMY!!"

Gracie's voice cut through Hannah's reminiscing and she almost jumped in her seat. How long had Gracie been yelling at her? She glanced up into the rearview mirror. "Yes, honey?"

"Look what I can do with my arms."

"Um, I'm sorry, Gracie, I can't really look at the moment. Mummy has to concentrate on the road."

"Yes but look, I can stretch them right up like this. When we're in the car and I'm all strapped in I can't do that. I can't reach that far. But look how far I can go now. I can touch up to the roof and the sky."

"Hang on, what do you mean, *when* you're strapped in. You're strapped in now . . . aren't you?" Hannah felt her stomach sway. Had she forgotten to do up Gracie's seat belt? She tried to twist around to take a look.

"No. Not today. Today my arms are free and I can *dance* in the car!"

"SHIT!" Hannah hit the indicator and pulled over to the side of the road. Once they were safely stopped, she sat still for a minute, breathing fast. She couldn't believe she had forgotten to do up the buckles on Gracie's car seat. What had she been thinking?

While Hannah did up the straps, Gracie said happily, "You said we could stop at the shops today."

"Did I?" Hannah asked distractedly. Her mind was on Gracie's small figure; she was imagining her tiny body being tossed around the car like a rag doll. *Oh God, imagine if we'd had an accident.* "Umm, I don't remember that. Grace, we're already past the shops, baby; maybe we could go tomorrow instead? It's really very late, in fact it's already your dinner time."

Gracie's tantrum lasted all the way home. But Hannah wasn't listening. She was thinking about what might have been. She hadn't had a car accident for a long time now. In fact, she'd only had one in her entire life. It was when she was still learning to drive. She had run into the back of another car at a traffic light. She had been checking her blind spot to change lanes. The owner of the car she had hit had been freakishly nice about it. She wouldn't even take Hannah's details, explaining that her car was so old and dented that another scratch didn't really matter. Hannah remembered thinking at the time that this was about karma. That she was going to have to make sure she did the same for someone else one day. Although she sort of didn't want to; after all, her car was quite nice, and wasn't it pretty expensive to get a dent in your car repaired, even if it did seem small?

But that was beside the point. The point was—she must be due for another car crash by now. That was how these things worked. The longer you went without having an accident, the closer you

came to having one. She must have been right on the verge of
one. And here she was, forgetting to strap in her three-year-old.
The thought of that delicate body flying up and hitting the roof of
the car, or being crushed by torn metal, made bile creep up her
esophagus.

CHAPTER 8

～～～～～

L iam opened his eyes slowly and lay still, enjoying the fact
that it was Saturday morning. That it was eight o'clock instead of five. He rolled over and reached out his hand to
stroke Hannah's arm suggestively.

"You know we can't have sex yet, right?" Hannah's voice
sounded hard and she remained facing the opposite wall.

"I know," Liam said quickly. "I was just . . . trying to be affectionate."

He paused before asking, "What do you want to do today?"

Hannah's shoulder shrugged under his touch.

"Hey, you know what I've been thinking? What if I invite my
parents to come up and stay for a few days? They're desperate to
meet Ethan and see Gracie again. And then maybe, while they're

here, they could look after the kids one night while we have dinner out or something?"

"Sure, sounds good." Hannah still hadn't turned to face him.

"Han," he said slowly, "is everything okay? Are you annoyed with me or something?"

"Just tired," came back the clipped voice.

Ethan began to cry from the other room then. "I'll get him for you," Liam began, but Hannah had already thrown back the covers and sat up. "It's okay," she said as she stood and left the room.

Liam lay back on the pillow and frowned. She seemed to be coping really well with the new baby—so why was she in such a bad mood?

Hannah sat in the darkness of the living room, the television quietly flickering at her as she gave Ethan his 3:00 A.M. feed. She was mentally going over everything that needed to be done before her parents-in-law arrived. When Liam had suggested that his parents should come and stay for a few days, her reaction had been mixed. She adored Liam's parents: Trish was like a cuddly koala bear, while his dad, Nick, was the typical Maltese father-in-law, always telling Hannah she was too thin, offering them more food, more money, a house! But as much as Hannah loved them, the thought of having them come to stay—of having them see what her day-to-day life with the children was like—was terrifying. Surely Trish, the archetypal, perfect mother, would see right through Hannah's charade, would instantly discover that she was a fraud as a mother. Perhaps she would want to whisk the children away at once?

As she chanted her way through her list of things to do, she noticed that her breathing was beginning to quicken again.

Make up spare bedroom.

Vacuum . . . everywhere.

Tidy the garden. Must get Liam to mow the lawn as well.

Grocery shopping, pantry is looking really bare at the moment. Get some of those wafer biscuits that Nick loves.

Her hands were becoming sweaty; she shifted them and tried to wipe them dry on Ethan's wrap. The movement disturbed him and he stopped sucking for a moment, his dark eyes darting up to look at her. She froze. *Please don't come off, Ethan, let's just get this feed done so I can get back to bed.* He returned to sucking.

Change Ethan's crib sheets . . . haven't changed them since he moved to the crib from the bassinet and that's been a few weeks now. Can't have Trish thinking I put the baby to bed on dirty sheets.

Laundry! Oh my goodness there is so much laundry to do. I've got to make sure I catch up on that before they get here.

Hang on, do we have enough pillows for all of us? Right. Check pillows—add that to the list.

Her breathing increased again. *There's too much,* she thought. *Far too much to do.* She kept discovering new things that needed to be done and each time a new task was added to the list, she was sure something else was slipping off at the other end. Her world was tilting dangerously sideways. The tips of her fingers tingled.

She didn't notice that she had started to shake until Ethan un-latched himself, opened his mouth and began to wail.

Please don't cry so loudly, baby.

She lifted him up and over her shoulder, rubbing his back, try-ing her best to calm him down. Eventually the sobbing subsided and she returned him to her lap. *Have you fed enough? Can we go back to bed yet? Which side did you start on, have we done both sides or just one? Dammit!* Why was it so hard for her brain to keep track of these simple things? Her chest began to feel tight and her breath started to quicken yet again. Meanwhile Ethan had closed his eyes and was beginning to breathe deeply. *You must be finished then,* she decided. And she crept down the hall to place him back in his crib. Once he was wrapped up she padded back to the kitchen, still feeling as though the air in the house seemed to be in short supply. Why couldn't she fill her lungs properly? Why was the kitchen off balance? She tried to steady her eyes on the smoothness of the kitchen counter, but it wouldn't work. Shouldn't that bowl of fruit be sliding down the slippery slope and onto the floor right now? Apples bouncing and rolling, banana peel split-ting. Shouldn't the fridge be crushing her right now? How is it still standing at that tremendous angle?

She snatched up a piece of paper and a pen and began to write down everything that needed to be completed over the next few days. Seeing each new item, right there in black ink, unable to fade away from her memory, soothed her. Her breathing slowed and the tightness in her chest slowly unraveled and vanished. The kitchen began to right itself and the fridge stopped looming over her, settling back on its haunches, no longer a predatory creature. *I can do this. As long as it's all written down, I can get it done.* Her list completed, she headed to the pantry, moved boxes of breakfast cereals aside and reached to the back for her new supply of chocolate. She was ravenous; she supposed she had forgotten to really eat anything that day again. She stood at the cupboard and methodically ate her way through two Mars bars and a king-size Twirl. Toward the end she started to feel sick, but she kept eating anyway, a strange feeling of pleasurable defiance creeping over her as she did.

A few days later, Hannah was running her eyes over her to-do list, making sure everything was set for when Liam arrived home from the airport with his parents in tow. Her eyes caught sight of the one item she hadn't yet crossed off: change Ethan's crib sheets. For some inane reason it had been so important to her to get everything on that list done before they arrived. And really, how hard was it to change a set of crib sheets, for goodness' sake? Why hadn't she just found a spare moment to do it? What was wrong with her? Ethan was on the rug in the living room just last night, having some tummy time—that would have been the perfect opportunity to have got it done. But what was she doing? She was sitting on the couch, just *watching* him. God, she was so lazy. Lazy and empty in fact. Because the reason she had been sitting there watching him was because she had been waiting for some kind of emotion to hit. Some remote feeling of affection for the cute little baby that was wriggling around on the floor at her feet, examining his own fingers as though they were amazing little creatures on the ends of his hands. She had sat there and watched him and become acutely aware of the fact that she was dead inside. That her limbs were logs of rotting wood. That her torso was a hollow trunk. And she had accepted this fact and simply shrugged. *Oh well, I have no soul. Wonder what I should cook for dinner tonight.* The realization was kind of a relief really. Now she could stop trying to figure out why she wasn't gushing over her adorable new baby. She could just get on with things instead.

The visit from Trish and Nick ended up being, for the most part, fairly uneventful. Hannah simply played the part of the loving mother. She was a machine. She cooked, she cleaned, she fed her baby, she played with Gracie, she rocked Ethan in her arms and pretended to look down at him with dewy, loving eyes—but behind her eyes was that empty, dark space.

The one day that her world threatened to become unstuck, when she almost dropped her cool, calm and together façade was when Trish offered to take care of the kids while Hannah took a walk to the store around the corner to pick up a few things. The problem came when she arrived back home. As she was putting away the few groceries in the kitchen, she was listening to Trish chatting away about what they'd been doing while she was gone.

"... and we played with Ethan together, didn't we, Gracie? We did round and round the garden and watched him gurgle and grin at us. And then Ethan was starting to seem tired so he went down for a nap and Gracie and I have been doing some finger painting, haven't we, sweetheart?"

Hannah was smiling politely as she listened to the blow-by-blow description of each thing her mother-in-law and children had done while she had been gone for all of twenty minutes and thinking to herself, *That's great, Trish, but I don't really care. I know you think that I do. Because most mums do care. Most mummies want to know everything their gorgeous little monkeys have been up to for every second of the day that they're out of their sight. But nope, not me. You could be telling me you took them out the back for a toke on a joint or up the road to the pub for a drink and a game on the slot machines, but I'd still smile and nod because I'm not really listening because I don't really care.* She was just about to start reprimanding herself for thinking such awful things when something that Trish said made her pay attention.

". . . Oh and I changed Ethan's crib sheets for you. I noticed there were a couple of little sickie stains on them and I thought you might like some fresh sheets in there for him. I popped the old ones in the machine with a few other things I could find. You don't mind, do you?"

Hannah's skin began to tingle unpleasantly. How had this woman come into her home and managed to do that one simple task? That one thing that she had been failing to do for the last couple of weeks—when she had been left alone for just twenty minutes?

Why are you reacting like this? she thought crossly. *Why does it matter that Trish was the one to do it? You wanted it done, and now it's done.* But she couldn't seem to make herself see clearly. Instead her thoughts were curdling and her hands were starting to tremble. An odd sort of feeling was rising up in her chest. She seemed to be swinging between two fierce desires. On the one hand she wanted to throw herself into Trish's arms, to thank her for doing that one thing that had been hanging over her head, to cry against her chest and let her be the mother that she no longer had. But on the other hand she felt ready to fly into a rage. She wanted to scream at Trish for interfering. She wanted to yell at her, "*I* was going to get that done. You didn't *need* to do it. You shouldn't have taken that one thing away from me. Now I'll never be able to prove to myself that I could have got it done. I'll never be able to prove that I'm not a failure!" But deep down underneath it all, a voice was saying quietly, "But you are a failure. And you already know it. Those thoughts you were having earlier prove that. You don't even seem to love your children any more. Either of them." And then suddenly a thought struck her, with complete clarity: *You don't even* want *those children any more.*

"Are you all right, dear? You look a bit pale." Trish's voice brought Hannah hurtling back to reality. Her whole body was shaking. She turned to look at Trish, pasted a smile on her face and said quickly, "Actually, I forgot one thing at the shops. Butter! Would you believe it? That was the thing I went out for in the first place, wasn't it? Do you mind? I'll just . . ." And without waiting for a response she rushed back out through the living room, ignoring the look of concern on Trish's face and slamming the front door behind her. Then she began to run up the street.

Nick pressed his Visa into Liam's hand. "Here you go, dinner's on us," he said, winking at the two of them.

"You don't need to do that—" began Liam; it was enough that they were babysitting so that he and Hannah could get some time to themselves.

"Ah, let your father treat you," said Trish, rocking Ethan in her arms, her eyes glinting. "We like to do something nice once in a while for you both."

"The pin is your mother's birth year," Nick added. They were ushered out the door then and they walked to the car in the driveway in silence.

Liam automatically hopped in the driver's side and Hannah circled around the car to climb into the passenger seat.

As they reversed out of the driveway, Liam gave a loud groan of contentment and Hannah looked over, startled. "What?" she asked.

"What do you mean what? We're free! Just the two of us for the night! Doesn't it feel great?"

"Oh," said Hannah. "Right, sorry, I thought you'd hurt yourself or something."

Liam glanced sideways at her as he negotiated out onto the road and then swung the car around and headed up the street. "You're worried about him, aren't you?" he asked. "Don't stress, babe, he'll be no trouble for Mum. You have to leave him for the first time eventually!" and he reached across to pat her thigh. Hannah looked out the window.

"I know," she replied. "Just hoping he'll eat okay for them," she said, "and that they'll be able to put him down to bed without too much hassle." But her voice sounded monotone as she spoke.

"Try not to think about it. We can call during dinner if you want, check up on him?" Liam tried.

"Yeah, sure."

They drove in silence then, and Liam tried to remember what the two of them usually talked about when they spent time together on their own. Why did he feel so nervous? As if it were a first date and he was keen to impress.

Why can't I seem to get through to you at the moment, Han?

They picked a busy Greek restaurant on Terminus Street and were given a table in a corner. Hannah was relieved to find the place buzzing with noise and movement. Maybe she could be swallowed up in all that buzz. Maybe she could find her personality hidden among it. Or maybe she could stay quiet and Liam wouldn't notice because everything else would fill the silence for her. Maybe she could sink into her chair and disappear and Liam could replace her with that waitress over there, the one with the long, dark, spiral curls and the olive skin and the unreasonably large breasts. She looked like the motherly type. As Hannah disintegrated into her chair, the waitress could seamlessly take her place. As she leaned forward, pouring the wine for Liam, she could carefully ease herself into Hannah's seat. *Watch out! I'm not completely dissolved yet; you're sitting on my head!* And then Liam would play with her cute, bouncy curls and he would be in awe of her massive chest and she would be entranced by his big brown eyes and he would take her home and Trish and Nick would say, "Nice time, love?" and he would say, "Fantastic! I found a new wife and mother for my children!" And Trish would beam as she gave her new daughter-in-law a welcoming hug and she would whisper, her voice a little watery, "Oh good choice, son! That Hannah was like a corpse on a trolley!" and Nick would say, "Great rack!" and they would all laugh together and Gracie would come running from her bedroom to throw herself into her new mummy's arms.

"Hannah. Hannah! *Hannah!*"

Hannah's eyes fluttered and she looked up in surprise. Jeez, she had been completely lost in that one. *Concentrate, Hannah. Participate in the world!*

"Sorry, yes?" she asked. She had no idea what he might have been trying to talk with her about.

"What do you want?" he asked.

She peered back at him in confusion. *What do I want? What do I want? Oh God, Liam, how do I even begin?*

"What do you want to drink?" he repeated—and he indicated the waitress who was standing by their table. Towering over it, in fact. God, she was ridiculously tall. And up close her breasts were like small mountains, shooting out from her chest and hovering over them. Hannah realized she was staring and quickly lifted her eyes to fix them on the waitress's face instead. The waitress raised her eyebrows as she waited.

"Oh right. Yes, um. Glass of wine," she said quickly.

"Any particular type or would you like me to guess?" the waitress responded as Liam said simultaneously, "Are you drinking tonight? I just ordered a beer—sorry, I assumed you'd be driving because you'll need to feed again when we get home."

Hannah felt flustered as she looked back and forth between the waitress and her husband. "Right, of course," she said. "Ah, I'll just have a lemonade?" and her voice faltered as the waitress rolled her eyes and scribbled on her notepad.

As she turned swiftly and left the table, Liam said hurriedly, "Sorry, you didn't need to change your order. I wasn't saying you shouldn't drink; I mean, you can have a glass of wine, can't you? When will he be due to feed again?"

"No, no, it's fine. Best if I don't, just in case he won't take the expressed milk for your parents. I wasn't thinking, that's all."

Through dinner, they talked about Liam's work, about Gracie's tantrums, about how nice it was to have Trish and Nick staying with them, about the weather, about the entrées—Liam's was nice but a little salty, Hannah's was better, maybe not enough sauce though—about whether or not they should have dessert. Should we be getting back, or do you think everything is fine? Should we have one each or choose something to share? They discussed the floods up in Queensland and Hannah pretended to know what Liam was talking about—she hadn't watched or listened to the news in weeks, she hadn't known that not only had there been floods, but inland tsunamis. She almost asked Liam how he knew about the floods, but at the last second, she caught herself as she remembered, *Oh right, you live out in the real world, don't you? You have discussions with other people, give your opinion, chat, laugh.* Mostly, Hannah kept her shoulders stiff and her smile fixed as she fraudulently joined in on their conversation. But at one point, she forgot that she was a cardboard cutout and she fell into her feelings. It was when Liam told her a story about one particular drowning victim in the floods. An elderly woman and her husband had been clinging to a tree as a swollen river rushed around them. An emergency rescuer had waded out to rescue them, but could take only one at a time. The woman's husband insisted that his wife be taken first. He promised her he'd be right behind her. But just after the woman was taken to safety, a new surge of floodwaters had rushed through and her husband had been washed away. They found his body a few kilometers up the river.

As Hannah heard the story, and pictured that elderly man, chivalrously putting his wife's life before his, she remembered something. *I am part of an entire world. There are other people with much greater problems than me—whole towns being swept away—and more importantly, sweet old men who sacrifice themselves for the love of their life. Pull yourself together, Hannah. Remember who you are.* And she cried for that man and for his family and for the wife who maybe wished she had been swept away with him.

Liam reached across the table to squeeze her hand and said, "Sorry, Han, I shouldn't have told you that story. This is meant to be a happy night."

And Hannah wanted to scream, *Why shouldn't we talk about him? Why shouldn't we cry for him and his family? Why should we have a blissful night out when his wife will never be able to feel joy again?* But instead she nodded and shrugged and rubbed at her eyes and told him not to worry. And soon she was torn cardboard and dead wood and sterile plastic again.

When the bill came, Liam had to admit that he couldn't remember what year his mother was born. *1959*, thought Hannah immediately. But for some reason she didn't tell him that she knew and she pretended to join in on Liam's jovial banter as he tried to work it out. Finally, he settled on paying for the dinner themselves seeing as he actually earned more than his parents did. Hannah agreed, and when they stood up to leave, Liam looped his fingers through hers and she tried to feel relaxed and comfortable with her hand in his, but instead it felt clunky and their bodies seemed to be out of sync and her skin felt sweaty and Liam's hand felt too cold, like a dead fish in her palm. She thought again about that elderly couple, clinging to that tree, and Liam's hand turned to rough bark and she squeezed it, suddenly and involuntarily.

CHAPTER 9

H e hadn't intended on having a drink with her. In fact, tonight, for once he was going to get home on time. But as he had headed out of the office, he'd bumped straight into her—quite literally.

"Hey, latte-boy!" she said with a smile as they stepped back from one another.

"Coffee-shop-girl," he responded cheerfully. There was an awkward moment as they both stood staring at one another. "Ahh, finished your shift for the day?" Liam asked.

"Yep. Actually, I was thinking of stopping in at Chance Bar for a drink. Why don't you have one with me? My treat."

"Oh," said Liam, caught off guard. "Well I was just about to . . ."

But she interrupted him. "Come on, one drink," she coaxed and then she started walking and Liam felt as though he had no choice but to fall into step beside her. "Okay," he said, "I guess one quick drink." And he thought as they headed down the street, *Who says you can't have a friendly drink with a member of the opposite sex? Completely harmless.*

Somehow one drink turned into two. And two drinks turned into three, and somewhere along the line, Liam began to realize that Paige (that was coffee-shop-girl's actual name) wasn't just flirting harmlessly with him, she was hitting on him. He had to put a stop to this. They were sitting opposite one another in a cozy booth. It was only a Tuesday night, but the bar was packed nonetheless.

"Hey, Paige," he said, trying to figure out how best to word this. "You know that I'm married, right?" he asked, twisting the wedding band nervously around his ring finger.

"So?" she replied.

"Well it's just that—I mean maybe I'm misinterpreting here— but I thought maybe you were expecting . . ." he drifted off, embarrassed. Maybe he *did* have the wrong idea?

But then her foot was against his leg under the table and she leaned forward to whisper suggestively, "I really don't care . . ."

On the same day that Liam was having a drink with a pretty girl named Paige, Hannah was in the car, driving. It had been a horrendous day, with Gracie throwing tantrum after tantrum and

Ethan refusing to sleep; finally Hannah had strapped both kids into the car and started driving. She had no idea where she was going, but it seemed to be the only way to settle Ethan and even Gracie cheered up when she realized they were going out. After an hour, both children had fallen asleep and Hannah continued to drive. Another thirty minutes later, she realized her legs were beginning to feel stiff and she started peering at road signs, trying to figure out where exactly they were. A couple more turns and she saw a sliver of blue in front of her. Instantly she was struck by the sensation of a memory, a feeling of anticipation and excitement. Almost immediately she figured out why. It was because when she was small, and her parents drove her up the coast for a holiday at the beach (long before they split up), there was always a competition to be the first one to spot the ocean. They would be winding through the hairpin turns, and Hannah would be peering out of the window, scanning the view through the gaps in the bush, and usually they would round one particular corner, right at the top of the hill above Gosford, and there it would be, way off in the distance, and if the sun hit it right, it would look like diamonds on the horizon and you had to be the first to shout out those five magic words.

I can see the water!

Hannah had to restrain herself from calling out in triumph. She pulled up by the beach, hopped out of the car and checked a sign. Brighton-Le-Sands. She had no idea how they had ended up here, but she gently woke Gracie, popped Ethan in the stroller and they walked down to a nearby fish and chip shop to buy some dinner. They spent the late afternoon and early evening on the beach. It had been a hot day, so she stripped Gracie down to her underpants and tank top and she ran around at the water's edge, splashing and laughing. Ethan sat unsteadily on the sand, his back propped up against Hannah's legs and his face set with concentration and wonder as he attempted to control the movements of his hands as his fingers ran through the soft, cool sand.

Later, when they had finished eating, she watched as thick, dark purple clouds spread across the sky. A wind whipped up around them and she gathered their things and raced back to the car with the kids as fat drops of rain began to fall. They sat in the car and watched the storm rage around them, Ethan on her lap and Gracie kneeling in the front passenger seat, her hands and nose pressed against the window. Whenever the thunder clapped, the three of them would huddle together, and for those ten minutes until the storm passed over, Hannah thought, *Oh, this is what it's supposed to feel like.* But then they were driving back home and the kids started to get whiny because they had been in the car for too long and the thought of everything that was waiting for her at home—cleaning, washing, putting the kids to bed—made her feel stressed and sick and she wished they could have stayed by that beach forever.

She didn't tell Liam about their impromptu trip down to one of Sydney's southern beaches. For some reason it felt as though she needed to keep it to herself; it felt like a magical time that she had shared with her children and if she tried to explain it, it might break the spell. She wondered if they could do that every day.

•

Liam was feeling tense. Tense and stressed and guilty and confused. Nothing had happened with Paige. He had extracted his
legs from her wandering foot under the table, paid the bar tab and
left. He had to leave his car in the office car park because he had
had way more drinks then he intended. The long train trip home
was suitably sobering, though.

You haven't done anything wrong, he kept reminding himself.
It was just a few drinks with a friendly person . . . a very friendly
person.

And anyway, could he be blamed for wanting some company from someone who actually wanted to talk with him? Who
wanted to touch him? Lately he felt like he was constantly trying
to keep up with Hannah. A couple of times he'd called on the way
home from work offering to pick up takeout for dinner. Hannah
always refused, assuring him she had dinner under control. The
other day he had gone to iron his work shirts only to find the
washing basket empty and all the shirts hanging in his wardrobe.
"You don't need to iron my shirts for me, babe, you have enough
on your plate," he'd tried to protest. "I don't mind," she'd replied in
a martyred tone that seemed to say the exact opposite.

Walking home from the station, he tried to think of what he
would say to explain the fact that he was arriving home so late—
and probably smelling like spirits. As it turned out though, he
needn't have worried. When he walked in the front door, Hannah
looked up from the couch. "Dinner's in the oven," she said. "I'm
off to bed."

"Han, I'm so sorry I'm late," he began.

"Don't be," she cut in, "I know you have to work long hours." And then she disappeared down the hall and Liam found himself wishing that she *had* smelled the alcohol on his breath, because maybe then they would have had a real conversation.

On Thursday night, Hannah was feeling a bit out of control. She had fallen behind on the housework today. She didn't have dinner sorted out yet. She looked up at the clock. *Shit, Liam's due home soon and I haven't tidied the kitchen yet and I still need to get the kids bathed and in bed.* She started the bath running (they couldn't possibly skip a bath tonight, she'd skipped it the night before) and rushed to check that Gracie had finished her dinner. She was sitting in front of her barely touched plate, eyes on the television; *In the Night Garden* was on, Upsy Daisy dancing across the screen.

"Gracie," she exclaimed in exasperation. "Why haven't you eaten your dinner? I've started your bath; I thought you'd be finished by now."

"Don't like it," said Gracie firmly.

"You liked cheesy pasta yesterday," Hannah replied, trying hard to stay calm.

"S'yuck."

"It's not yuck, it's a yummy dinner. Please, *please* will you just eat it up?"

"Yuck, yuck, yuck," Gracie chanted, picking up a piece of the pasta between two fingers and examining it with revulsion.

"Stop it," Hannah said quietly. "Stop saying that. It's not yuck, I cooked it especially for you because yesterday you said you loved it."

"Yuck, yuck, yuck, yuck, yuck, yuck," Gracie continued to sing tunelessly.

"Stop it," Hannah said again. Anger was boiling deep in her gut, dangerously threatening to erupt. Gracie's voice was like a vegetable peeler, scraping away layers of her skin. "Gracie, *please*. Stop saying that right now." Hannah clenched her jaw. *Stay in control, stay in control.*

"Yuck, yuck, yuck . . ."

"STOP IT, STOP IT, STOP IT!" As Hannah began to scream she lost control of her body; she picked up Gracie's plate and hurled it against the wall. The plate smashed and pasta and vegetables flew everywhere. Ethan, who had been lying on the floor happily playing with his toes, burst into tears. A second later Gracie joined in with him. "My food is on the wall!" She sobbed uncontrollably. "My food is on the wall! Get my food off the wall!"

"I'm sorry," Hannah whispered, looking from the broken pieces of the ceramic Peter Rabbit dish to her two crying children to the smears of food across the wall. Some had even splattered right up to the ceiling. She collapsed onto the floor and buried her face in her hands. "I'm sorry," she cried through her tears, "I didn't mean it. I don't know what's wrong with me."

As all three of them continued to sob, Hannah reached into her pocket and pulled out her phone. This had to end. She couldn't go on like this. She typed a text message with shaking hands:

please, please, could you please just come home on time tonight. In fact, could you come home now? Right now. I really need you.

She would send this message to Liam and then she would sit here, on the floor, surrounded by the mess and the broken pieces of the little plate that had been her own before it was Gracie's. She would sit here by her crying children and she would wait. And when Liam came home he would see all of this and he would finally know the truth.

She was just about to press send when her phone beeped with a text. She opened up the new text instead.

So sorry, babe, but it's going to be a late one tonight. Probably won't be home before midnight so better have dinner without me. I'll eat takeout at the office. Love you.

Hannah stared at the message with burning eyes. What would have happened if she had sent hers first? Would he still have stayed back anyway? And what would he do if she still sent the text anyway? Would he drop everything and rush home? Maybe. But then again, maybe not. His work was important, after all. It didn't matter though, because she hadn't sent it and she wasn't going to, and she certainly couldn't sit here on the floor until midnight. This was a second chance to pull herself together all on her own. To fix things before Liam ever found out what was going on.

She wiped her tears away and looked around at the scene. She stood up. "Come here, sweetheart," she said, picking Gracie up from her chair and hugging her close. She walked over to Ethan and scooped him up with her other arm and then she sat down on the couch with the two of them, stroking Gracie's hair and rubbing Ethan's back until they had both settled down.

She didn't remember that she had started the bath running until ten minutes later. When she realized, she leapt up and raced to the bathroom. But by this time most of the bathroom was flooded. The floor mat was soaked through and bright yellow rubber ducks floated by across the tiles.

A thought struck Hannah. What if she had put Gracie *in* the bath and then forgotten to turn off the taps? If she could lose chunks of time so easily—if she could forget to give Gracie lunch, or strap her into the car—wasn't it possible that she could let something much, much worse happen? The possibilities crept up her spine and she pressed her fingers hard against her temples.

Hannah, you need to do better.

By the time Liam arrived home, a little after one, all evidence of the mini-disaster that had occurred there that night had vanished. Once the kids were in bed, Hannah had mopped the bathroom and scrubbed at the living room wall until all the food was gone. She had dragged a chair over and stood on it so she could reach up to the ceiling and clean that too. She had cried quietly as she cleaned and had thought to herself, *When is it all going to end?*

•

When Liam left the office, Paige was actually waiting for him, leaning casually against the wall, checking something on her phone. "Hey there, latte-boy," she said when she saw him. "I was wondering if you were ever coming down."

Does she even know my real name? Liam wondered distractedly.

"Coming for another drink?" she asked.

He opened his mouth to decline, but somehow the wrong words came out. "Why not?" he said, and they walked together down to the pub.

He drank far too much again. At some point he sent Hannah a text, telling her that he was working late again, telling her he loved her. He pressed send with a slightly sick feeling in his gut. And when Paige took him by the hand and led him out of the pub and into a cab, he followed her blindly. As they climbed into the back of the taxi, he tried to keep his mind blank. Tried to convince himself that this wasn't his fault. How was he supposed to say no when she was coming on so strong? How was he supposed to turn down the prospect of having a warm body pressed against his when his wife kept turning the cold shoulder on him?

It was as they were crossing the harbor bridge that Paige slid across the back seat of the cab and began to stroke his neck. She was leaning in and her breath smelled of creamy cocktails and then she was kissing him. And he was kissing her back. That's when he saw it. His eyes opened, just for a fraction of a second, and in that moment he saw the bright lights of Luna Park. The place where he had met his wife. All of the emotions that he had been squashing down came racing back.

What the fuck was he doing? He *loved* Hannah.

He pulled back from Paige and as the taxi left the bridge he said quickly, "I'm sorry, but I can't do this."

He had the driver drop him off in North Sydney and he walked to the train station feeling revolted with himself, but resolved to figure out what was going on with Hannah. There was something she wasn't telling him and he needed to find out what it was.

When he arrived home though, at quarter past one, Hannah was fast asleep. *Saturday,* he told himself, *I'll sit down with her on Saturday morning and we'll talk this all out and we'll figure out what's going on.*

Friday afternoon and Hannah was heading back home from picking up Gracie from preschool—late, yet again. She touched the back of her head tenderly and felt a small lump there. When she had been placing Ethan back in the car, he had decided that no thank you, he did not want to get into the car seat again so soon. He was actually quite capable of exerting a surprising amount of strength for such a small baby and he had arched his back and screamed and wriggled and writhed as Hannah tried to strap him in. When she had finally managed to snap the buckles together, she'd pinched the skin of her thumb along with them, causing her to jump back and violently smash her head on the roof of the car.

As they made their way through the traffic, Gracie asked her to put on one of her nursery rhymes CDs. As the music filled the car, Hannah began to think about the past few months.

What the hell has been going on with me?

"Old MacDonald had a farm . . ."

I don't think I can do this any more. I really don't think I can.

"And on that farm he had a chicken . . ."

What if I'm not meant to be a mum?

"Eee-eye-ee-eye-oh . . ."

What if I was never supposed to be a mother or a wife?

"With a berk-berk here and a berk-berk there . . ."

What if they really would all be better off without me?

"Eee-eye-ee-eye-oh . . ."

"Eee-eye-ee-eye-oh . . ."

The familiar taste of salty tears reached her lips and she looked down at the CD player and jabbed at it to stop the music. To stop these crazy, frightening thoughts. The button jammed and she slammed her hands down on the steering wheel in frustration.

She looked back up from the stereo just in time to see the red light right in front of her as she crossed into the intersection, and the black four-wheel drive flying toward her from the left at a good seventy kilometers an hour.

The following morning Hannah sat in the back of the taxi and told herself yet again that she was doing the right thing.

"Going on a holiday are you, love?" The taxi driver peered at her through the rearview mirror.

"Umm, yes. Sort of," she replied.

"Where to?"

"Uh, the airport."

"No, I mean where are you going after I drop you off, you know, up in the . . ." He motioned a plane taking off with his hand.

"Not sure yet," she said quietly.

"Right then." The taxi driver seemed a little taken aback by this and fell quiet.

Hannah looked out of the window and tried not to cry. She had cried enough these past few weeks. But she had no other choice. Yesterday afternoon when she had driven straight through that red light, when that four-wheel drive had had to screech its brakes as it swerved to avoid her, when she had risked her children's lives, all because she was busy throwing a little tantrum because she couldn't get Gracie's damn nursery rhymes CD to stop playing—she had known.

I have to leave my family.

Before I do something to hurt them.

Because what if the next time she stopped concentrating, the other car didn't swerve in time? Or what if the next time she threw something against a wall it rebounded and hit one of her kids? Or what if Ethan was being damaged because of the love she was incapable of providing him? Or Gracie was being disadvantaged because she wasn't interacting naturally with her, or taking her out to the park or helping her to make friends with other children? What if she let Ethan drown in the bath, or lost Gracie at the shopping center, or any one of a million different possibilities? It wasn't safe for her to stay.

It was clear that she had no right being a part of these two amazing kids' lives. She had to leave, had to get out of the way. Liam could meet someone else, find a new wife, a new mother for their children, a mother that would nurture and nourish them. Someone real. Someone alive. Someone who wasn't made of broken spare parts. Of hollow wood. Of plastic and rubber and rusted metal cogs.

Last night she had packed a large backpack and hidden it around the side of the house. This morning was Saturday. She told Liam she was taking a quick walk, that she needed the exercise. She gave him a kiss on the cheek and then snuck into the kids' rooms. Both Ethan and Gracie were still fast asleep. She paused at each doorway and gazed down at their sleeping forms. Her heart felt empty. A small part of her hesitated, though, and thought, *Maybe I'm wrong, maybe I could still stay, maybe I could just be careful, try harder, concentrate more.* But she remembered the risks, the danger to such innocence, and she hardened her bones, encased her heart in a stiff, mesh cage, closed her eyes and turned away. She left a note on the kitchen table and she walked out the front door.

The taxi had been prebooked to meet her at the corner. As she lugged her backpack up the street to meet it, she thought these two things:

I am doing the right thing for my family, I am setting them free.

And,

I am an awful, evil person.

When Liam found the note, he knew before he even read it. *I waited too long*, he thought, *I waited too long to talk to her.* And he sat down at the kitchen table and cried.

She was using Facebook as an excellent source of distraction in order to delay writing her weekly email home. Riley knew she needed to get it done soon, though. The Internet café she'd found had slightly more expensive rates than most. She was about to close the window and open up her Hotmail account when she noticed a page called "Letter to Simon" that a few friends had liked and shared. Wondering what it was, she clicked on the link and read the description first.

It had been posted by some guy called James who explained that he was searching for the right Simon that the letter he had reproduced part of was intended for. Apparently there was no address on the letter, just the words Simon and The Aella. *Riley frowned. That name—The Aella—was very familiar. She scanned the contents of the letter and then gasped. She quickly reread it and found that her chest was thudding. While there were hundreds of comments from other people claiming they knew who Simon was, Riley was certain that she knew who the real Simon was: her brother.*

Her fingers trembled as she hurried to write a private message to James to find out if she would be able to get hold of the entire letter.

PART THREE

London
Once More

CHAPTER 10

~~~~~~~~~

India arrived at Hannah's building as an older man was heading out the front door with his two small terriers on leads. She caught the door just before it banged shut and then began to climb the stairs to Hannah's flat on the top floor. When she reached her door, she began to knock, and then she knocked again, and again. No answer. Was she out? But an anxious feeling was creeping over her. Instinct was telling her that something was wrong. She tried the handle and found it unlocked.

When she stepped inside, what she saw took her breath away. On the other side of the room, the window was open wide, and crouched on the windowsill was Hannah, ready to jump. India's stomach turned and she launched herself across the room. In four wide strides she had reached her, and just as Hannah began to lean forward, as she was reaching the point of no return, India's hand closed around the back of her shirt. Summoning all of her strength, she yanked her backward. Hannah's head slammed against the top window pane above her, and then her knees buckled and she folded in on herself as India dragged her roughly back through the small opening of the window and into the flat. They both fell to the floor and lay still for several seconds; then India rolled over and slapped Hannah hard across the face.

"What the fuck was that, Hannah, what the hell were you *doing*?" She was kneeling in front of Hannah now, her eyes wide with terror as she clasped her hands onto Hannah's shoulders and shook her frantically. "FUCK!" she screamed and specks of saliva landed on Hannah's cheeks. India let her go then, collapsed back onto the floor, put her head into her hands and started crying.

"Jesus," breathed Hannah. They both lay on the floor like this, flat on their backs for at least five minutes, catching their breath, trying to understand what had just happened.

Eventually Hannah spoke. "You just saved my life, India."

"And you were just about to throw it away," India responded. She was furious with Hannah. Didn't she realize how precious life was? Did she know that for a second when she had stepped into Hannah's apartment and seen her out there on the ledge, she had thought, *There is no way I am going to be able to cross that room in time?*

"I'm so sorry, India," said Hannah. "I'll tell you everything, I'll tell you whatever you want to know."

India stood up shakily. She looked down at Hannah with

contempt in her wet, puffy eyes and wiped the back of her hand across her nose, sniffing noisily.

"Don't bother," she said and spun around, then strode from the apartment, slamming the door behind her.

India spent the entire night walking the streets of London—probably not the safest thing she had ever done, but she didn't care. She was fuming, she was confused, but most of all, she was terrified. Hannah's problems were much, much worse than she could ever have imagined. What if she couldn't save her? What if Hannah's issues were beyond her? Obviously the girl needed help—professional help. What if she tried to hurt herself again? God, what if she had climbed right back out on that window ledge as soon as India left? As the sun rose and the hazy light began to filter between the buildings that surrounded her, India began to feel guilty. She probably shouldn't have left Hannah in that state. What she needed was compassion—not judgement—but India hadn't been able to help it; she had been so angry that Hannah had been preparing to toss her perfectly healthy body out of the eighth floor of a building.

India started to head back toward Hannah's flat—even if she had no idea how to handle this, she needed to make sure Hannah was okay. She would figure the rest out as she went along. As she passed a pub, India caught sight of herself in the large front window. Her short blue hair was sticking out at odd angles, her clothing looked crumpled and dark crescents accentuated her eyes. Her arms and legs felt weak from the constant walking through the night.

When she reached Hannah's place and pressed the front door intercom, she stood waiting, smoothing her hair down in a nervous gesture. *She'd better bloody well be there.* Hannah buzzed her in almost immediately, and India climbed the stairs feeling wary. When she reached Hannah's floor and knocked, the door was answered within ten seconds; Hannah stood in front of her looking like hell—she looked like India felt.

When India spoke her voice was stiff, formal. "I just came to see that you're okay. Didn't know if maybe you had a concussion from banging your head. Couldn't live with myself if I'd left you to die on your apartment floor, especially after . . ."

Hannah nodded, then lifted her hand to gingerly touch the back of her head. "Um sure, yeah I'm fine, thank you. Just a lump and a bit of dried-up blood. Least of my worries . . . Look, would you please come in, let me explain?"

India hesitated—she was still angry—but curiosity won and she relented. She stepped inside and walked over to the window; it was still open. She peered outside, reliving the previous evening, and then she reached up, placed her hand on the top of the window frame and forcefully slammed it shut. She sat down at the small table where Hannah rarely ate her meals and Hannah took a seat opposite her.

"So," India said, "what were you doing out there?"

Hannah paused. "The truth is I don't really know what I was doing. I didn't climb out there with the intention of jumping—at least I don't think that I did. I was just trying to escape, trying to find my way into another world. And then I started thinking, about everything, and the next thing I knew, it seemed like letting go would be the only choice."

India frowned. "Go back to the beginning, Hannah," she said, her voice hard. "I need to know from the start. Why are you here? What made you come to London?"

Hannah looked down at her hands. She took a deep breath and then, finally, she told India the truth. "I left my family, India. I abandoned my children. I have a three-year-old daughter and a baby son. Just under two months ago, I walked out on them and my husband and I came here to London because that was the first flight available when I arrived at the airport."

India stared at Hannah, her eyes burning with accusation. "You left your children? Why? What possible reason would you have to do that?"

Hannah began to cry. "I don't know," she started to say, but India reached out and grabbed her hand.

"No," she said. "You don't get to cry. You don't get to sit there and expect sympathy from me. Pull yourself together and enlighten me, because I don't get it." She knew she wasn't being compassionate, but she didn't care. All she could feel right now was empathy for those children—and the familiar sting of abandonment that she had felt all her life.

Over the next couple of hours Hannah did her best to explain to India how she had come to leave her family. She told her how she had found motherhood to be such a shock when she first gave birth to Gracie, how she had struggled at times, but Liam had supported her through it and when things were finally going along fine, she had fallen pregnant again. How she had been terrified of another big change, but that she had been determined to succeed. How at first she had thought she was doing okay, but slowly things had started to crumble around her and still she continued to deny that anything was the matter. She tried to make India understand that in the end leaving seemed to be the best decision, for the sake of her children. They weren't safe with her. She had done this for them.

When she finally finished India narrowed her eyes at Hannah. In a flurry of movement she slammed her fist down on the table between them. "BULLSHIT, Hannah!" she snapped. "You think you did them a favor? You think they're better off without you? Well you're wrong. You think your little girl isn't crying herself to sleep at night, wondering where her mummy has gone? You think your baby boy isn't desperate for you to hold him in your arms? You think they're not wondering: What did I do wrong, why doesn't she love me, why doesn't she want me? That little girl is probably spending hours, sitting by the river, wondering about her mum, trying to figure out why she didn't care enough to stick around, or why her dad didn't even want to meet her, didn't want to hold her in his arms, see what she could become. Why she wasn't worth it." India hadn't meant to turn this into something about her own past; she barely even realized what she was saying until the words tumbled out.

"I'm sorry," Hannah whispered, biting her lip to stop the tears from starting again.

"Yes, well, I'm not the one you need to say sorry to."

Hannah nodded. "I know. I know that you're right, but I can't go back now. I can't ever go back. I don't deserve them and they're better off without me. I know you think I'm making up excuses, justifying what I've done, but I'm not. They're not safe with me."

"You can get help, Hannah. See a psychologist or a psychiatrist or someone. You can come back from this; you just need to be pre-pared to help yourself first. You realize there's a simple answer, don't you? You've got postpartum depression—obviously. That's all. No big deal, you idiot. Isn't there something like one in four women who get it? Or I don't know—I'm not sure what the stats are. But the thing is, you can fix this. Start by calling them. Now," she added firmly.

Hannah looked back at India warily. She shook her head. "I can't," she said desperately. "I'm not ready for that."

"You can and you will," said India firmly. "Your little girl needs to hear your voice. It's the least you can do. You can tell her that you love her, so that she knows." India folded her arms and stared at Hannah.

Hannah hesitated, and then she shook her head. "No, I heard from Liam last night, a text message. He hates me. He never wants to see me again."

"Hang on, take me back a step here. You've been in contact with your husband? How is that possible?"

"When I first got here I sent him an email, trying to explain what I'd done. I told him I was overseas, but not where. I gave him a contact number, but I said it was just for emergencies, you know, for in case something happened with the children. I guess I should have known that he would ignore that. At first he used to call me over and over, every day. I stopped picking up the phone most times. But once or twice I gave in and I answered."

"Wow. You're not really very good at running away, are you?"

"What do you mean?"

"Isn't it obvious? Hannah, this just proves to me that you need to go home to your family. You never meant to stay gone, did you? It was . . . I don't know . . . a cry for help or something, wasn't it? You didn't know how to tell anyone you were in trouble, so instead you made one dramatic, attention-grabbing gesture. You wanted them to see how bad things were, but you also *wanted* to be found. Otherwise you would have never made contact. Think about it—how many people have you heard of who disappear from their family, only to send an email with a contact number for 'just in case'?"

India laughed then, suddenly and loudly. "You're a walking contradiction. You think that leaving was the right thing to do, that you were doing it for your family, while at the same time you hate yourself for doing the unthinkable. But here's the good news—you can come back from this. You just have to listen to me. Okay?"

Hannah felt her resolve collapse under the weight of India's stare. She nodded miserably.

"Good," said India. "Then here's what you need to do. If you don't think you can have this conversation over the phone then you need to book yourself a flight to Sydney. You need to GO HOME. Go back to your family. Yes, it's going to be hard, yes it'll be a shock when you turn up on that doorstep—but they need you, babe."

India waited for a few minutes, watching Hannah sit chewing her fingernails, considering everything that she had just been told—and then she exploded. "For fuck's sake, Hannah, it's your family. It's a no brainer."

Forty minutes later, India had helped Hannah pack all of her belongings into her backpack. They booked the flight over the phone for later that afternoon and India took the keys to the flat, promising to drop them off to Hannah's landlord and explain why Hannah was cutting the lease short. Then they stood out the front of the building waiting for the taxi that would take Hannah to Heathrow.

"I have to say, when I imagined all the reasons why you were here in London—what it was you were running away from—I never thought it would be this. I can't believe you're a mum, Han." India stood with her arms wrapped around herself, her foot scuffing against the ground.

"Most days I can't believe it, either," Hannah said in a sad voice.

India grabbed her by the shoulders and turned her so they were face to face. "I know you think you're a bad mother, you think you're a failure—but I'd put money on it that you're not. One day all of this is just going to be a ditch in your past, a time where you hit bottom, ended up in your own personal hell. But when you come out the other side, things are going to be *good*. Okay? Trust me."

Hannah nodded; once again she was fighting back tears. As the taxi pulled up to the curb, they each leaned in and hugged one another, hard—and when they finally pulled apart, India was crying too.

"Tell your family hi from me," said India, as Hannah climbed into the taxi.

When the cab pulled away and Hannah was gone, India stood still for a few minutes. For the first time in weeks she was feeling lost. For the past few weeks, figuring out what was wrong with Hannah had been her driving force. What would she do now? She supposed it was finally time to leave London.

As she walked away down the road, heading for the tube station, she reached into her pocket and her fingers closed around the piece of paper with Hannah's address in Sydney that she had given her, asking her to promise to stay in touch.

I'll try, Han, she thought a little sadly.

Simon was reading the letter through for the fifth time. It was so out of the blue—he had assumed after their last conversation that he was never going to hear from her again. But now here was this letter—telling him she had a secret, talking crazily about scratching away layers of her skin. Asking him if he truly loved her. And what was the bit about not being sure if the next letter she sent would "actually make it to him"? God he wished he had a contact number for her. He needed to talk to the girl, find out what it was that was tearing her up inside. He needed to answer her questions, to reassure her that everything was going to be okay. So when the phone rang, it felt like fate.

He snatched up the receiver by his bed just knowing, *knowing* it would be her.

"Si," she breathed into the phone and he felt his muscles unclench, his body relax.

"India!" he exclaimed, and he wanted to say, *I knew it, I knew it would be you on the phone*—but it seemed stupid and so he didn't speak, just waited, wondering what she would say next. Wondering how he could convince her to tell him exactly where she was, how he could just be with her.

"I'm leaving London," she said eventually.

"And coming here?" he asked, knowing the answer before the words even left his mouth.

"No. Don't know where I'll go next. Maybe hitch a ride and head north."

"I got your letter."

"You did?" She sounded surprised, excited.

"Yeah, what's this about having a secret then?"

"Oh," she said, "I thought you meant . . . I thought you'd got the next one."

"No. Only one. When did you post the next letter?"

"I didn't. I don't like to post my letters, Simon. I like to send them out into the world and see if they get to you. I give them to travelers and I ask them to pass them on. It's like an international game of Chinese whispers—except the messages can't change, because they're there in ink, waiting to get to you."

That's what she bloody well meant by wondering whether or not the letter would get to him.

"India," he said carefully, "exactly how many letters have you sent to me like that?"

There was a pause and when she spoke her voice sounded tight. "Oh, a few," she said. "Maybe nine or ten I guess."

"Are you kidding me? Do you realize all this time I thought you'd pretty much forgotten about me? Why didn't you *post* them?"

"I don't know," she said in a small voice.

"Look. Why don't you just tell me your secret? We can talk it through. Whatever it is, I can help you with it. I don't like to think of you scratching so hard at your skin that you're tearing it to shreds. Your skin is lovely; please don't do that to yourself. *Please*, tell me."

"No."

"All right, maybe this will help. You wanted to know me? Here are the answers to your questions. My favorite movie is *Crash*. I love it because of that one particular scene, when the little girl jumps into her father's arms to protect him from the gunshot and your heart jumps into your mouth and then there's no bullet and it's the most beautiful moment of relief you've ever experienced. When I was a baby I had no hair, completely bald until I turned two; my mum was considering buying me a toupee when the first wispy curls finally appeared." He paused to take a breath and then added, "Are you still there?"

"Yes," she whispered.

He continued on. "I'm allergic to cut grass—so obviously that's not my favorite smell. My favorite smell is your skin after you've swum in the ocean. It's a mixture of sea-salt and gardenias. Did you know that? That your skin naturally smells like gardenias? Well, I suppose it might not be natural. I suppose there's a chance that you wear perfume. But now whenever I walk past the gardenias that grow on that hill above the wharf, and there's a wind blowing in from the ocean, I find myself turning around expecting to see you there, standing behind me, smiling your huge smile."

He heard a muffled, tearful sounding laugh come through the receiver, but he didn't stop talking. "The last time I cried was the 2006 soccer World Cup, when Gianluigi Buffon saved a goal in extra time, a save that was crucial to taking Italy to victory for the first time in twenty-four years. It was *awesome*. The last time I laughed so hard that my stomach hurt was when a couple of eighteen-year-old tourists drank too much on our boat and one of them fell overboard. After I stopped laughing I realized that he really couldn't swim very well and I had to jump in to rescue him. The last time I stubbed my big toe was last week. I did it on purpose against my coffee table after I read your letter, so I would have a specific time to tell you when I finally got to speak to you. Do you realize how hard it is to make yourself intentionally stub your toe? Your foot is screaming out, 'No, no, why the hell do you want to do that?' And it's exceptionally difficult to follow through, but I did it—for you.

"And your most important question of all: Am I truly in love with you? Hell yes."

There was silence then, and for a second Simon was worried that she had hung up. But then she spoke. "I'm staying at the Wanderers Hostel in Earls Court," she said, and her voice was rushed and wavering, all at the same time. And now she did hang up.

Simon sat still on the edge of his bed, his heart thumping. It had worked; she'd finally told him the truth. He was going to be able to see her again.

After a few minutes, he had gathered his thoughts and was ready to get moving. First he needed to figure out his travel plans. In the morning he would speak to his boss. He headed out to the local Internet café to check train timetables and to catch up on his emails before he left.

He looked into his travel plans first, then logged into his gmail account. An email from his sister Riley caught him up on the latest family news. She was planning on flying back home in a week or two and she wanted to know when he'd be back in Sydney. Apparently it was a bit of a problem that neither of them had been back to meet their new nephew since he was born six months ago. That wasn't really an issue he wanted to deal with just now—although he had been thinking lately of the return flight ticket to Sydney that was stashed at the back of his mind, waiting to be booked in—but he wasn't ready to return home to Australia. Especially not if he was about to embark on something new with India. He shot off a reply, telling Riley a little about India, explaining her quirky way of posting him letters—Riley would get a kick out of that—but he stopped short of telling her he was just about to take off for London to see her again. What if it didn't work out? He didn't want to look like an idiot. He finished off the email with a promise that he'd think about coming back home soon.

Eventually he logged off and headed back to his rented room to pack, a slight spring of excitement in his step as he went.

Poor Simon never had a chance. Even if he'd stood up and walked straight out his front door and stepped onto a plane the second that India had hung up on him, he still wouldn't have got there in time. The problem was her stomach. The moment she'd told Simon where she was, it had begun to twist. It had started churning and knotting and surely that wasn't a good sign. So India wrote him another letter, left it with the girl at the front desk, heaved her backpack onto her shoulders and left.

Dear Simon,

I'm so sorry. I thought that writing you that letter was the answer. I thought that once my words were somewhere safe—that they'd landed in your hands and you'd begun to breathe them in and started thinking of something to say back—then everything would be okay.

But what could you say really?

Nothing.

So I was wrong. Forgive me for running from you. For your sake I hope that my letter never does reach you. I hope that my words have been crumpled. I hope they've been trodden on, ripped to shreds. I hope that they have been whipped out of some traveler's hand, that they've flown into the ocean, become sodden and heavy. I hope that they've sunk to the bottom and been swallowed by a hundred-year-old turtle named Sam.

Love,

India

She took a bus that was headed north and tried hard not to feel guilty. After all, she hadn't exactly told him to come and see her. She didn't know for sure that he would even turn up. Maybe after she hung up the phone, Simon had thought to himself, *What is that girl on?*, shrugged his shoulders and turned on the television. Maybe he headed straight out to a club and picked up a pretty American girl and they're still dancing right now, grinding their hips together, with his lips brushing against her shoulder.

But thinking about that made India want to punch the seat in front, so she stopped. In all honesty, though, she knew this wasn't the case. She knew that Simon was probably already making arrangements to come and see her—and *that* made her want to bang her forehead against the bus window.

Come on, India, stop it. You're an independent, grown woman. You don't have to answer to anyone. No regrets.

But her pep talk wasn't working, because deep down she knew that she hadn't played fair with Simon.

Simon was nervous. His boss was going to hate him, he was certain of that. There was no one to replace him and he felt bad. But he couldn't pass up this chance to see her again. He needed to know what her secret was and to help her with it, whatever it turned out to be. He squared his shoulders before he knocked on Angelo's office door.

"Come," called the voice from inside.

Simon pushed open the door and stepped into the room. "Angelo, we need to talk," began Simon.

"Is about girl?" Angelo asked in his thick Greek accent.

"Yes, actually, it is," said Simon.

Angelo paused as he picked up a paper cup on his desk to take a sip. A second later he spat the liquid back into the cup with a disgusted look on his face. "This," he announced, "is not coffee. Has been here on my desk all morning. It is ex-coffee. Blah. Cold. Now, as for Simon and his girl. I know. I see it. Your face, it's different. All mopey, all the time. Wah, wah, why doesn't girl like me? Go."

"Umm, excuse me?"

"Go. You go and find girl. And come back happy. I give her job too."

"Really? You don't mind if I take off? What about the boat, how will you manage on your own?"

Angelo shrugged. "These things, they work out. My wife, she is good woman. She will help. Go."

When Simon continued to hesitate, Angelo picked up a stapler from his desk and hurled it at him. Simon ducked and then hurried out the door before his boss could throw any more stationery at his head.

She was sitting in a cramped café in a small town outside of Manchester when she realized something. India wanted to go home. The guilt about what she had done to Simon was making her feel lonely—lonely and homesick. And while there was no one waiting for her back at her home in Gingin, there were acquaintances, old friends who would welcome her back. It would be good to see a friendly face.

Most surprising was how much she missed Hannah. She hadn't expected that. God she hoped Hannah's reunion with her family had gone well. On an impulse she decided to write Hannah a letter, something to check in with her. As she considered what she should say, she thought back to their first meeting and an idea struck her. She was going to have to use up a fair chunk of her savings, but why not? She had decided she had had enough of traveling now anyway, and she wanted to do something nice for Hannah—it might help to appease her guilt over Simon.

When she had organized everything for Hannah's surprise, she hesitated over how to word the letter. In the end, she lied about where she was and how the idea had come about. For some reason she didn't want Hannah to think of her, here in this tiny, rainy town, feeling lonely and lost. She wanted Hannah to think of her as some bohemian traveler, flitting around the world, continuing to make friends and hopping across borders on a whim.

After she posted the letter she booked her last plane ticket home.

Simon had to take a bus, a train and a boat to get himself over to London. He would have loved to have flown, he wanted to be there as quickly as possible, but his savings account didn't have the funds to cover it just now. That's why it was such a kick in the guts when he arrived at the Wanderers Hostel. Several backpackers were hanging around at some undercover tables out the front. Simon scanned their faces briefly as he passed by, but when he couldn't pick out India's face in the group, he headed on inside.

He approached a desk where a bored-looking girl in a white tank top and bright green flares was folding sheets from a laundry basket by her chair.

"All right, love?" she asked as she pretty much just balled up a fitted sheet and added it to the pile of linen.

"Hi, I'm looking for someone who's staying here. India Calder?"

"You Simon then?"

Simon nodded, a smile beginning to form on his face. The

girl leaned forward and reached under the desk. When her hand reappeared she was holding an envelope. "She said to give this to you if you showed up."

Simon's face fell. "She's gone, hasn't she?"

"'Fraid so," the girl replied, not unkindly. "If it helps, she did look sort of tortured about it," she added. Then she returned to her sheets. Simon walked slowly back out onto the street, where he tore open the envelope with trembling hands and read the letter inside. He was angry. No, that didn't cover it—he was pissed off. Fed up. He'd just traveled for a day and a half to get here and the bloody woman had taken off on him again. God, he was a moron.

Never again, he thought as he crumpled the letter in his fist and headed down the street to look for a pub where he may as well drown his sorrows. *Never again would he let himself fall that damn hard and that damn fast for a girl.*

Maybe it was time to give up and go back home to Sydney after all. Maybe he was bloody sick of traveling.

James smiled as he read the message on his Facebook account. He didn't even know why he cared so much about this, but for some reason, he did. It felt vital that this letter make it to the right Simon, and it looked as though he'd finally received a genuine message from someone who believed they knew the right one. Someone who knew what The Aella *meant. A boat, huh? He should have thought of that.*

He typed out a message to Riley, arranging a place they could meet so he could hand over the letter. Who knew, maybe this Riley would be cute, maybe this could be the start of something. His Facebook profile photo was of his childhood pet dog, so he couldn't tell what Riley looked like, but he sounded sweet.

James found himself looking forward to their rendezvous.

PART FOUR

Sydney as the Seasons Change

CHAPTER 11

When Hannah's plane landed, she hung back and allowed most of the other passengers off first. A part of her wanted to just stay in her seat. Curl up and hide. Wait for the plane to turn around and take her back. She hadn't realized how comfortable she had become in London.

So what now? When she got off the plane, walked through the airport and hailed a cab—then what? How did she begin to walk back into her life? Did she just turn up on the front doorstep?

Finally she stood up and began to head down the aisle—after all, she really had no choice.

From the airport she took the train to the city then walked down to Circular Quay. She was procrastinating, she knew—but really, she needed to prepare herself properly for this, and Circular Quay was the first place that came to mind. She wanted to see the harbor. She wandered up and down the curving footpath that followed the water's edge with her backpack hoisted up on her shoulders and drank in the Sydney air. Storm clouds were gathering in the south, but the wind was surprisingly mild considering it was almost May. Soon, though, winter would begin its battle with summer for custody of autumn and the weather would turn icy.

Eventually she stopped by a pay phone. If she couldn't bring herself to just turn up at their home, then she may as well start with a call. She stepped up to the phone, found the right money—extracting the familiar dollar coins from among the last few pounds and pence she had in her wallet—and dialed.

Hannah stood still, listening intently to the crackling sound of the phone ringing. It rang six times before there was a click as someone picked up.

"Hello?" It was a woman's voice. Hannah didn't move, her entire body tensed.

"Hello?" repeated the smooth voice. And then she heard it, the voice of a small child in the background, the voice of her small child. "Mummy!" called the voice. She sounded happy. Happy and carefree. She had been wrong. She could never return to her family. Even if what India said was true, if she had never meant to stay gone . . . it was too late. She hung up before she could hear that woman's voice again. That woman who had taken her place, just as she had intended that someone would. But she simply hadn't thought it would happen so soon. She burst into tears.

He's already met someone else. Already replaced me. And my Gracie is actually calling her mummy. Instinctively she placed her hands against her gut, where pain had flared up, as though she had run flat out and now she was trying to soothe a stitch. But she was standing dead still, she couldn't have a stitch, the pain wasn't physical.

She didn't want to think any more. She didn't want to keep crying, her eyes felt drained. Instead, she needed to keep moving; it was the only thing she could think to do. Her children were okay. Just as she had planned, they were happy now. Her family had moved on. They were safe. India was right—she had sent that email to Liam with her new phone number as a way to keep some sort of link with her family. But that was selfish and stupid. She needed to close it down. Needed to stay away. She should have known when Liam sent her that text message that they truly were through.

She looked out across the water and saw a ferry slicing effortlessly through the churning foam toward her. A ferry. *Good. Fine,* she thought blindly. Buying a ticket to somewhere, anywhere, felt like the only option—just something to get her moving. She felt sick. She had made such a mess of everything. When she had boarded that plane to Sydney, it had felt like the right thing to do. But now that she was here, she had no idea what to do next.

Liam had met someone else. She let those five words hang for a moment in the air around her. Let them settle on her shoulders. Tried them on. Attempted to understand them. But they wouldn't fit right and a small part of her thought, *No, surely she had it wrong, surely he hasn't really moved on so soon?*

But then she realized that Ethan would have already forgotten her. And Gracie would begin to forget, soon. And how could they ever forgive her anyway? She understood everything now. India was right—she had been suffering from postpartum depression. She had tried to deny this fact and hide her true feelings and eventually she had believed that running away was her only choice. She saw how senseless it all was. She should have asked for help. But it didn't change the fact that it was too late. And it didn't change the fact that she was still messed up in the head. Beyond repair. That she was a danger to everyone she touched. That she was a walking disease. And as much as she was wishing for Liam to come striding toward her—to gather her into a hug and tell her it was all going to be okay, that he could fix everything— that wasn't going to happen.

Liam sat down on the bed and placed his head in his hands. It still seemed to hit him like this every now and then—this startling realization that his wife was gone. That Hannah had left him—alone with their two children—and he still didn't understand *why*. Why hadn't she talked with him? Why hadn't she told him that she was unhappy? He could have helped if he had just known. He would have done anything for her. Taken time off. Moved to . . . anywhere. For God's sake, he would have sold his damn business if that were what it had taken. All she had to do was *say* something, instead of being this bloody superwoman all the time. And now it had come to this.

There was guilt as well, though. Guilt for the part that he had played in all of this. Deep down, he'd known that something wasn't right—and what did he do? He let her continue to push him away and he kissed another woman. He should have tried to talk with her sooner.

He stood back up determinedly. There was no point sitting here thinking over it all again; he'd covered this ground enough in the past month or two. And if he didn't get moving, he wouldn't have Gracie ready in time to be picked up for the birthday party. A small girl from Gracie's preschool had invited her along to her fourth birthday party at Luna Park. It was the last place where Liam wanted to be, so when another one of the mums had offered to pick Gracie up and take her along for him, Liam had jumped at the chance.

Right, what did he need to pack in her backpack for the day out? He tried to work his way through his mental checklist—*spare change of clothes, drink bottle, snacks*—but at the sight of the bedside clock, tick, tick, ticking away, the minutes sliding effortlessly past, he lost his concentration.

"Dammit!" He turned and kicked their dressing table, hard. A small glass ornament of a ballerina wobbled and then fell, smashing on the tiled floor. That was Hannah's. He'd given it to her on her twenty-fifth birthday. He swore and was about to bend down to pick up the pieces when Ethan's cry began to echo down the hall. He huffed in frustration and turned to walk down the hall. At the same time as Ethan's cries increased in fervor and volume, the doorbell rang. *Perfect*, he thought bitterly. *You know what,*

Han? I bloody well get it, I get what you were going through. I just don't know why you didn't tell me.

Liam pulled open the door with Ethan screaming in his arms.

"Oh, darling, what's up?" said the preschool mum immediately, turning doe-like eyes on Ethan.

Liam racked his brain, trying to remember her name. *Donna? Diana?*

"Hi, Diane," Liam said uncertainly, standing back so she could step inside.

"Deanne," she corrected. "Just call me Dee though. Can I take him?" she added, reaching out for Ethan. Her own little boy was hiding behind her legs, squinting up at Liam distrustfully. Liam hesitated and then allowed Dee to extract Ethan expertly from his arms. She began to sway back and forth, cradling Ethan, and he stopped crying almost immediately.

"Where have you been all my life?" Liam joked with a sigh of relief at the blissful silence. He immediately regretted his words though when he saw Dee jerk her face up toward him, a wolfish glint in her eyes. *Oh shit, Dee wasn't one of the divorced mums, was she?*

"Let me go and find Gracie. She's hiding in her room for some reason," Liam said quickly, and he headed down the hall to see what was going on with her.

Opening Gracie's bedroom door, he scanned the room and then spotted the lumpy shape hidden under the covers on the bed. Liam walked over and sat down, pulling back the quilt. "Grace honey, Dee and Cody are here to take you to the party. Time to go."

"Don't want to," Gracie replied.

"What do you mean? You've been looking forward to this. You'll have a great time!"

"Nope. Not going."

"Why don't you want to go, sweetheart?"

"Want to stay here with you."

"Are you kidding me? How much fun are you going to have here at home with me? Ethan and I are going to be doing boring stuff, like . . . like eating vegetables!" he said.

"I like veggies," said Gracie stubbornly. "Don't like Cody's mummy," she added.

"Why not?" Liam asked in surprise.

"When she picks up Cody from preschool she always wants to blow my nose or brush my hair."

Maybe Dee *was* planning on moving in on their family? Or maybe he was getting carried away and she was just trying to help out. Ever since Hannah had vanished, all sorts of people were constantly coming out of the woodwork offering advice and wanting to get involved—be that mother figure that his children apparently so desperately needed.

"Right," said Liam, trying to think of how to solve the situation. But he had a feeling that there was only one solution. "Will you go to the party if Ethan and I come too?" he asked tentatively.

Gracie's face lit up. "Yes!" she exclaimed at once.

"All right, let's get moving then. Looks like I've got to pack a few more things and we're already running late. Will you help Daddy get organized?"

"Mmmm," said Gracie, already leaping out of bed to reveal herself fully dressed in party mode, shoes and all. *Hmm, was this her plan all along?*

The phone began to ring from the kitchen and almost immediately he heard Dee's voice call down the hall, "Shall I grab that for you, Lee?"

Lee? What the hell? No one ever shortened his name. And then he stifled a laugh as a thought crossed his mind. If Deanne was planning on making a move on him, was she expecting that they become some sort of cutesy rhyming couple—Dee and Lee?

"That's okay," he called back. "The machine can get it." But a moment later he heard her answer the phone anyway. *Ah.* Gracie suddenly reached out a hand to grab Liam's arm. "Mummy!" she exclaimed.

"What?" Liam said, confused.

"That must be Mummy on the phone, calling to see if she can come to the party too!" And before Liam could stop her, she turned and dashed from the room, calling down the hallway, "Mummy! Mummy!"

"Gracie, wait!" he said weakly, his heart breaking for her.

Dammit. That was his own stupid fault. In the early days when Hannah had first left, he jumped almost every time the phone rang. "Hannah?" he would say into the receiver as he snatched it up, certain it would be her. So sure she would be phoning to tell him where she was, to say that she was ready to come back home. He hadn't realized that he must have been doing that right in front of poor Gracie.

Back out in the living room, Liam smiled apologetically at Dee who had already hung up the phone. He placed a protective arm around Gracie's shoulder as she stared from Dee to the phone and back again, a suspicious frown on her face, as though she thought Cody's mum must have done something to make Hannah vanish from the other end of the line. "Change of plans," he said. "Looks like I'm going to be bringing the kids in after all. I'm so sorry you came out of your way to pick up Gracie for no reason."

"You're coming to the party?" Dee asked, looking positively delighted. "That's great. We'll drive together, shall we?"

"Ahh, no—car seats," said Liam quickly. "You don't have a seat for Ethan and I don't have one for Cody."

"Oh," said Dee, her face falling for a moment, but then she rallied. "Never mind, we'll meet you there. Need a hand getting out the door?"

"No, no, you go. We'll be right behind you." Liam reached across to take Ethan back and began herding Dee and her son toward the front door. At the last second, he remembered the call Dee had picked up for him. "Oh, who was on the phone?" he asked.

"No one there, they just hung up. Wrong number maybe?"

Hannah wondered now as she headed down the wharf where the ferry was going to take her next and what she would do when she arrived at her destination. Hop straight back on another ferry? And then another and another? Could you live like that? Constantly in transit? Did the ferries even run through the night? Would someone kick her off eventually?

When she was little, her dad had made fun of her once for the way she pronounced ferry.

"Dad! Me and Mum took a fairy to Manly today!"

"You took a *what* to Manly?"

"A fairy!"

"Oh-ho! Rode on a *fairy*, did you? Flew you there with her pretty pink butterfly wings, did she?"

"Stop teasing her, Jack, you know what she means."

Now as she stepped on board the ferry she imagined responding to her father, *Fuck off, Dad.* Wow. Where had that thought come from? She loved her dad. Even with that sliver of blame over her mother's death. But truthfully, no one made her mum step in front of that train. People got divorced—that was life. Sure she had felt jealous at times, had worried that her dad had replaced her with his three new stepchildren, his ready-made family, but she had got over that, hadn't she? It was her mum who made her angry the most. Hannah had been pregnant with her mother's first grandchild when Anne had decided to take her own life. How could she have done that? The hypocrisy of this wasn't lost on her.

Hannah took a seat outside on the ferry and rested her head in her hands. Her mind felt too full, too confusing, all these thoughts and feelings clamoring to be heard. She wanted to clear it all out, but when she closed her eyes she saw faces. Mum. Dad. Liam. Gracie. Ethan. India. All glaring at her, asking her, *What's next, Hannah? What the fuck are you going to do now?*

Hard drops of rain began to fall and Hannah stayed outside, allowing herself to get drenched as the storm got into full swing, soaking her clothes through, plastering her hair to her face. The ferry took her to Cremorne Point, South Mosman and Old Cremorne before finally arriving at Mosman Bay, the last stop before it would swing around and return across the harbor to Circular Quay. She was just wondering what she should do, stay on or hop off, when a voice exclaimed, "Hannah! Is that you?"

She looked up to see a woman staring at her, one foot hovering above the plank that stretched across to the wharf. She was holding a newspaper over her head to protect her hair from the rain and her eyes were widened in amazement.

Hannah squinted through the rain at her. "Amy?" she asked.

"Oh my God, it is you! Come on, quick, the ferry's about to move off again." Amy dashed over to where Hannah sat and grabbed her by the arm. Hannah was too stunned to resist; she allowed Amy to drag her and her backpack off the ferry and onto the wharf. They stopped once they were under cover and sat down together on a bench seat.

"Jesus, Hannah, what are you doing here? Do you have any idea how worried everyone has been? I thought Liam said you'd run off overseas somewhere? Are you back? I mean, are you back at home, with your family?"

Hannah stared at her stepsister, unable to form an answer. She felt as though she had been caught doing something dirty in public, like picking her nose and then licking her finger. She had forgotten that being back in Sydney meant there was a very real possibility of running into someone she knew. She had thought that she would be invisible still, like she had been in London. And did it have to be Amy? The girl who Hannah had aspired to be for such a long time. The girl with the perfect life—*her* perfect life. And look at her. She was wearing a stylish black pencil skirt and a cream blouse along with stiletto heels. Her hair was tied back in a sleek blond ponytail and her makeup was flawless. The humiliation of what she had done, of how she must have looked, of the awful person that she had become, set in and she started to cry.

Amy placed a tentative arm around her shoulder. She let her cry for several minutes before standing and pulling her to her feet. "Right, you'll catch pneumonia if you stay in those wet clothes any longer. I'll take you back to my place and you can have a hot shower and change. *Then* you can tell me what's going on."

Amy lived in a gorgeous townhouse, a five-minute walk from the ferry wharf in Mosman. Her husband was the art director for a massive advertising agency and she had one perfect, angelic baby, who was looked after by a nanny when she went to work two and a half days a week as a graphic designer for a firm which was in constant competition with her husband's company. Hannah could just imagine the spritely, intelligent arguments they would have during the evenings after work, over who stole whose client or who came up with a concept for a particular campaign first.

Hannah took her shower in the most modern bathroom she had ever set foot in. A giant showerhead cascaded scalding hot water over her and the bathroom filled up with plumes of per-

fumed steam from Amy's frangipani scented shower gel. When she
stepped out of the shower, she wrapped herself up in the luxurious
bath sheet and stood in front of the large mirror. She couldn't see
her reflection; the mirror was steamed up and she was too afraid
to wipe it clear for fear of leaving streaks in an otherwise pristine
room.

When she was dry and dressed in some of Amy's clothes—
her backpack had been soaked through as well—Hannah walked
downstairs to the living room, wondering what her stepsister was
going to say to her. Amy had changed her clothes too. She was
now wearing skinny Levi jeans and a deep red top, her hair was
down and she was holding her plump, rosy-cheeked baby boy on
her hip. Even the baby was wearing designer clothes—Ralph
Lauren overalls and a smart checkered shirt.

"Make yourself comfortable," said Amy. "I made you a pepper-
mint tea, I hope that's okay?"

"Of course," Hannah replied, her voice quivering. She sat
down on the white leather sofa, tucking her wet hair behind her
ears before placing her hands awkwardly on her lap.

"I can't believe how lucky it is that I ran into you. I mean, I
wouldn't normally be in at work on a Saturday, it's only because
Luke's away for the weekend that I decided to do a half day at the
office. Otherwise I would never have been on that ferry."

"So," continued Amy, "how about I start, tell you what I know
and then you can fill me in on the rest." She popped her son into a
baby swing and switched it on. He began to rock gently back and
forth, serenaded by instrumental lullabies. "This is Harrison by

the way," Amy added as she took a seat on the couch next to Hannah. "He's six months," she added without being asked. "Not sure if Dad would have told you about him?"

Hannah nodded, "Yeah, I heard."

"Ah. Right, so this is what I know about you. Liam called Dad when you first vanished. He was frantic, didn't know where you'd gone. Why you'd left. Said you left a note, saying that you'd run away overseas somewhere. None of us could understand it at first. But I had an idea. I know I've never known you well, but it seemed pretty clear to me. You've been suffering from post-partum depression, right? Maybe even post-partum psychosis. I know because my mum went through it with all of us. Wasn't called PPD back then though; Mum was just told she was having a mental breakdown. Luckily she got through it on her own, left my dad—my first dad—when I was ten and later she met Jack. But when I was pregnant with Harrison she told me all about it. Wanted to warn me in case I suffered from it too—it's supposed to be genetic. She explained how there were times when she wanted to run away from it all.

"Anyway, when I heard about you and started to think that maybe this is what you were going through too, I went to see Liam. I spoke to Mum first, asked her what she thought and she agreed. She wished that she had chatted with you about her PPD too, wished she had been closer to you, that maybe if she had she might have picked up on the signs. But she's always known the part she played in splitting up your parents and has expected you to hate her for it, especially after what happened with your mother . . . later."

Hannah was keeping her eyes down as Amy spoke, her mouth clamped shut. She flicked her eyes up momentarily, though, to take another look at Harrison. He was grinning across at them from his swing, leaning forward slightly, as though eager to hear the story as well. Amy continued with her retelling of the recent events.

"Obviously I didn't know Liam well, either; in fact, the only time I've even met him was at your wedding. But I wanted to see if I could help in some way." Amy paused here, and Hannah got the feeling that she was nervous about what she wanted to say next.

"Hannah, he was devastated. He blames himself, you know. For not picking up on the signs. You've got to call him. He's missing you like crazy."

Hannah nodded. "I know. I know that he was at first anyway. But he's moved on now, right? Met someone else. And that's for the best anyway. That's what my plan was; those kids deserve more, much more . . . than me."

Amy stared at her in surprise. "What are you talking about? Are you insane? Of course he hasn't met anyone. Jesus, Hannah, it's only been a couple of months. What makes you think that anyway?"

"It doesn't matter, I just know what I heard, okay? Listen, thank you for everything, the clothes, the tea . . . but I think I should go, get out of your way."

Amy looked startled by Hannah's sudden decision to leave. Her composed demeanor became flustered as she jumped up from the couch. "Uh, wait, no—you can't go yet," she said, flapping her arms at Hannah.

"No, really, you've done enough. I've got to figure out what I'm going to do next, where I'm going to go. I need to think. Please, Amy, don't tell anyone you saw me, okay?" Hannah was already reaching for her backpack, which was still sodden from the rain.

"Hannah, WAIT!"

Hannah stared back at Amy, taken aback by her yelp.

"You can't leave yet because . . . because I've already called Liam. I'm sorry. It was while you were in the shower. He didn't pick up though, must be out . . . and I don't have his mobile number. But I left him a message, told him you were here." Amy began to chew on her fingernails as she waited for Hannah's reaction. "I'm really sorry," she said again. "I felt like I had to," she added.

Hannah hesitated, unsure of what to say. Her head was clamoring with thoughts fighting to be heard. *Stay, Hannah. Stay, you could see him again.* If she stayed, he might come straight here when he received the message. Maybe there was a way, maybe there was a chance to sort it all out. But at the same time doubt was tugging at her fingertips. *What if he doesn't want to see you? What if he doesn't come rushing around here? Because remember, he hates you now.* And he has every right to. After all, there was that text message. His final words to her, washing his hands of her, giving up. Seeing those words in her mind again was like having cut glass slicing at her bones.

No. Hannah was too afraid to stay and find out.

Liam finally had both the diaper bag and Gracie's backpack organized. He gathered up Ethan, took Gracie by the hand and led her out the front door. As he pulled the door shut behind him, he heard the phone inside begin to ring again. They were already running at least half an hour late for the party and it might just be a wrong number again. *Too bad, machine'll have to get it. If they really need me, they'll try my mobile.* And then he strapped the kids in, hopped in the front seat, and reversed out of the driveway.

Forty minutes later, Liam winced as the car entered the Lane Cove tunnel. "Uh oh," he whispered under his breath.

On cue, Gracie started wailing. "I don't like it in here. I want to get out of here. Daddy? Daddy! I want to get out of this tunnel." He wasn't sure when or where she had developed this intense dislike of driving through tunnels, and he wondered briefly if this was something brand new that Hannah had never even experienced with her. The thought made him angry. She shouldn't be missing out on any of this stuff.

"S'all right, Gracie, we'll be out in the sunshine again in a sec. Okay?"

"Daddy?"

"Yeah, hon?"

"Please can we get out of this tunnel?"

Liam sighed. "Sure thing, Grace, we'll be out any minute now."

"Yes, but I said please. So can we please get out of here NOW?"

"Ahh, yes, my mistake, I forgot that you'd said please. All right, Gracie. Hold on, let me just see if I can process that request for you, it'll just be one minute, okay?"

There was a pause and then Gracie said politely, "Okay. Thank you, Daddy." Liam glanced in the rearview mirror and smiled. A moment later the car glided out into the sunlight and Gracie applauded from the back seat. "Oh, well *done*, Daddy!

"Daddy," Gracie added suddenly.

"Yep?"

"When we get to the party, will we see Mummy there?"

Liam felt a thud deep in his gut and his hand flew up from the steering wheel to pinch the bridge of his nose. He had to cough wheezily before he could respond. "I really wish I could say yes, baby, but no. We won't see Mummy there. But hopefully soon, okay?"

"Please can we see Mummy there?"

"What about this—we'll see all your friends. That'll be nice, won't it?"

"But I said *please*," Gracie wailed.

"All right, Grace. Here's what I'll do, I'll process your request, okay? But it's going to take a little while. Lots of paperwork, red tape, you know? Might have to get a few interns on the case, approval from some higher-ups—that'll take time. But I'm going to get right to work on it, okay?"

There was silence from the back seat. Gracie seemed to be carefully considering what her father had said. Eventually she responded. "Right," she said firmly. Then, after another pause, "Good luck, Daddy."

Liam raised his eyebrows in surprise at the grown-up statement. Then he laughed. "Thanks, honey, I'm gonna need it. Hey look, you see that?" he added then, pointing out through the front windscreen. "That's the city skyline up ahead, means we're nearly there."

Riley had had to fly from the UK to Spain in order to meet up with James, but it was worth it. She knew this letter would be important to Simon. She knew how Simon felt about India. The fact that he'd even mentioned India at all in an email to her was a definite sign. Besides, she wanted to deliver it to Simon in person, so it was sort of on the way. They were meeting at a restaurant at 10:00 P.M. James had suggested they have dinner, and Riley figured why not. She could see from James's profile photo that he was cute. Her first impression when she spotted him at an outdoor table was that he was even more good-looking in person. Her second impression when she waved and headed his way was that he was not thinking the same thing.

She sat down in front of him and James stared for a few seconds before asking politely, "Sorry, but can I help you?" Riley hesitated, thrown for a moment.

"I'm Riley," she replied. "Aren't you James?"

"You're Riley?" James's shoulders slumped. "Sorry—I just thought you were a guy, that's all."

It clicked for Riley, "Oh, nope. Afraid not." She smiled. "You were hoping to meet Mr. Right, hey?" James nodded reluctantly.

Riley laughed. "So was I actually."

CHAPTER 12

Hannah was walking briskly up a steep hill. *What now, Hannah? What now?* Coming back to Sydney had been stupid. Of course Liam had moved on. Of course she was going to run into someone she knew; it had just been a matter of time, hadn't it? Still, did it have to be so quick—on both accounts? She sneezed, and then she sneezed again—five times in a row. *Great, probably going to get sick cause I got caught in that storm. Maybe I'll get lucky, maybe I will get pneumonia. Maybe I'll be so sick that I'll end up in hospital with it. All weak and pale, but beautiful, still beautiful of course. And then . . . maybe Liam will come. Would that be enough? Enough for him to want to forgive me? If I was near death?*

But that's not what's going to happen. Instead I'll just get a normal common cold. The tip of my nose will go all red and flaky. I'll have a hacking cough and a sweaty fever and there'll be no one to look after me and I'll be miserable and unattractive (because of the red nose) and I'll wish for someone to rub Vicks on my chest and make soup for me and it won't happen because I won't deserve it. Oh hell, Hannah, what have you gone and done with your life?

She had walked all the way through the back streets of Mosman and had found her way up to Military Road now. She spotted a city bus and ran for the stop up ahead, then flung her arm out to flag it down.

"Just made it, huh?" chuckled the bus driver as she hopped on.

"Looks like it."

"Lucky you weren't out there trying to catch a bus about an hour ago. HUGE storm, should have seen it. Wouldn't have wanted to get caught in that. Most of my passengers looked like drowned rats. Ha!" The driver grinned at her as she handed over money for the fare and then continued to chat as she took a seat near the front.

"Day seems to be coming good now, though. Bit of sunshine peeking through over there. Doesn't feel much like winter's coming at the moment, eh?"

"Guess not."

"You a local, love?"

The personal question took Hannah by surprise. "You mean the North Shore?"

"Nah, I mean are you a Sydney girl? Or a traveler. Saw you had that big backpack. But no accent. I mean, no foreign accent. You sound Aussie, you from another state?"

Hannah shifted uncomfortably in her seat. She had thought catching a bus instead of a taxi would mean no questions. No awkward conversations. Why hadn't she taken a seat further up the back?

"Um, I'm from Sydney actually." And she looked pointedly out the window, hoping he might stop questioning her. Instead he turned to look at her, dangerously taking his eyes off the slowing traffic up ahead.

"Huh. So what's with the luggage then?"

Hannah attempted to curb the irritation from creeping into her voice as she responded. "Been overseas," she said.

"Oh yeah? Where'd you go? Never left the country meself. Always wanted to travel, though. Those pyramids, they must be something, right? Did'ya see the pyramids over there? And the Statue of Liberty, that's another one I'd like to set my eyes on. What about her? You see her on your travels?"

"Nope. Neither. Went to England."

"Ah! England! The mother country. I've got English heritage, that and a bit of Maltese actually. Don't look it, though, do I?"

Before she could stop herself, Hannah blurted out, "My husband's Maltese."

"Really? What's the surname? Never know, could be that we're related, right?" And he chuckled again.

"Privitelli."

The driver frowned and rubbed his chin thoughtfully. Eventually he said, "Nah, don't know any Privitellis. Sure it's a good name, though. So where's your husband then? Didn't he go overseas with you?"

Hannah kicked herself for having mentioned Liam at all. How was she supposed to answer this?

In the end she settled for a simple "No."

"Why's that?"

Jesus!

"It's complicated."

"Ahhh. Having problems, are you? I'll tell you something, love, and I'll give you this advice for free. If a marriage is worth saving, you'll know. My wife and me, we went through some problems. Divorced, fifteen years ago now. Shouldn't have given up so easily, though. And that was my fault, I accept that. I didn't work at it hard enough, you know what I mean? You see, everyone has their ups and downs. So what is it anyway? You fight over money? Kids? You want them, he doesn't? Sex? Lotta people fight over sex, don't know why—such a simple act—but it causes big problems."

Hannah stood up abruptly. "Actually, this is my stop up here."

"Oh. Really?" The driver looked disappointed. "Well, nice chat, love. You take care, all right?"

As the bus pulled up at the stop, and Hannah made to step down the stairs, he shot an arm out to stop her. "Hey, let me tell you one more thing. My wife and I, we got back together, had a second wedding and all. Another big white dress. Never know how things might work out in the end, even if it seems bleak now."

Hannah nodded and gave him a tiny smile as she stepped down onto the street. *That was different. I think I just got the friendliest bus driver in the bloody world.*

She looked up as the bus pulled away from the curb and tried to get her bearings. Thanks to the all-consuming conversation with the driver, she hadn't paid any attention to where she had hopped off. As she spun around on the spot, looking for something familiar, her eyes caught sight of a splash of color. It took a moment for her brain to catch up and then her vision blurred and her stomach heaved. It was the giant smiling face of Luna Park. She was just down the street from Milsons Point train station.

"Isn't he just exquisite?" gushed the woman at the cotton candy stand.

Liam smiled politely and shifted Ethan from one arm to the other. "Exquisite, yes—but also surprisingly heavy for his age."

He was hoping she might take the hint and move things along; he wanted to go and sit down, take a breather for a few minutes before it was time to rejoin the party. He had been proud of how he had managed to successfully extricate himself from the main group. Once they'd arrived, Gracie had forgotten all about her fears of being there without her dad and had raced off to join her friends. There were no other dads accompanying their children, just mums—mums intent on telling him how he should be dealing with Gracie's tantrums, when he should be starting Ethan on solids, what sort of sleep patterns he should be enforcing and all sorts of other shit that he had no interest in whatsoever. As far as he was concerned, he was doing just fine with his kids so far. When he'd mentioned finding somewhere quiet on his own to give Ethan his bottle, Dee had been quick to offer him her company, but he'd been able to decline, even if it had taken a fair bit of force.

The cotton candy woman missed Liam's subtle hints and continued to coo at Ethan. "He's got your eyes, you know. Adorable."

Liam's smile became fixed as he restrained himself from correcting her. *Actually, you twit, they're his mum's eyes; anyone can see they don't look anything* like *mine.*

Liam walked away feeling agitated. He was quite close to the spot where he'd first laid eyes on Hannah. He still remembered that moment clearly. Remembered spotting her walking away from the roller coaster, recalled how what he'd first noticed about her was her eyes. Oh okay, so that was bullshit; what he noticed first were her great breasts—perky, round, just the right amount of cleavage showing to get him feeling quite aroused. But then he'd looked up and noticed her eyes. It was the cheeky spark that attracted him. That's what caused him to be so bold when he'd approached her. He had the sense that a normal pick-up line wasn't going to work on this girl. Instead he'd stepped right up to her, acting like they were friends who had planned to meet rather than complete strangers. And she'd made that crack about how he ought to have picked up that paper cup and he'd immediately thought, *This is going to be fun.*

So then how had it all gone so wrong?

•

Hannah walked steadily toward the train station, her shoulders aching from the weight of the backpack. *So, Hannah, what happens when you reach the station? Going to get on a train, or going to step in front of a train? Seems like such a small difference, doesn't it? Step on, step in front. On, or in front? On. In front.*

On. In front. Her brain was filled with those three words, just tumbling around, piling on top of one another; over and over and over they asked her, *On? In front?*

At the station she bought a ticket. So that seemed like a good sign. She hadn't been here to this station since her mother had taken her own life. And now as she walked slowly down the platform, she found herself wondering what her mother had been thinking when she had come here. Whether she herself was now walking the exact same path as her mother. She took notice of her surroundings carefully. She saw the sparkle of the sunlight glinting on the specks in the concrete. Noticed the grime of grease on the tracks. Felt the air pressing against her skin. Felt pressure on her lungs. Tightening around her throat. Where had she stepped off the platform? Was it here, by the staircase? Was it over there, near the ticket booth? Did her blood splatter up from the tracks, onto the concrete of the platform? And how well would they have cleaned it? Would they have scrubbed at it with bleach until all remnants of her mother were gone? Or could there still be faint traces of her?

Did she know when she came here? Was it a plan? Or was it

a spontaneous decision? Most people thought spontaneity was a good thing.

In the distance she heard the sound of a train approaching. And she wondered about that old saying and how true it really was: *Like mother like daughter.*

Liam found a bench seat and sat down to give Ethan his bottle. After a few minutes of trying to figure out if he could feed Ethan and also eat the cotton candy he'd just bought at the same time, he gave up and rested the pink and yellow cloud of spun sugar on top of the stroller instead. He watched Ethan's eyes follow the colorful shape of the cotton candy as it passed over him. "Nope," Liam said quietly, "I might be a man and according to all these preschool mums, therefore incapable of looking after my baby son—but one thing I do know is that you don't give cotton candy to a newborn. Sorry, kid."

But then Ethan's eyes caught sight of his bottle of milk and he practically dived on the teat. Liam leaned back on the seat as Ethan fed and watched the groups of people pass by. It was a different sort of crowd from when he'd first met Hannah here eight years ago. A lot more families and young children—or maybe he was the one who had changed and he had just started noticing the family types more. He spotted a young couple who he guessed might have been on a first date—or at least in the very early stages of their relationship. The guy was trying to win her one of those giant stuffed toys by tossing rings across a water canal and attempting to land them around old style milk bottles. Each time he missed the red flush on his neck would creep a little higher. Liam was feeling bad for the guy, but then the girl stepped in close, grabbed him by the shirt and kissed him, hard. Even if the guy couldn't see it, as far as Liam was concerned, the message was clear—that girl didn't give a crap about some stuffed toy, all she wanted was him.

Hannah stood on the train, watching as the doors slid shut and they moved off, away from the station. In the end, the decision had been made for her. A little old lady had approached her as she stood, toes lined up against the yellow paint strip on the platform. She had coughed to get Hannah's attention and when Hannah turned to look at her, she had expected a sweet little old lady voice—to match her sweet white-curled-hair appearance. But instead the voice had been clipped. "I'll need your help getting on the train. This walker is really very heavy. Much too heavy for me to lift up over the gap on my own. But mind you're careful with it." And she had indicated the steel walker she was leaning heavily against.

"Sure, no problem," said Hannah.

"Of course it's not a problem. I wasn't *asking*, dear."

Once on the train the woman had wrenched the walker out of Hannah's grip as she moved off to sit down without so much as a thank-you. Hannah now stood by herself, wondering if she needed to be grateful to the old woman for saving her. But really, she knew that she had had no intention of killing herself. Just as she hadn't really meant to lean forward from her flat window that night.

Like mother like daughter? Pfft. Fuck that.

No. It was time to make a change. It was time to step up and take back her life. The train was headed out west. She was going to go home. She was going to step right up to her front door and she was going to hug her children and she was going to kiss her husband. And if that woman who had answered the phone answered the door, this time she was going to ask her who the hell she was.

Liam smiled as Gracie came barreling toward him. She thrust a stuffed elephant in his face. "I won it!" she exclaimed, breathless.

"Well done, hon," Liam replied, lifting Ethan up over his shoulder so he could burp him.

Gracie was followed by Dee and Cody, along with one more mum and her two little girls.

"Where's the rest of the party?" Liam asked.

"Gone," said Gracie matter-of-factly.

Dee leaned in to explain. "Our birthday girl ate too much and threw up everywhere, had to go home early—the party sort of disintegrated from there." Then she looked pointedly at the other mum, the last one standing. "I guess we should all call it a day then," Dee said brightly.

"Oh, okay, yes I suppose I should take these two home," said the other mother awkwardly.

"Coming to the train station?" she asked.

"Oh no, we both drove," Dee replied a tad smugly, standing her ground firmly. Liam gave the other mum a desperate plea for help with his eyes, but she smiled sympathetically, said her good-byes, and backed away with her two children under Dee's hardened gaze.

Left alone, Dee turned her attention to Liam. "What say we take this lot into the city for an early tea by the harbor?" she asked.

"Ahh, you know what," said Liam falteringly, "I was actually thinking I might hang around here a bit longer, you know, make the most of the entrance fee now that we're here. Have some *family* time." If he had placed any more emphasis on the word family it would have been like hitting her over the head with a blunt stick.

Dee's face remained unfazed. "Darling," she said, "there was no entrance fee. It's free."

"Oh you know, figure of speech . . ." said Liam, his voice petering out nervously.

But Dee just giggled as though Liam was the funniest person she had ever met. "Well anyway, that's perfect; you see I was just saying to Cody we should explore a bit more before we have to go home. Come on," she added, her eyes flicking toward a shooting game nearby. "You can win me a giant teddy bear with your rifle skills!"

What rifle skills?

"I'm not really much of a shooter," he said quickly.

"What?" she exclaimed, with a peal of artificial laughter. "I bet you're just being modest! Hey, Gracie, don't you want to see Daddy win that giant toy over there?" Dee appealed to Gracie, and Gracie looked back and forth between her dad's face and the huge teddy bear—clearly torn.

"That settles it," said Dee, as though Gracie had responded by jumping up and down with excitement and begging to go over to the game. "Let's go!" And Liam felt as though he had no choice but to place Ethan in his stroller and obediently follow Dee over to the heavily decorated stall.

He couldn't believe how badly he wished that it was eight years ago still and he was here with Hannah, flirting outrageously, the air thick with sexual tension, his skin fizzing each time his hand touched hers.

The train ride seemed to be over so quickly. One minute they were crossing the bridge, the next they were underground, and then suddenly, suburbs were flashing past. Redfern. Auburn. Parramatta. Seven Hills. She watched as backyards with Hills Hoist clotheslines, gray buildings splashed with graffiti and milk bars rushed by. When her stop arrived, she stepped off the train with trembling legs. It felt as though all of the confidence that she'd gathered back at Milsons Point had been hemorrhaging since about Strathfield.

What if he slammed the door in her face?

What if Gracie hated her now?

What if Ethan couldn't remember her?

But her feet took control and her body was forced to take the familiar route home. Down Carson Street. Left onto Rooke, right at Prescott. Cut through the walkway between Prescott and Potter Avenue. And finally, left into Amber Place. There it was, just up ahead. Her home.

That's your family, Han. Right there, behind those white bricks and gray cement. On the other side of that door, your family is waiting for you—whether they know it or not.

Of course, she was wrong.

All that preparation. All the strength it took to lift her hand and knock. And no one came to the bloody door. Eventually she found the spare key, hidden in the garden, taped to the bottom of a frighteningly ugly garden gnome—and she let herself into her house. It was the smell that hit her first. It was so familiar, that smell; if she was asked to describe it, she wasn't sure that she could—but it smelled like home, and it brought the memories rushing back. She saw herself vacuuming the living room furiously, determined that Liam not know she wasn't coping. Saw herself sitting on the sofa in the darkness, feeding Ethan in the dead of the night, eyes fixed on a silent, flickering television, mind blank. And she saw herself huddled in the kitchen pantry, with just the light from the cupboard spilling out into the room, as she steadily ate her way through chocolate after chocolate, until she felt sick enough to vomit.

She had to shake her head to push those memories away, to stop herself from being suffocated by them. Instead she let the straps of her backpack fall away and dropped the pack to the floor, feeling relieved to be free of its weight on her shoulders.

Now what? Did she wait for them to come home? Cook dinner for them, greet them at the front door and pretend she'd never left? She snorted at the thought. She walked slowly through the house and wondered if perhaps it was actually best this way. Almost as if by spending time in their house on her own, she could ease herself ever so gently back into her life again. Step by step.

In her bedroom she gazed at the bed and she thought about her and Liam, and how they had always liked to sleep together, back before sleep became a precious commodity constantly interrupted by tiny people demanding her attention. They'd start with her head on his chest, her legs curled around his legs, and Liam would be constantly puffing his cheeks out as he tried to blow strands of her hair away from his face because they would tickle his nose. And then after five minutes, she'd turn over, and he'd stay flat on his back and she'd slide her hand up under her pillow and find his hand waiting there and their fingers would entwine together and that's how they always fell asleep.

In Ethan's room, Hannah's eyes traveled from his crib to his changing table to his baby-blue wardrobe and the sense of loss and of longing, longing for a relationship that had never even seen the light of day, tugged so strongly at her body that she had to turn away and squeeze her eyes shut tight.

Then Gracie's room. Hannah barely caught sight of her white

and pink cupcakes bedspread, the teddy bear sitting crooked on her pillow, before the tears welled up and she wanted to scream out loud: "Hannah, what did you *do*?" Before she closed the door, she quickly crossed the room and then gently righted the crooked teddy bear so that it sat, tall and confident on her daughter's bed. Finally she headed back up the hall and into the kitchen. That's when she saw the invitation on the fridge. She double-checked the date.

Unbelievable. That's where they were right now. At Luna Park for a birthday party. Dammit, how could she have been so close?

She checked her watch. Could she get all the way back there and catch them in time? Or should she wait here for them to come home?

No. She was supposed to be taking her life back. She left the house at a run.

"Ooh, shall we go on the ferris wheel next?"

"Yeah sure, we'll just find a carnie to look after Ethan for us, shall we?" Liam knew he was being rude, but he couldn't help it. Subtle didn't work on this woman. She'd dragged him from one meaningless game to another. And she was one of those people who liked to touch you—a lot. There was constant arm grabbing and neck stroking and even, once, butt squeezing. Honestly, it was starting to become uncomfortable. Imagine if *he* was coming on that strong with a woman! He'd be sued for sexual harassment. Or at least he'd have been slapped in the face by now.

He imagined responding to Dee's advances with a slap in the face and then trying to explain to a police officer that he was only trying to stand up for himself. Obviously he would never do that, but God if that woman ran her glossy, manicured talon of a fingernail down his arm one more time . . .

"Maybe we should just—" he began, but Dee interrupted him— an occurrence that was becoming all too frequent.

"Let's give you one more chance to win me that giant bear. I know you'll never forgive yourself if we go home without one!"

We? Go home? What the fuck?

And he was too taken aback to respond as she led him over to yet another game that was designed to relieve him of as much of his cash as possible, usually in exchange for a plastic keyring or a bloody fridge magnet.

Stepping in through that giant smiling face hadn't been as hard as she had expected. She was focused now. She was strong. She was going to find her family.

For the first five or ten minutes, as she searched through the park, she was avoiding it—that place where she had met her husband. But eventually, it was as though she was being drawn toward it and she gave in, allowing her legs to lead her to that familiar spot, as though a hook was attached to her navel, guiding her steadily toward it—just near the roller coaster. Up until now, she had been keeping her eyes open wide, scanning the crowds, searching for her family—but now, when she was sure she had the exact place, she closed her eyes and tried hard to transport herself back. Tried to change the sounds she could hear, the feel of the air on her skin. Pictured Liam as he was that night, walking toward her—shy but confident. His hair was a little longer back then, messier. God he was sexy.

She had to get him back. She had to get her family back. She had to make this right.

And that's when she heard it. A child's voice screaming out in delight, "Mummy!"

She whipped her head up so fast that her neck twinged.

That sounded like. Oh God, it is.

Gracie.

It was Gracie who saw her first.

Liam was lining up his next shot, thinking how stupid this was. Thinking how Hannah would never demand that he win her a giant teddy. Wondering how in the hell he was going to get rid of Dee—and more than that, wondering how he was ever going to get his family back together—when Gracie suddenly screamed out, "Mummy!"

What?!

Before he could stop her, before he could take in the scene in front of him, figure out who it was that she'd seen, Gracie had torn away from him and was running through the crowds of people.

It can't be. It can't be her. She must have just seen someone who looked like Hannah and now he was going to have to console her when she realized. Leaving Ethan in his stroller with Dee, he took off running after her.

That's when he saw her. She had turned at the sound of Gracie's scream and she was looking right at him and it was her face. It was Hannah.

Before she knew it, Gracie had flown into Hannah's arms and bowled her over. As Hannah landed with a thud on the ground, she could barely believe it. It had finally happened. Gracie was here, in her arms. Before Hannah could find them, her little girl had spotted her first. And right now, the rest of the world was receding around her and it was just Hannah and her baby girl, held so tight in her arms. And she was thinking to herself, *I will never, ever leave you again* as her tears streamed down her cheeks and into Gracie's hair.

When she finally looked up, she saw Liam standing above her, staring at her incredulously.

"Umm." Hannah took in a deep breath, unsure of what to say—of how to begin a conversation like this.

But then Liam had dropped to his knees next to Hannah, and he had wrapped his arms around the two of them, and he was hugging her just as tight as Gracie had and both of them were crying, and Gracie was laughing. "Daddy! You're squashing me!" she giggled, but it took several seconds before Liam registered what she had said and let go.

Eventually he leaned back and spoke. "God, Hannah, I don't

know what to say. Where do I even start?" His voice sounded hurt and Hannah began to feel scared. When Gracie had flown into her arms just now, and then Liam had followed suit, she had been instantly filled with euphoria. Tiny sparks of hope for forgiveness from her family had flared and she had had visions of slipping seamlessly back into her life. Now she was coming back to reality—it wasn't going to be that easy, was it?

That's when Dee appeared above them, pushing Ethan in his stroller, her own son by her side. She was staring at Hannah in shock.

"What . . . what are *you* doing here?" she spluttered. Hannah realized then how odd they must have looked, the three of them on the ground in a tearful embrace. In fact, she saw now that several people were eyeing them curiously as they walked past. Hannah resisted the urge to respond to Dee, who she recognized from Gracie's preschool, "Well, what are you doing here?"

Was Dee the woman who had answered the phone? Was Dee here *with* her family? And why was she pushing Ethan in his stroller? The stroller that had once been Gracie's. The stroller that Hannah could so clearly remember picking out with Liam when she had been pregnant that first time. They had raced strollers up and down the aisles of Babyco until a staff member had icily suggested that perhaps speed wasn't the feature they should be looking for in a stroller and they had nodded meekly, but in the end they had still chosen the one that Hannah had won the race with.

"Should we move somewhere out of the way? So that we can . . . talk?" Hannah asked in a small voice.

Liam nodded and stood up, then helped Hannah to her feet. Gracie was still clinging to Hannah's neck, which Hannah was relieved about. She didn't want to let her go yet either, and she kept her arms wrapped around her as she stood. They moved over to a bench seat and Hannah was acutely aware of how her heart was beating like a bass drum as she sat down and tried to prepare herself for the conversation that was coming. But first they needed to get rid of Dee. She couldn't have this talk with an audience.

Luckily, Liam seemed to be thinking the same thing. "Listen, Deanne, I really appreciated all of your help today, but . . ." he was obviously hoping she would take the hint and just leave. Unfortunately, she didn't.

"But," she said in confusion, her eyes on Hannah, an accusing tone in her voice, "where did you come from? How are you here? You can't just be back."

That's when another woman appeared behind her. Hannah looked up to see another one of the mums from Gracie's preschool, Jenny, with her two daughters by her side. "Hi," she said brightly. "We hung around for a bit because our train wasn't for a while." Then she caught Hannah completely off guard by reaching out to clasp a hand on her shoulder. "It's so good to see you back, Hannah," she said in such a genuine tone that Hannah almost wanted to cry again. She didn't even know that Jenny knew her name. Then Jenny turned to Dee. "I think we'd best leave them to it, shouldn't we, Dee?" she said firmly. "I'll walk you to your car," she added. Then Jenny guided the livid-looking Dee and her son away, throwing an encouraging smile over her shoulder at Liam and Hannah as she left.

Finally, Hannah was alone with her family. Gracie was still on her lap, Ethan was asleep in his stroller, and Liam was sitting next to her, looking like he had a thousand questions he wanted to ask but—like her—he had no idea where to start.

So instead, they didn't speak. Instead, Liam put his arm gently around Hannah's shoulders and they sat like that for thirty minutes. Long enough to watch the sun set. Long enough to see the sky change from a pale blue, to a fiery orange with swirls of pink and finally, a deep, dark blue with pinpricks of stars beginning to appear.

As it began to get cold, Liam spoke. "Come home," he said, his voice thick with emotion.

"Come home with us and we can talk about everything tomorrow."

Angelo was tipping the cup of coffee into the pot plant outside his office when the young girl appeared in front of him, pushing sunglasses up onto the top of her reddish-brown hair and squinting in the sunlight at him. At first he had jumped; he thought it was his wife, come to reprimand him for pouring his coffee out.

"I keep telling you, Angelo, this plant is fake. Fake. No water and definitely no coffee." Now he touched the leaves suspiciously; they certainly looked real.

"Umm, excuse me?"

The girl's voice startled Angelo; he'd almost forgotten she was there.

"Yes? How I can help you?"

"I'm looking for Simon. He works here, right? On your boat, The Aella?*"*

"HA!" Angelo leaned forward to slap his knees and laugh uproariously. "You are girl! You come here looking for Simon, just as he goes to search for you! HA! Yes, very pretty, now I see why he is so sad. Always wah, wah, wah is our Simon. Ha." He finished with a quiet chuckle, wiping tears of mirth from his eyes.

"No, no, no—I'm not that girl. I'm Riley, Simon's sister. He's gone somewhere?"

"Oh." Angelo looked disappointed. "You are sister. Very embarrassing for me. Very embarrassing." He turned to walk away, back into his office, shaking his head a little dolefully.

"Sorry, my fault, should have explained who I was first,"

Riley called out hurriedly. "Can you please tell me where Simon's gone?"

Angelo turned back; he still looked glum about his failed joke. "Gone to London to find girl, left . . ." he checked his watch ". . . three, maybe four hours ago." His face brightened then. "Hey! You look like nice girl, you need job?"

CHAPTER 13

The following day they did talk. About everything. Liam called Amy and asked if she would mind coming to look after the kids for them, and they went out to a coffee shop so they could have the discussion on their own.

When Hannah had said good-bye to Gracie there was a heart-breaking moment where she had hugged her tight and whispered, "You will come back again, won't you, Mummy?"

Hannah had felt a flush of heat behind her eyes and she had to concentrate very hard to keep her voice steady as she had responded to her daughter. "Yes, I promise, Gracie, I'll be back."

On the drive to the coffee shop they remained silent. Hannah felt so confused. They had spent the night wrapped up in one another's arms. Never before had Hannah spent an entire night sleeping in that one single position. It was as though neither of them were prepared to let the other go—just in case. And as they fell asleep, Liam had whispered fiercely in her ear, "Don't ever leave me again, Han. Please. Don't ever, ever leave me again." And then he had pulled her in close, and begun to cry into her shoulder. Hannah's body had felt weak with relief. He still loved her— despite everything, despite that message he'd sent her, despite what she had done to their family. They had both fallen asleep with tear-streaked cheeks.

But what now? What was he going to say to her? And how was she going to explain everything to him?

When they arrived at the café, they both continued to avoid starting up the conversation, waiting till they had placed their orders for their cappuccinos and then waiting until the coffees had arrived. Waiting until there was no chance of interruptions before they began to speak.

It was Liam who broke the silence first. "What made you come back?" he asked, as he stirred sugar into his cup. He was trying to sound casual, like he was chatting with a friend about why they'd decided to come home early from a holiday, or what made them return to an old job. But his eyes were intense when he looked up from his coffee to wait for the response.

"It was a friend," Hannah said slowly. "A girl I met in London. She made me see reason. Convinced me I could make everything right again. I flew back to Sydney, I was going to come straight home. But then . . . I called the house first, and . . . a woman answered. I had started to back out. I thought you must have moved on."

"God no," said Liam. "That was just bloody Dee. She was there to take Gracie to the party, but then . . . we all ended up going. I told her not to answer the damn phone." Liam hesitated then. "There is something I have to tell you, though," and his voice was heavy with guilt.

"I kissed another woman." The words came out in a rush and Hannah felt their sting, felt her skin turn cold.

She kept her eyes down and when she spoke, her voice was raspy. "When?" she asked. "Was it while I was gone because, you know, I left you . . . so I can't really blame you for doing that."

"That's the awful part," he said. "It was two nights before you left. I'm so, so sorry, Hannah. I know it will sound like a cliché, but it meant absolutely nothing. I was going to tell you—that day. I was going to have this big talk with you. I knew that something was wrong, but I'd been in denial about it. But when I kissed that girl, it's like it woke me up—made me see how bad things really were. I was going to sort everything out. Tell you the truth and make you tell me what you were really feeling. But then . . . it was too late. You were already gone."

Hannah stayed quiet, trying to gather herself, trying to figure out how she felt about all of this. What was the right reaction? Was she allowed to be angry with her husband for kissing some-one else? Or did everything she had done—walking out on her family, running away from them—negate that? Were they even now? Or did a simple kiss not even compare to what she had done? Or should she not be looking at it like this? It wasn't really about making comparisons, was it? About scoring points—or losing them, as it was. This was a marriage, not a competition.

There were so many questions she wanted to ask. *Who was she? Why did you kiss her? How did it happen? Is she prettier than me? Do you still love me?* But instead, she needed to say her bit. "Listen, Liam, I did a terrible thing, to you and the kids. I don't know how to explain it to you, but I'm so, so sorry."

Liam seemed taken aback; she supposed he was expecting her to say more about his confession. He reached across the table and took her hands in his. "It's not your fault," he whispered. "I need to say sorry too. I'm sorry I didn't see what was going on with you. I should have picked up on the signs. You had postpartum depression and I completely missed it. Or maybe . . . maybe that's not true. Maybe I was ignoring it. Maybe I wanted to believe things were really as good as you were making out they were. I should have been there for you. I should have made you talk with me sooner."

Hannah nodded. "And I should have said something too. I should have told you I was struggling. I don't even know why I was trying to hide it now—it all seems so stupid."

"Look at me, Han," said Liam then, leaning in close. "We're going to get through this together now, okay? All of it. We're going to get you whatever help you need." He paused then, before saying carefully, "Han, I noticed that . . . that you haven't actually held Ethan yet. Don't you . . . you know, want to?" he asked.

Hannah looked back at him, startled. Then she slowly shook

her head. "It's not that I don't want to," she said shakily. "I'm scared to hold him, Liam. I know it sounds awful, but I'm terrified that I'm going to get sucked back down into that black hole. I think I just need to get . . . better first." Hannah hesitated before adding, "Do you think I'm some kind of monster? I mean, what sort of mother leaves her newborn baby for almost two months and then doesn't want to hold him when she comes back?"

"No," Liam said firmly. "You're not a monster."

"But that's not what you thought the other night, though, is it? That message you sent me. The one where you said you were done with me . . ."

"Please, please don't believe a word of it," Liam cut in quickly. "I didn't mean it. Truthfully, I got angry. I was fed up. I was missing you and Gracie was missing you and I didn't know what else to do, I was just so . . . frustrated. I thought maybe if I got mad, I could wake you up, you know? Shock you into coming back home. Maybe like reverse psychology or something stupid like that.

"I didn't mean a thing that I said in that stupid text message. I love you, Hannah, and I've never bloody stopped loving you, even when I was as mad as all hell with you for leaving us."

"I love you too," said Hannah, as the relief washed over her.

Despite their heartfelt reconciliation, over the next few weeks things remained somewhat tense between the two of them, even awkward, as they attempted to figure out how to pull their family back together. And it seemed as though it was going to take

some time before Hannah could form any sort of relationship between herself and Ethan—he was just as wary of her as she was
of him. In fact, the first time that Hannah held him, two days
after coming home, he screamed so much that she handed him
straight back to Liam and fled from the room, hyperventilating
with fear that her baby was never going to forgive her for what
she had done.

The one person who had welcomed her back with open arms
was Gracie. She treated Hannah as though she had been on an
extended holiday, showing her every drawing and painting she
had created while Hannah had been gone and curling up on her
lap each evening, absentmindedly playing with Hannah's ponytail as they watched *In the Night Garden* before bed. If it weren't
for Gracie, Hannah's whole being would probably be disintegrat-
ing, flecks of her soul scattering throughout Sydney. But Gracie's
instant, unadulterated forgiveness was like a thick glue, pasting
her back together.

They were talking about moving house as well. Maybe back to
Leichhardt, where Hannah could remember having been so much
happier. It was all up in the air at this stage, but the prospect of a
new start was keeping Hannah optimistic about the future.

There had been one horrendous day, though, when Hannah
had found her letter. The one she had left Liam when she first
walked out. She had discovered it folded up in Liam's top bedside
drawer and it felt like a piece of the past was reaching out and
dragging her down. All that Hannah wanted was to forget about

that part of her life. She wanted to block it out, pretend it never happened. But here was this letter that she could so clearly remember writing, hunched over their dining room table the night before she left—so sure that leaving was simply the only option.

But the letter's discovery had led to one good thing. Liam had found Hannah sitting on the edge of their bed and he had sat down next to her and gently taken the letter out of her hands. As they sat side by side—Liam holding the letter in his hands, Hannah staring at the wall, afraid to move, afraid to speak, concentrating hard on stopping her hands from flying out, snatching the letter back from Liam and tearing it to shreds—Liam had said something.

"You think you weren't a good mother? You think you couldn't bond with Ethan, or that you didn't feel anything for our kids? If that were true then you wouldn't have been able to write these things, Hannah. Look at it."

And he held out the letter and waited. As Hannah read what she had written, pushing past the first few horrific lines where she told Liam that she was leaving him, she saw the messages that she had left behind specifically for her children to read one day.

Dear Gracie,

When you were younger, about two, you liked to put things behind your back to make them vanish and then you would hold your hands out and exclaim, "Where's it gone?!" You were like a tiny, little magician! So once you hid a coin behind your back and said, "Where's it gone?!" But then when you went to find it, it really was gone! We searched everywhere, in your clothes, on the kitchen floor, in the hood of your sweater and it was just gone! So I was very impressed with your magician's skills. Anyway, later when I was undressing you for your bath, I took off your diaper and there was the coin. I couldn't stop laughing and you smiled shyly at me, as though you weren't quite sure what it was that I found so funny—but then you started laughing too, and I hugged your small body close and almost didn't want to let you go for your bath.

Once, I was at the shops with you, you were standing with your arms folded and stamping your little foot about something that you wanted and a stranger stopped to say to me, "Oh, she's getting a real, little personality of her own, isn't she?" And I remember thinking to myself—*Well, of course she has her own personality, she's her own person, isn't she?* But lately it's got me thinking—what sort of a person will you be when you grow up? Will you keep changing and changing? Will you hit your teenage years and become grumpy and wear dark eyeliner and want to paint your room black? Will there be just one stuffed toy from your childhood that you'll hang on to and keep hidden, in the back of your closet? And will your dad be able to cope with these changes, all on his own?

And so there's just one thing that I wanted to tell you, for when you reach your high-school years, because I think you'll be the type of person who is friends with everyone, I think that you'll be kind and caring and you won't get lost in the politics of high-school girlfriends—but just in case, maybe you could listen to this song on the first day of year seven: "Caught in the Crowd" by Kate Miller-Heidke. Just listen to the lyrics and think about what they might mean to you.

Because I know that you will be amazing.

Dear Ethan,

You gave your first-ever smile to your big sister. She was dancing around the house in her rainbow-colored skirt and you were lying on the floor, supposed to be having some tummy time, but I had to roll you onto your back because you hated lying on your tummy. Gracie started spinning around and around right next to you and I could see your blinking lashes as you watched the twirling colors. Then she threw herself down onto the carpet and lay right next to you, with her face pressed so close to yours that your noses were almost touching. All of a sudden this beauti-ful grin spread itself across your face, and the more you smiled, the more Gracie smiled, and the more you smiled again! Then Gracie leapt back up and continued to dance and the whole time I had been standing in the doorway watching. Watching and smiling because the two of you were simply beautiful.

On the night that I went into labor with you, it was raining. Hot, but raining. It was funny, because I hadn't noticed the rain until I stepped out the front door, and then we saw big, fat droplets, splashing on the front porch. I remember driving first to Rita's place, to drop off Gracie, and when your dad hopped out of the car with her, Gracie leaned back in to say, "Mummy, will the new baby come with anything?" And I was confused for a second, and then she said, "You know, like a teddy bear or a pretty book?" And I laughed and promised her that yes, the new baby would have a gift for her. But truthfully, we'd forgotten to get something, so I had to send your dad straight into the gift store when we arrived at the hospital, because I didn't want to forget and I so wanted Gracie to be happy the first time she met you. Everyone tells you about sibling jealousy when you're having a new baby. Funny thing is, when Gracie did finally come to the hospital and meet you, she couldn't care less about the stuffed toy, all she wanted to do was crouch on the bed next to me while I held you, and all I could hear was her snuffly breathing as she gazed at you in amazement.

You were born with the most incredible amount of hair. Great, thick tufts of such dark, dark hair. One of the nurses brought in a troll doll (they're these little plastic dolls with crazy tall, brightly colored hair that were big in the eighties) that she had at home and gave it to me because she thought it was such a great joke. I'll keep it forever you know, that funny little doll with its shock of purple hair.

When Hannah finished reading she leaned into her husband's shoulder and she felt a slice of hope. Maybe he was right. Maybe her heart wasn't empty.

Liam and Hannah were driving home from one of their sessions with Elizabeth—Hannah's new psychologist. Elizabeth had been helping them to tackle one problem after another—Hannah's food issues, her need to strive for perfection, all of her fears and insecurities. But today had been more of a couple's therapy and at the end of the session, Elizabeth had leaned forward and announced happily, "Right, I'm forewarning you—next session we're going to take a look at your sex life, so be prepared!"

So now the car seemed filled with tension as they both avoided talking about what Elizabeth had said. Hannah was driving and Liam was keeping his eyes fixed on the passing world through the passenger window. But Hannah eventually broke it. "So you think we're supposed to do homework for the nest session?" Liam looked over at her, momentarily confused, but he realized what she meant and they both started to laugh. The tension dissipated and they began to relax.

"Do *you* want to . . . you know, do any homework?" Liam asked.

"I don't know, do you?" Hannah responded shyly.

"God, look at us, together eight years, married for four, and we're acting like teenagers about to do it for the first time. I guess it's been a while, though, right?" Liam suddenly spoke very quickly, "It has been a while, hasn't it? I mean, you didn't meet anyone in London, did you?"

"No!" Hannah almost let the car swerve off into the shoulder in her rush to reassure Liam. "Absolutely not, I could never!"

"Sorry, just checking."

"That's okay, but you believe me, right? You trust me?"

"Of course," said Liam, and he meant it.

"And you? It was never more than that one kiss . . . right?" Hannah sucked in her breath as she waited for a response.

"I promise you—that was it, one stupid kiss."

"Good."

They drove on in silence for several more minutes. As they finally pulled into their driveway, Hannah turned off the ignition and looked at Liam. "Tonight, kids in bed, dinner and then you and me: homework," and then she hopped out of the car quickly before Liam could respond, but as he watched her head toward the front door, she glanced back at him, still in the car, and he saw that she was smiling.

A few days later, Hannah was wandering along the footpath, pushing Ethan in his stroller, keeping an eye on Gracie as she trotted ahead, stopping every now and then to pick up interesting stones or examine ants crossing the path. They had spent about an hour at the playground around the corner. Ethan had sat on a picnic blanket, gurgling at his toys, while Hannah had pushed

Gracie on the swings, caught her at the bottom of the slide and spun her on the roundabout. Ethan still cried whenever Hannah held him, but Hannah had accepted that enduring his disapproving wails must be her punishment. Perhaps he would never love her? Elizabeth had tried to assure her that this was not in fact the case and that such thoughts were not conducive to her recovery—but she couldn't help it; Ethan practically dived out of her arms whenever Liam was in sight.

As they neared their house, Hannah heard the roar of a motorbike coming around the corner. "Look, Gracie, here comes the mail carrier. Wonder if she'll have any mail for us!"

Gracie beamed; she loved waving to the mail carrier each afternoon. They sped up so that they could reach the mailbox at the same time as the letters arrived. Their mail carrier lifted the visor on her helmet and smiled at Gracie. "You want to take this from me, sweetheart?"

Gracie looked ecstatic as she collected their mail and then they waved as the bike puttered on up the street and Hannah and the kids headed inside.

"What have we got? Anything interesting?" Hannah asked as she lifted Ethan out of the stroller and then quickly deposited him onto the rug in the middle of the living room floor, just as his bottom lip was starting to quiver.

"Nah," said Gracie, "it's just junk." And she chucked the mail onto the couch in perfect imitation of her father. Hannah suppressed a laugh as she picked up the letters to see what they actually were. She leafed through a few bills and then stopped as she found a bulky envelope with an airmail stamp. She flipped it over and a smile spread across her face. It was from India!

Tearing the envelope open, she sank into the couch to read the letter.

Dear Han,

Just a short one to say hi. I was in New York last week, and I started thinking of you. Remember when we met, you told me you were training for the New York marathon. Ha! You great big dork. Anyway, thought I'd make an honest woman out of you (see enclosed tickets, there's only three, Ethan would fly for free, right?). You've got about five months to train up for it—if I can, I'll meet you there, okay? To be honest, I don't know where I'll be by then, but for now, I'm thinking about spending some time by the river, so I can tell that little girl to stop crying for her lost parents and move on. I wish I could give her a hug.

Love,

India

x

Hannah smiled as she touched the writing gently with her fingertips. *Oh India.* Then she checked the envelope. Hannah gasped—inside were three plane tickets to New York. She couldn't believe that India had spent so much of her savings on her. And then she saw a letter, confirming Hannah's entry into the New York marathon for November that year.

Hannah laughed out loud.

Hannah was putting sunscreen on the kids. Gracie was obediently standing frozen in front of her, lips pursed, eyes scrunched as Hannah spread the cream across her face. Liam appeared behind her and she immediately handed over the tube. "Good, you can do Ethan."

They were about to head out to Leichhardt. They were going to take a look at a few places they were considering buying and then head over the bridge to Drummoyne to take the kids on the bay walk. Afterward, dinner at Birkenhead Point. It was one of those perfect winter days, early on in June, when the air was crisp but the sky was clear and blue and if you stood directly under the sun you could pretend that summer was just about to appear—instead of it being months away.

Liam took the sunscreen and sighed. "Are you asking me to do it because you have your hands full with Gracie or because you're afraid to touch Ethan?" he asked.

"Umm, first reason," she replied.

"Humph," he said, distrustfully.

"Look, he still screams whenever I hold him. He hates me, Liam. It's okay, I've accepted it, but it's just easier for everyone if you deal with him and I deal with Gracie, right?"

"Hannah! No, he's your son. We can't split the kids up into teams! You have to keep persevering with him."

"You're right, you are absolutely right . . . But not today. Soon, promise." Hannah smiled hopefully at Liam and he shook his head as he sat down on the couch with Ethan on his lap and began smothering his skin in the cream.

The phone rang then and Liam made to pass Ethan over to Hannah so he could go and grab it, but she sidestepped around him and raced for the kitchen to answer it herself.

"Hello," she said into the receiver.

"Hi, love." The voice was slightly gruff, maybe even nervous.

"Oh, hi, Dad."

Conversations with her father were usually quite short and sweet, so Hannah paused as she waited to see why it was that he had called.

"So listen. Carol's suggested we have a family dinner. Everyone's so pleased that you're back and that you're okay. Your stepsisters and stepbrother will be there. It's next Saturday night. Can you make it?"

"Umm . . ." Hannah hesitated, but before she could respond, her father cut in.

"Wonderful," he said, as though she had happily agreed. "Carol will be so happy that you're coming."

Hannah took down the details of the restaurant and hung up the phone. She stood still for a moment, wondering how she felt about seeing her whole stepfamily, wondering what they would think of her and what she had done. Liam appeared in the doorway.

"Ready to go?" he asked.

"Sure," she nodded.

"Who was on the phone?"

"Dad. He wants us to go to dinner next Saturday. It'll be a whole family thing."

Hannah followed Liam back through to the living room and picked up the diaper bag while Liam carried Ethan and took Gracie by the hand. "What do you think?" he asked as they headed out through the front door, locking it behind them.

"Can't say I'm in love with the idea. What if it's really awkward? What if they hate me? It's not like I was ever that close to them to begin with—imagine what they think of me now."

They strapped the kids into the car and hopped into the front seats. "Look, have a think about it over the next few days; if it's really making you uncomfortable, then we can always politely decline. But I doubt anyone will have a problem with you. They'll understand that you were going through something tough. Amy was good to you—wasn't she?"

"Yeah . . . I guess."

Halfway around the bay walk, they took a break and sat down on a bench to rest. Ethan was fast asleep in his stroller and Gracie was pedaling her trike in circles as she waited for her parents to get moving again.

Liam was resting the tips of his fingers gently on the back of Hannah's neck, his eyes on the silver-edged water in front of them.

"Tell me more of what I missed while I was gone," said Hannah suddenly.

Liam turned to look at her, surprised. "You sure you want to talk about that? You won't find it too upsetting?"

Hannah nodded.

"Oh! I know something you missed. I can't believe I forgot to tell you about this. We got a pet bird."

"What do you mean? I haven't seen any bird."

"Yes well, that's because he only lasted twenty-four hours. I was trying to cheer Gracie up one day while we were at the shops. It was an impulse buy, beautiful cockatiel, cost over a hundred bucks. Got it home, set him up in his cage, had a big talk with Gracie about taking care of pets—she was thrilled, she named him Gary, by the way. Next morning she got up before me. When I came out into the kitchen the cage was empty. I asked her, 'Gracie, where's Gary?' 'He's just having a play date with his friends,' she says. Turns out she saw a flock of birds in the backyard, so she decided to take Gary out of his cage and release him out the back door. Needless to say, I decided we could replace Gary when she's a little older."

Hannah laughed. "I can't believe I didn't know you guys bought a bird." She shook her head. "Dammit, there's so much that I really did miss."

"See, I knew we shouldn't start talking about this. It's just going to upset you."

"No," Hannah said firmly. "They're my children; I need to know what happened in their lives while I was gone. Tell me more."

As they stood up and began to walk again, Hannah pushing Ethan's stroller and Liam guiding Gracie with the handle at the back of her trike, Liam filled Hannah in on one story after another. The week where Ethan decided bath time was torture and screamed for the entire duration of each and every bath, from the moment Liam began to undress him until he was dry and fully dressed once again, and how Gracie would put her hands over her ears and sing loudly to try and drown him out, which just added to the noise and commotion.

The day that Gracie ran away from Liam in the supermarket and he panicked because he thought he'd completely lost her, but it turned out she had sat herself down on one of the lower shelves and opened up a box of Weet-Bix to eat. A bemused-looking older couple had spotted her and pointed her out to Liam.

Liam paused before telling her the next story. "Han, there's one more thing that happened while you were gone. I haven't told you about it because I was worried it would upset you . . ."

He hesitated and Hannah nodded at him reassuringly. "You can tell me."

"A few nights after you left, when I guess Gracie was starting to worry about where you were, she came into our room and found your nightie under your pillow. She told me she wanted to wear it to bed, and I started to say, 'No, it's too big for you, it won't fit.' But she was adamant. Anyway, she ended up wearing it to bed every single night from then on. If it needed a wash, I had to have it dried and back to her within the day so she could wear it again that night. The first night, after we found you at Luna Park, I saw her sneak the nightie back into our room and under your pillow again. As though she thought, *Right, I don't need that any more, I've got the real thing back.*"

Hannah turned her face toward the water, her neck slightly strained. She didn't want Liam to see how upset she was.

"Liam," she said quietly, "I don't think I'll ever be able to forgive myself for what I did."

"Yes you can," Liam said firmly. "Because you know what? Gracie's forgiven you and Ethan's forgiven you and I know that you think he hasn't because he keeps crying when you hold him, but that's going to change, okay?" Liam stopped walking and flung out an arm to stop Hannah as well. He turned to face her, grabbed hold of her hands and said firmly, "And I forgive you, Hannah."

It was Sunday afternoon and Liam had popped out with Gracie to take a look at another place for sale in Leichhardt.

Hannah and Ethan were sitting on the floor of the living room together. The windows were open wide and a pleasant breeze was drifting in through the curtains. Hannah could smell jasmine on the wind. Jasmine made her sneeze. But it also smelled pretty, so she didn't mind. It was early June, but there was a distinct feeling of an Indian summer in the air, and it was filling Hannah with hope.

Maybe I will be able to connect with Ethan, maybe we'll fall deliciously in love with one another, the way all of those celebrity mums always describe the moment when they first meet their newborn babies.

Maybe this place that Liam is looking at right now will be perfect for us, and we'll move there and be deliriously happy and we'll fall deliciously in love (all over again) too.

Maybe I could just pick him up right now, ever so gently, and he won't scream.

Hannah leaned forward and carefully lifted Ethan up off the carpet and onto her lap. She held her breath. Silence. For ten glorious seconds, Ethan sat comfortably on her lap without a sound. Then his lip began to tremble, his mouth opened and a great wave of wails came cascading out.

Well, I guess that's progress, isn't it?

Hannah tried to settle her nerves as they drove along Military Road. Certain situations still made her feel anxious, and tonight was definitely top of the list.

"You know we don't really need to go, we could grab a takeout pizza and go straight back home if you like? Or catch a movie or . . . anything you want." Liam glanced across at her, a worried expression creasing his face.

"Nope, I said we'd be there. And I should. It's been such a long time since I've seen any of them—apart from Amy of course. Just, maybe be prepared to leave early . . . if that's okay?"

"Of course it's okay. I'll fake a call from the babysitter if you like?"

"Thanks."

They arrived at the restaurant and Hannah steadied her breathing before stepping out of the car. Liam came around to her side and pulled her into a quick hug. "They're family, Han. No one will be judging you; they all know what you've been through."

Hannah gave him a weak smile before they headed inside. She spotted her dad first, grinning across at them over the heads of the other patrons in the restaurant, easy to pick out thanks to his penchant for brightly colored shirts and ties. He gave them an overexaggerated wave to get their attention.

"Yeah, Jack, we see you," Liam muttered under his breath, and Hannah laughed quietly, jabbing Liam in the ribs. He pretended to double over in pain and for just a second, she felt as though they were the old Hannah-and-Liam, the couple that joked around and were affectionate in public (without being excessively mushy) and were secure in their love for one another.

Maybe it is a window into our future, she hoped, *and not just a reminder of the past.*

Her stepmother, along with Amy and Amy's husband, Luke, were already at the table, either side of Jack. Hannah smiled awkwardly at them as they approached the table. She moved to sit down, but Carol jumped up from her chair and grasped her shoulders before she could make it to her seat. Up close Carol smelled of strong, flowery perfume, and Hannah noticed the edge of a foundation line under her chin and the several gray strands on her head defiantly creeping through the orange hair dye.

"Hannah, I'm so, so sorry about everything you've been through. I know that I'm not your mother—and I know that you would never want me to try and take on that role in your life—but I still should have been there for you. And if it's okay with you, I'd love to become a bigger part of your life. What do you think?"

Bloody hell!

Hannah was lost for words for a moment, overwhelmed by her stepmother's pre-prepared speech.

"Ahh, sure, Carol, of course," she responded eventually. "Thank you," she added. Carol then gave her a quick lipsticky peck on the cheek before finally allowing her to sit down.

"Jeez, Mum, you don't want to start with a bit of small talk or anything first?" Amy joked, throwing Hannah a sympathetic look.

"I wanted to make sure the air was clear, that's all," said Carol, looking a tad miffed. "We've been very worried about you, sweetheart," she added to Hannah. "And if you ever need someone else to talk to, you make sure you call, okay? Because I've been through it all before, and I know it's tough. My goodness, when Amy was born, it was awful. She looked nothing like me—spitting image of my ex. And he was not an attractive man, let me tell you. And the set of lungs she had, it was as though she couldn't stand me. A nurse would be cradling her and she'd be placid as a lamb and then they'd hand her over to me and she'd start screaming like a banshee. It was as if I was the devil incarnate. I actually said to the nurses, 'You keep her; she could be your display model for the maternity ward.' Incidentally, they didn't find my comment all that amusing. Stern breed, those midwives. Anyway, we got along eventually, didn't we, Amy?"

"Wow, thanks, Mum," Amy responded, ignoring her mother's question.

"Ahh, my wife, the ugly duckling," Luke joked, ruffling her hair.

"Stop it!" said Amy, batting his hand away. "And I've seen the pictures. I was a cute baby thank you very much. Massive ears, I'll give you that, Mum, but I grew into them—thank God."

"Little Dumbo," Carol replied affectionately.

Hannah glanced at the two remaining empty chairs and Amy spoke up, "Just waiting on our eternally punctual siblings," she joked. Hannah nodded. Her other stepsister and stepbrother were the two that she was most nervous about seeing. She didn't feel as though she knew them at all. What if they thought her behavior over the past few months was absolutely disgraceful? What if they hated her and dinner became a debate over her right to still be a parent, possibly fueled by several bottles of wine and culminating in someone's ocean trout and parsnip mash being thrown in her face (it was a seafood restaurant, so best bet it would be fish). Imagine how long it would take to get the smell out of her hair!

Hannah realized that while she had lapsed into this daydream the conversation had continued around her. Liam was chatting with her father about soccer. Jack had absolutely no clue about soccer, but he liked to pretend to know what was going on when he spoke with Liam; generally he threw around generic phrases like "solid side they've got this year," and "good to see Smith is back in the game, isn't it?" Liam generously refrained from pointing out that there wasn't and never had been a Smith in his favorite team and just nodded along with his father-in-law. Amy and Luke were taking it in turns to sip from their glasses and guess which flavors they could taste in the red wine.

"Raspberry," said Luke firmly.

"No, no, oak!" cried Amy.

"Ahh, thought I picked up on some earthy, wooden tones."

"You did not, you're just copying me."

"Here they come," said Carol suddenly. "Our prodigal children, for once both back in the country at the same time," she added brightly.

Hannah's toes curled in her shoes and she focused her eyes on the lower halves of their faces as she said hello to her stepbrother and stepsister, afraid to catch their eyes in case they were filled with contempt or disgust. Liam sensed her stress and gave her knee a squeeze under the table. Unfortunately, he managed to hit a pressure point, causing her knee to jump violently and smash into the bottom of the table. Several water glasses trembled and a wineglass tipped over, sending a deep red stain across the white tablecloth.

"Ho!" exclaimed Jack. "Look at the commotion you two cause when you walk into a room! Troublemakers you are, that's what I've always said." He chuckled happily while his stepchildren rolled their eyes collectively. Hannah stopped panicking about the scene she had caused and focused on her family instead. She had never noticed it before, but she suddenly realized that her dad was just as eager to impress his stepchildren as she had always been. She softened and relaxed. *Ah, Dad, you big old goof. Don't worry, they love you, I can tell.*

She finally allowed herself to look straight into her step-siblings' eyes and discovered that what she saw there was ... nothing. Not contempt, not disgust. To be honest, the look on their faces could probably only be described as bland indifference. And then she figured out why. They had their own lives, their own issues. What did they care about a stepsister who had gone AWOL for a few months and was now back with her family? To them, it was probably a vaguely interesting story about someone they really didn't know all that well.

As Amy turned to greet her brother and sister and the three of them hugged and laughed and chattered as they all sat down, Hannah watched them and was struck by that familiar stab of jealousy from her childhood. What she wouldn't have given to have been a part of their close-knit relationship when she was growing up. *Oh get over it, Hannah. So you were an only child, big deal. You want a relationship with your stepfamily then make it happen. And stop whining about it.*

"So," said Carol, cutting through Hannah's thoughts as she brightly addressed Hannah and Liam, "Simon's just spent two years working in the Greek Islands and Riley's been traveling around the UK."

She tried to curb her agitation as she dialed the number. She sup-posed it wasn't really his fault that she'd shown up at the Greek Islands expecting him to be there. But really, they'd only just been in contact a few nights before—he might have mentioned he was planning on leaving. It would have been nice to know he was intending on going home to Sydney too.

Anyway, it didn't matter—they were in the same city now. She would finally be able to pass on this bloody letter. She hoped he was going to appreciate it.

Dean answered the phone and her irritation dissipated fur-ther.

"Hey, Dean, how're you doing?" Unconsciously, a sweet, girl-ish tone was creeping into her voice.

"Ella?"

"No. It's Simon's sister, Riley." Her bad mood was returning.

"Oh! Sorry, Riles, you sounded like Ella. Hey, welcome back to Oz."

"Yeah thanks. Is Simon there?"

"Sure thing, hold up one sec."

There was a clunk and then the muffled sound of a voice yell-ing out. A moment later her brother came on the line.

"Si. We need to meet up. Can you be at Vertigo Bar in New-town in like, an hour?"

"I guess so. What's up?"

"I'll tell you when I see you." There was a pause and then Riley added, her voice a little sulky, "So Dean's still with Ella then?"

PART FIVE

Taking Flight

CHAPTER 14

India was seated between two fat men. She knew it was rude to refer to someone as fat, but really, they were enormous. One was in a business suit. The buttons of his lime green shirt strained over his stomach and a few belly button hairs poked out between the gaps. The other man wore a white polo shirt that could have doubled as a tent, and khaki shorts. She felt as though she were seated between two versions of the same person. *This is me on the weekends, when I play tennis and try not to die of a heart attack. Over here is me during business hours, see my smart suit jacket? I had to have it specially made, it's a size extra, extra, extra, extra large.* She closed her eyes and pressed her legs together so that her bony knees dug into one another. Shame she was trying not to drink; a few vodkas would go down quite nicely right about now, then she could fall asleep in a drunken stupor, wake in Perth when polo-shirt man started trying to squeeze past her out into the aisle.

In the end she fell asleep anyway. And apparently she must have been tired, because she slept right through dinner. When she woke the plane was dimly lit and full of snores. Leaning forward, her neck felt excruciatingly stiff. Quietly she unclasped her seat belt and stood. She considered the space between business-suit man and the seat in front of him. There was no way she could slip through without waking him. A chuckle from the seat behind drew her attention. She looked over to see a young man with long ginger hair that flopped rather sexily into blue eyes, grinning at her.

"Bit stuck, are you?" he whispered.

"Seems like it," she hissed back.

He stood up and leaned forward to take a look. "Way I see it is you've only got one option," he said.

"Oh yeah? And what's that?" she asked.

"You're going to have to take my hand and climb over the back of the seat."

India stifled a giggle. "Are you kidding me? I can't do that; I might get in trouble from a flight attendant."

He looked up and down the aisle. "No one's looking. Come on, you'll have to do it quick before someone comes."

India relented. "Oh all right, fine!" She placed one knee on her seat, reached across to take his waiting hand and began to clamber over. They both had to suppress more laughter as her bottom brushed against polo-shirt man's face on the way across, but eventually she was safely in the row behind and her ginger-haired savior was stepping out into the aisle to let her past.

"Thanks," she hissed as she stretched her arms luxuriously.

"Any time," he responded, his eyes twinkling flirtatiously at her.

Huh, I think he might be hitting on me.

"I'm Jonas," he added then, reaching out a hand to shake hers.

"India," she supplied politely.

"What a gorgeous name," he exclaimed.

Oh dear, now he's getting just a bit too smooth.

"Can I take you for a walk, India? Perhaps we could stretch our legs together?" India was about to decline, but Jonas pressed a hand to the small of her back and began guiding her down the aisle.

Bit sure of yourself aren't you there, Jonas?

He chatted quietly with her as they circled the plane, up and down the aisles. His conversation seemed to vary between clichéd compliments—*wow, you have the most amazing legs, India*—and flattering facts about himself—*so you see I'm the youngest accountant to ever make partner in the history of the company.* India found him revoltingly amusing. When they came to a stop outside the toilet door, Jonas placed one hand on the wall above her and leaned in close to whisper in her ear. "Look, I think we both know there's an attraction here. So here's what I'm suggesting. Let's get it out of our system right here and right now." And his eyes flicked up to indicate the toilet door behind them.

India smiled. She imagined the two of them disappearing into the tiny space together. She saw herself pushed up against the wall, her skirt yanked up around her, underpants tugged to the side. Jonas with one foot braced against the toilet seat, thrusting in and out with gleeful enthusiasm. She had to bite the inside of her cheek to stop herself from laughing. The thing was, once upon a time, she would have taken him up on his offer. Not because she found him at all appealing. But because she liked sex, and she had no problem with using a man simply for the orgasmic high he could provide her—or could try to provide as the case sometimes was.

She liked the fact that she was a sexually liberated person. She liked the fact that she did what she wanted, when she wanted, with whoever she damn well pleased. But yet again she was finding herself thinking of someone else. Simon. Bloody Simon. And what he had said to her on the phone—before she had left London in a panic. She couldn't get the sound of his voice saying those words out of her mind. *Am I truly in love with you? Hell yes.* She realized then that Jonas was still waiting for her answer, staring at her expectantly. Carefully, she stepped out from under his gaze and then pushed open the toilet door and, holding her arm out, she indicated that he should go in first. He looked like a confident, self-satisfied wolf as he stepped inside—she could swear he was just about smacking his lips in anticipation. Then she gave him an overexaggerated wink as she shut the door on him. As his face disappeared, she saw him nod in understanding; he clearly expected her to come in and join him in a few minutes.

Back in Jonas's seat, India fell asleep again almost immediately. She didn't wake until the plane was descending into Perth. When they had landed and were allowed to depart, Jonas gave her a filthy look as she was making her way down the aisle, but she just smiled and shrugged as she continued on past. *Sorry, buddy, but you must know that you're a bit of a wanker.*

Simon placed the phone down on its receiver, stood up and stretched, cracking his stiff back as he did.

"Heading out," he called to his mate Dean, who was letting him stay on the couch. He could have moved back in to his parents' place, but it felt wrong after so much time away from home. Besides, with parents came questions. *Are you going to stay in Sydney? Do you have any money left? When are you going to get a job? When are you going to get your own place?*

Dean grunted in response and Simon pulled the apartment door closed behind him and jogged down the stairs to the street. He was heading to a bar in Newtown to meet Riley. Mostly he got along fairly well with his eldest sister, but he wasn't particularly looking forward to today's catch-up. For some reason she seemed really annoyed with him for coming home to Sydney without consulting her first. Apparently she'd been trying to reach him for a few days—even went to the Greek Islands to see him. But come on, he was a grown man—he didn't generally feel the need to run his travel plans by anyone, least of all his big sister. How was he supposed to know she had been trying to track him down?

When they'd spoken on the phone just now she'd sounded irritated, her voice clipped as she arranged for them to meet up. He
reached the bar first and ordered a drink while he waited.

When Riley finally arrived and came charging through the
bar toward him, Simon regarded her warily. "So what's with all
the urgency, what's going on?" he asked, swirling the liquid in his
glass so that the ice cubes clinked together. "You're very pale,"
he added before she had the chance to respond. "Too much time
spent in dreary England methinks. You need to get yourself some
sun, girl."

"Simon, shut up. I'm here about India, that girl you're clearly
in love with."

Simon immediately sat up straighter. "What about her?"

"That weird mail system you told me about, you know, the way
she gets travelers to pass her letters along? Well, I've got one of
her letters for you. And the thing is, it's got some fairly major
news in it. I haven't read the whole thing, just the bit that was
posted on Facebook. But I wanted to give it to you in person."

Simon was momentarily confused. *Her letter had been posted
on Facebook?* But he didn't want to start asking questions about
that right now. He knew which letter she must have: the secret.

"Where is it?" he asked sharply.

"Right here." Riley pulled the slightly crumpled envelope out
of her handbag and passed it over. She watched as Simon tore it
open and pulled out the letter, then pretended to be examining
her fingernails while she waited impatiently for him to read it.

When he was finished his hands were visibly shaking. Without a word he held the letter out so that she could read it in full too. He waited until she was finished before he spoke.

"Riley, what the hell am I going to do? I have no idea where she is now. I spoke with her on the phone, just before I left the Greek Islands. She finally told me where she was staying. But when I got there, she was gone again."

"And you don't know where?"

Simon thrust his head into his hands. "No! Fuck, fuck, fucking hell. I was so angry with her for taking off on me. I thought she was just some stupid girl that broke my heart. Dammit, why did she have to be so secretive about everything?" The outburst caused several people at the bar to look their way, and Riley reached out to squeeze her brother's arm, attempting to placate him.

Simon drained his bourbon and stared down at the letter that Riley had placed on the bar in front of him. *What the hell was he supposed to do now?*

India was avoiding going back to Gingin—but she knew that she was going to have to head out there eventually. It was getting dark, and cold. And she really hadn't been feeling all that well since she stepped off the plane. Probably the jetlag she supposed. As she meandered around the streets of Perth, avoiding catching a bus back to her childhood home, she caught sight of a homeless couple, backs propped up against a building, a cardboard sign resting by their feet, an upside down hat waiting for coins from strangers. They were quite young and India couldn't help but wonder how it was that they'd ended up in this situation. And then she saw the track marks on the girl's arms and she felt a surge of anger. Drugs. That was what caused people to ruin their lives.

Was that what her parents had looked like? All those years ago, living on the streets of Perth. India knew so little about them, but now she realized just how much she wished she did know. What did her mum look like? Did she have any thoughts for the baby that was growing inside her as she continued to shoot up? Did she get to lay eyes on India before she died? *Elyza*. That was her mum's name. And that was all she knew about her.

As India headed toward the bus station, she tried hard to picture her mother. Tried to imagine what she might have been like, the color of her hair, the smell of her skin. When she reached the station and sat down on a bench seat to wait for her bus, she closed her eyes and imagined.

1992

Elyza rolled back her sleeve with shuddering fingers. Her lank, grimy hair hung in curtains around her face. It used to be blond when she was a little girl; now it was dyed permanently black, but her pale roots showed the truth. Her eyes were dull and bloodshot. Used to be turquoise; she knew that because someone had told her once. A boy? A school friend? Her neighbor? Sparkly turquoise, like a stone from the bottom of the ocean, they'd said. Her mum once told her she had wild Irish eyes. "If a boy ever tells me that, I'll marry him," she had declared, pleased. Later, a boy-

friend told her she had "fuck me eyes." It wasn't nearly as romantic, but she fucked him anyway. She wore navy blue trousers and
a cream dress shirt that she'd picked up at the Salvation Army.
As she tugged at her sleeve, she considered the shirt. Who did it
once belong to? Where did they wear it? A job interview? A baby's
christening? A funeral? What would they think if they knew who
wore it now? Would they cry if they saw how it had been torn and
stained? Grease. Blood. Dirt. Yellowed under the armpits.

She took the length of ragged material that had been clenched
between her teeth and wound it around her arm, just above the
elbow, where she tied it tight. Then she searched for the perfect
vein with practiced fingers, tapping, caressing. She squeezed
her hand into a fist and pumped it a few times to get the blood
moving.

There's one, fat and pale blue, popping out from the trans-
lucent skin around it. Perfect.

Her other hand scrabbled in the dirt by her feet for the needle.
Her fingers closed over smooth plastic and she lifted up the
syringe to briefly examine its contents. She spat on it and used the
saliva to clean some of the dirt off the needle's point. Then just
before she plunged it into her skin, she took a moment, one single
second, to consider her swelling belly that strained against the
pearl-colored buttons of the shirt.

I'll make this the last time, I swear it.

An empty promise to make herself feel better.

Seconds later, euphoria was coursing through her body and
the brief moment of guilt vanished. She fell back against the wall,

allowed her eyes to roll up into fluttering lids, dropped her arms by her side and smiled a lurid, gaping grin of pure joy, her jaw slack.

An angry voice yelled out, interrupting her blissful solitude.

"You took it all? ALL OF IT? What about ME?"

Dale materialized above her. Dirty blond hair flopping over his eyes. To strangers he looked thin, weedy, innocuous—but Elyza knew the clothes hanging off his small frame hid surprisingly powerful and muscular limbs. He was a good fighter; he looked after both of them. But you didn't want to be on the receiving end of his ability to pound anything—an enemy's face, a rich guy's gut—into pulp and mush. And right now he looked furious as he frantically searched among their possessions for more, tossing aside empty syringe after empty syringe.

"Bitch," he spat and backhanded her across the face, hard.

But Elyza just laughed. That would sting tomorrow, and a shiny purple bruise would blossom. But right now, it didn't matter. Right now, nothing mattered. Not the freezing cold of the night that had been numbing her toes. And not the strange warm sensation between her legs, sliding down her inner thighs, making them feel sticky, causing the material of her pants to cling to her skin. Not even the weird cramps she was feeling in her lower back, had been feeling for the last few hours now.

And not the metallic smell of blood that seemed to be surrounding her tonight.

When Elyza came round, it was to the sound of loud, urgent voices.

"Jesus, what have we got here?"

"Junkies. Sal's trying to get the father to talk, tell us what she's taken. I'd say she's been in labor a good few hours, maybe even all day. Obviously she had no clue. Don't know how long she's been hemorrhaging though."

"Thanks, we'll take her from here."

Elyza's eyes rolled around wildly. Bright lights flashed past above her, making her blink rapidly. Minutes went by. She was being rolled down a corridor. She was being transferred to a different bed. Her clothing was being snipped away by flashing scissors, sterile silver. She was surrounded by brisk, efficient people with masks covering their mouths and noses. Just their eyes were visible. Judging eyes. She could only hear clipped half sentences:

". . . Nope, too late for a caesarean. Take a look, it's crowning."

"Jesus, you think she's going to be able to push? Look at her, she doesn't even know . . ."

"Forceps, now."

A coaxing voice: "All right, honey, can you hear me? On the next wave you're going to have to give us a big push. Ready . . ."

Now more impatient, snappy: "Come on, Elyza, help us out here, for Christ's sake, kid, your baby needs you . . ."

For the next few minutes, all that Elyza was aware of was intense pain and immense pressure bearing down on her pelvis. Then eventually a slippery sensation between her legs, as though a slithering squid had just materialized between her thighs. A moment of silence followed. Then all hell broke loose.

"She's not breathing. Let's get her on the table . . ."

The crowd of people that had been surrounding her moved away to surround her baby girl instead.

As Elyza felt the world start to slip away, she quietly begged God not to let her daughter die too. A final act of compassion for her baby—even if it was just with her thoughts.

The last thing she heard was the sound of her baby crying. As the relief cascaded through her body, she tried to call out one last request, but the words died in her mouth.

Name her India, please.

The ironic thing was that even if one of the doctors or nurses had heard these words, they probably would have ignored the request, perhaps pretended not to have understood. They weren't all that forgiving of drug-addicted mothers who were still shooting up when they were in labor.

India's eyes opened with a flutter. She hadn't realized she'd fallen asleep while waiting for the bus. She sat up groggily and then looked up at the clock to check the time. Good, at least she hadn't missed her bus. Still ten more minutes until it left. She could feel wisps of a dream, tugging at the edges of her mind. What had she just been dreaming about? A girl in an alleyway? A hospital? But as she tried to remember, the pictures became more and more blurred and after a few seconds, they'd vanished altogether.

On the bus she wondered what it would be like to be back in Gingin. She supposed she was going to have to take on her old name again and that made her feel a little sad. She would miss India.

Changing her name had been a spur of the moment decision. It wasn't that she had anything against the name her grandmother had given her. Lily. It was a nice enough name. But something inside her had wanted to become someone new. Almost as if she could hide from the person she used to be, that person who had just battled with cancer. She wanted to start fresh. Her first thought was that she would change her name once a month, constantly reinvent herself—new name, new personality, new hair color! But as it turned out, the first name she chose stuck.

India. It was pretty and it suited her and it felt right. She had picked it by spinning a globe, closing her eyes and jabbing her finger at one of the countries. She was meant to be choosing which country she would fly to first. But when her finger landed on the tiny letters in the middle of the diamond-shaped mass of land, she looked at it and thought, *You know what? I actually really wanted to start my travels in Brazil, but how about we compromise and I'll take it as a new name instead.*

And that was how Elyza got her dying wish and India got her new name—one small connection between mother and daughter that India would never even know about.

Simon was sitting on the beach, glaring at the happy couples around him, sharing picnics, feeding the seagulls (which was stupid, those birds were a damn menace), and in the case of one particularly expressive couple, kissing in an excessively passionate way.

"Get a room, guys," he muttered in agitation as he lifted the hood of his jacket to protect against the wind and pulled the drawstrings tight.

"How's it going?" The voice came from behind him and he looked up to see Riley standing, shielding her eyes from the sun.

"Shit," he replied. Riley sat down beside him and he stared out at the ocean. "I have absolutely no way of tracking her down. I'll probably never see her again. Almost wish I'd never seen that damn letter."

"Sorry," said Riley, and Simon realized that she sounded a bit hurt.

"Not your fault," he said with a sigh. "It's okay, I don't really mean that. I just wish I could talk to her, that's all."

"You staying in Sydney for good now?"

"I guess."

"Well, look, I know you're probably not in the mood for it, but Dad wants us to have a family get-together. And we probably should go—after all, we are actually all here in the one country for a change. Saturday night at Sails Restaurant in Manly. You'll be there?"

"Sure, whatever."

Riley gave her brother's neck a quick affectionate squeeze. "You'll be all right," she said.

"It's not me I'm worried about," he replied, and his voice sounded like it had been shredded by a steel grater.

•

Simon almost didn't go to the dinner—but Riley turned up at Dean's place and forced him out the door and into a taxi. "What's the deal with Hannah again?" Simon hissed at Riley as they headed into the restaurant. "She sick or something?"

"Postpartum depression," Riley whispered back. "She ran away from her family for a couple of months I think. Now shut up about it," she added as they reached the table.

Once they were seated, Carol seemed to feel the need to intro-duce the two of them as though they were international stars or something. "So," she announced, cutting across the conversation, "Simon's just spent two years working in the Greek Islands and Riley's been traveling around the UK."

Liam politely turned to Simon and Riley. "Wow, guys, sounds great. Bet you've got some wonderful travel stories."

Simon shrugged and turned to his sister. "I guess," he said.

Riley smiled at Liam and Hannah. "Don't mind him," she said, flicking back her hair. "He's wallowing in self-pity over a broken heart. I practically had to drag him here tonight. Let's order and then we'll tell you the whole story. It's like a romantic movie, you'll probably all cry," she assured them.

"A love story with a crap ending," Simon moaned.

Amy stretched an arm around her brother. "There, there, sweetie, you'll be all right."

They ordered their meals and Hannah looked across at Simon. "Simon," she said, her voice shaking slightly, "tell us about this amazing love story."

He sighed dramatically and leaned back in his chair. "I met this girl," he began. "She was the epitome of a free spirit. Literally moving from one country to the next on a whim. Gorgeous. Absolutely stunning, in an 'I don't give a fuck what anyone else thinks' sort of way." Carol interrupted here to huff disapprovingly at her son's language. Simon ignored her and continued. "Never met anyone so comfortable in their own skin, so easygoing. We kind of just hit it off, you know what I mean? Spent every minute together for three weeks straight. I thought, *Fuck me, this is the girl I want to marry.* And I know that seems fast, but trust me, I just knew.

"Then one day, I wake up and she's gone. Leaves me a letter saying she's sorry but she has to keep moving, she has her reasons. Over the next few weeks, I hear from her once—this weird drunken phone call—and then out of the blue, I get a letter from her, telling me she has this secret that she's dying to share, but she doesn't know how to tell me. And then she calls again and apparently she's written me another letter, telling me the secret. Here's the catch, though, she hasn't actually posted the letter. She's given it to some random traveler and asked them to keep passing it on until it reaches me."

He mistook the look of bewilderment on Hannah's face for shock at the concept rather than surprise at how familiar this whole story was beginning to sound to her. "I know, insane, right?" he said, shaking his head.

Riley interrupted then. "All right, this is where I come in," she said, waving at Simon to be quiet and leaning into the table. "That letter—the one with the secret? I got hold of it. Someone published part of it on Facebook, looking for the recipient. So I went to Spain, met the guy who had it—actually, at this stage I thought that I was going to become a part of the love story myself; you know, end up with the guy who had the letter, right? Uh, no. Turns out he was gay. But seriously, how epic would that have been? Totally poetic. Anyway, I got the letter, and I start chasing Simon. Long story short, missed him at the Greek Islands by a few hours, finally caught up with him back here in Sydney and gave him the letter."

"But that's where the story turns to crap. I don't know where she is now. So it's all for nothing." And Simon rapped his knuckle against the side of his head in irritation.

"And the letter?" Carol asked breathlessly. "What did it say? What was the big secret?"

Simon opened his mouth to respond.

"The Atlantic salmon with risotto?" said a waitress brightly.

"Oh really?" exclaimed Carol in disgust. "What a time for the entrées to come out."

The waitress's smile became a little fixed as she placed the oversized plate down in front of Luke.

"And the chili prawn linguini?" she asked, a little more tersely.

"Mine," said Hannah, offering the waitress an apologetic smile. They waited until the rest of the meals were distributed and then the cracked pepper was offered, which Carol declined on behalf of the entire table, despite the fact that Riley and Liam had both already started to nod yes. The waitress shrugged at them as she left.

"And," said Carol, as soon as she was gone. "What did the letter say?"

CHAPTER 15

~~~~~~~~

Dear Simon,

So here it is. The letter that holds my secret. The one that needed to be shared but that I'm too afraid to speak out loud. It's a confession really. You see, I've been lying to you, and I've been lying to each and every person that I meet on my travels. And worst of all, I lied to my grandmother, just before she died.

When we first met, I told you about my battle with cancer. I generally tell most people that I meet about it, because I like to feel empowered and I like to remind people that they can do anything, that they can do extraordinary things, if they put their minds to it. I like to inspire people with my success. And I like the way they look at me when

I tell them that I fought cancer and I won. They give me a look of admiration, and it somehow makes me stronger, tougher, taller even! It gives me a buzz that courses through my veins.

But it's all bullshit, because Simon . . . I didn't win.

Cancer beat me. I had stage IV lymphoma. Most people respond well to treatment, but there are a few who just don't. I guess I was one of the unlucky ones. When I found out that the chemo hadn't worked, I couldn't bear to tell my grandmother the bad news, and so I lied to her. Told her it was all a big success and that I was getting better and that everything was going to be okay. I knew that she wasn't well and I had the idea that she was hanging on, waiting to see that I was going to be all right before she could let go. I was right, you know. She died just days later. But it was peaceful and I knew she was happy.

I hated lying to her, though. I mean, I didn't feel bad about the actual lie, because it was a good lie, right? But it was the deception in general that felt wrong, you know, sort of evil in a way.

As I began to meet people, I didn't feel like I could admit the truth to anyone, because why would some stranger deserve to know the truth about me if my own grandmother, the woman who raised me, didn't know? And what's the point in telling people the truth anyway? Because then all I would get would be looks of sympathy instead of admiration. Do you know what those looks of sympathy do to you,

Simon? They eat away at you. They make you feel weak and powerless. They make me feel sick, sicker than I already am.

I saw that look in the faces of the doctors when they told me that the chemo hadn't worked. I wanted to scream at them, "Stop looking at me like that. Stop feeling sorry for me. Don't you know you're sucking the life out of me with your eyes?"

I changed my name, can you believe that? India's not even my real name, it's Lily. But I kept thinking it was Lily who got cancer. It was Lily who tried to fight but failed. It was Lily who lied to her grandmother. I didn't want to be her any more. I wanted to be someone else, someone stronger, braver. I became India and I ran from my hometown and I started traveling the world and meeting new people and I had this strange sort of confidence, where I could talk to anyone, say whatever was on my mind. Do whatever the fuck I wanted—because I wasn't me, I was a new person; being India, it liberated me.

And then I met you.

Sorry, that sentence required its own space. Because you see, meeting you changed the game. I fell for you and I loved being with you and I loved fucking you and laughing with you and lacing my fingers through yours. But that wasn't part of my plan. How could we be together when I know that there's a finish line up ahead? I could see the way you were looking at me; your eyes had future etched in them. And a future with me isn't possible.

Hey, maybe we'll meet in another life and this time I'll be healthy and you'll be a rock star and we'll have fifteen plump little babies and we'll settle down in Texas once you finish touring and you'll take up knitting and you'll knit fifteen scarves for our fifteen babies to keep them warm in winter and I'll learn to do acrobatic horse-riding.

See you there.

India-Lily

xxx

P.S. You see what I did there with my name?

Simon finished reading out the letter and then folded up the piece of paper to return it to his pocket. He looked to see what everyone thought. They were all suitably shocked and upset—but it was Hannah's reaction that took him by surprise. She looked as though she had been winded; her mouth was gaping as she tried to speak. Finally the words came out.

"Simon," she said, leaning forward across the table, "I know where she is."

Simon stared at her in confusion. "What do you mean? How could you possibly know that?"

"Because I know her. I met her in London. She . . . she looked after me, helped me out while I was over there. But here's the thing, she sent me a letter a week or two back, and I think I know exactly where she is now."

Simon stared at Hannah. "You really know where she is?" He

pushed his untouched plate away as though ready to sprint from the table as soon as Hannah gave him a destination.

Liam looked over at her. "I didn't know she'd told you where she was in her letter?"

"She didn't—not precisely, but I could tell. She said she wanted to spend some time by the river with the little girl who used to cry for her parents. She's talking about what she did as a child, and she used to live by a river in her home in Western Australia. Gingin Brook, that's where she is."

Now Simon really did stand from his chair. "She's back in Australia again?"

"Yes. I think so." Hannah looked hesitant now. "I mean, I'm pretty sure anyway."

"Goodness, Simon!" exclaimed Carol. "Sit down. It's not as though you'll be able to get a flight this minute. Have dinner, and then when you get home you can book a flight for tomorrow."

"One step ahead of you, Mum," said Riley. She had pulled out her iPhone and was swiping her thumb across the screen and frowning. After a few seconds she turned to Simon. "Last flight tonight is at 8:00 P.M.; if you leave straightaway you can make it. I'm booking it now."

Carol looked flabbergasted. "Can you *do* that?"

"Of course I can. Pass me your credit card, will you," Riley added, looking up long enough to smile sweetly at her mother.

Carol begrudgingly passed it across. "It's for love, Mum," Riley reassured her as she tapped in the details.

"Yes, well, I suppose so."

As they waited for Riley to confirm the booking, Hannah looked across at Simon. "I can't believe it," she said. "India actually told me that the guy she was writing to was called Simon, and that he was working in the Greek Islands. God, she even described you to me. But I never even thought of you. Had no idea you were over there. What a terrible stepsister."

"Don't be stupid. How could you have known?" said Amy. "And even if you did, how many Simons do you think there are in Greece? There's no way you would have thought of the connection."

"Doesn't matter anyway," said Simon. "Main thing is you're helping me out now, big time."

Riley looked up from the phone and stared across the table at Hannah. "What is it?" Simon asked impatiently.

"I was just thinking," said Riley, her eyes boring into Hannah. "If you had never run away from your family, Simon would never have been able to find India again. It's like your family had to suffer for their love to have a chance."

"Wow," said Amy. "Sorry, Hannah. This whole family can be a bit blunt sometimes. You'll get used to it now that you're going to be hanging around a lot more," and she looked pointedly at Carol.

"Oh!" exclaimed Riley. "Is Hannah going to be Mum's new project? Wonderful. You know I was always so jealous of you growing up, Hannah. You had your own room in your own house, no annoying little sister and brother to share with. I was sort of in awe of you, wished I could get to know you better. It'll be nice to start seeing you more often."

"Yes, yes, that's all very nice," Simon interrupted. "But have you booked the flight, can I go?"

"All right, here you go," Riley replied, glancing back down at her phone. Riley gave Simon the booking number and he jumped up from his chair.

"Sorry to race off from dinner, guys, but if I lose her again, I don't know what I'll do." He looked over at Hannah. "Thank you," he said. "Thank you, thank you, thank you. And I'm sorry to be the one to give you the bad news about India's cancer."

Hannah nodded. "It's okay," she said. "Will you just hug her for me, and maybe tell her I'm here for her, if she needs anything?"

"Will do," he said, pushing his chair into the table and grabbing his wallet.

"I guess it was considerate of you to order the oysters," said Carol. "Makes it much easier to split your dinner between us. Let's see, how many are there . . ." and she began muttering to herself as she calculated how many oysters each of them should get. Simon turned and raced off through the restaurant and out the front to catch a taxi.

Simon willed the taxi driver to hurry up.

He willed the line at the check-in desk to move.

He tried his best not to become impatient as the woman at Virgin Air questioned him on why he was traveling with absolutely no luggage.

He did his best not to sprint down the corridor onto the plane.

And then he willed the pilot to take off, now, now, now.

India was willing Simon to come and find her.

She wished that she had told him the truth sooner.

She wished she had never left him.

She sat on the back veranda of her grandmother's home—her home—and she wondered where he was right now.

She wondered if he was thinking of her, if he was missing her, if he had ever received her letter.

She watched the water rushing by, fueled by a heavy downpour, and willed the racing currents to bring Simon to her, now, now, now.

When the plane landed in Perth, Simon was thankful he had no luggage to wait for. He bolted out of the airport and jumped into the first cab he spotted. It was a fair drive and the ride would be expensive—but it was worth it; he needed to get there now. God he hoped Gingin was a small town, because if he had to, he was going to knock on every door of every house in it.

When the driver let him out on the main street it was teeming with rain. Simon strode straight into a pub across the road and over to the bartender. "Hi, can you tell me which way to Gingin Brook?"

"Ah sure, but it's probably better to take a look at the river in the day . . . and maybe when it's not pouring rain." He was tall and potbellied, with a friendly face.

"I'm sure it would be, but I need to find someone. She used to live by the river and I'm hoping to track her down."

The bartender frowned. "You do know it's past midnight, son?"

Simon kept his irritation in check; he didn't want to look like some sort of crazy stalker. "I know, but I just flew here from Sydney and it's important I find her straightaway. She's sick."

"What's her name?"

"India . . . well, but her name used to be Lily; she grew up here with her grandmother."

The bartender raised his eyebrows in surprise. "Lily Calder? I know who she is, but she left here almost a year ago, a little while after her grandmother Caitlin passed away. Poor kid must have been devastated to lose her. Just took off. I haven't seen her back though. But if you really think she's here, just head down Clara Street and you'll come to the river. Turn left, follow it along for about a kilometer or so and the first house you come to was theirs. Just been sitting there empty since she left. Little redbrick cottage."

Simon grinned. "Thank you," he said, turning to leave.

"You want to borrow an umbrella?" the bartender called after him.

"Nope, I'm good," Simon yelled back as he disappeared out the door.

He headed down Clara Street at a jog, dismayed to discover

that the bartender had failed to mention Clara Street was in fact several kilometers long. God, how could he be so close and still so damn far from her? He was terrified of losing her again. What was he going to do if she wasn't there? He finally reached the river and turned left. He picked up the pace now he was getting closer.

When he saw the redbrick cottage up ahead, he broke into a sprint.

India stood up from the white wicker chair and stepped down the stairs from the veranda, toward the river. The rain had slowed to a soft patter and she wanted to stand in it for a few minutes before she went inside to bed. Coming back here had been the right choice. Each moment she spent here made her feel more and more at peace with herself, with her destiny. It was right to die here, in her home, and not in some strange country where she had no connections to anyone or anything.

Simon reached the front door and started knocking. He could see one light on inside, but no movement. No one answered. He paused to draw in some ragged breaths; his run here had taken it out of him. Then he stepped back from the front door and jogged around the side to check the back of the house, near the river. She had to be here, *had* to.

•

India spread her arms out, closed her eyes and turned her face up to the sky, enjoying the sensation of the rain on her skin, savoring the peace around her. She had a feeling she had only just made it back home in time.

"India!" At the sound of her name, India's eyes flew open.

That sounded like . . . It couldn't be. Could it?

Simon?

When Simon saw her she was standing in the rain, her arms thrown out wide and her eyes closed, her face tilted to the sky. He stopped to gaze at her.

God, you're beautiful, India.

Then he called out her name.

When she saw him, she didn't know whether to laugh or cry. How was this possible? How had he found her? But then again, *who cared*? She let her arms fall by her side and smiled at his rain-soaked form. "Simon," she whispered. "You got my letter, didn't you?"

He nodded and stepped toward her. "Of course I did," he replied, reaching a hand up to wipe raindrops from her face. Then he cupped her face in his hands, leaned in and kissed her gently.

They stood in the rain, kissing for several minutes, until eventually a crack of thunder interrupted them and they finally broke apart, laughing. India took Simon by the hand and led him up the stairs, inside the house and straight to her old bedroom.

That night they made love, and it was slow and tender and intense. And then they slept together, wrapped up in one another's arms.

The following morning, Simon couldn't wake India up.

CHAPTER 16

S imon was sitting in the hospital waiting room, his head resting in his hands. The image of India's face when he had woken that morning crept into his mind again and he tried to shut it out. Tried to remember her how she had looked the previous night instead, standing out in the rain.

When he'd seen her that morning, he had known almost straightaway that something wasn't right. She was too pale. Too still. He'd woken up, and before opening his eyes, he'd taken a second to relish the moment. He had found her. They were together at last. And he was going to convince her to fight for her life; they were going to fight together. Then he had rolled over, opened his eyes, and seen her face. Blue tinged lips. When he touched her, her skin felt cool.

"India? India!" He'd gripped her by the shoulders and tried to wake her. But her head just lolled to the side. Was she breathing? Was there a heartbeat? He didn't know. He needed to calm himself enough so he could check. He needed to stop his own heartbeat from drumming in his ears. He leaned in close; she was breathing, but it was fast and shallow.

He had sprinted to the phone and dialed triple zero. The wait for the ambulance had been agony. He cursed himself for not knowing any first aid. As he waited, he begged her to wake up, a poor replacement for CPR.

When the ambulance arrived, he did his best to explain her situation, but he didn't know enough about her condition. He felt inadequate, like he was failing her in her time of need.

At the hospital, it took hours before someone would speak to him. And even then he had to lie and say that they were engaged for them to agree to discuss her with him—but they needed to do tests before they could really tell him what was going on.

A nurse stepped in front of him. "You can go back in now," she said, not unkindly.

Simon tried to give her a smile, but the expression felt more like a grimace so he just nodded and followed the nurse to India's room. He scrubbed his hands outside her door and then headed inside. The sight of her pale face, the tubes crisscrossing around her, her slack jaw, made his stomach lurch and he had to turn away and jam his fist against his mouth. When his stomach had settled again, he walked over to her bedside and pulled a chair close. He gently took hold of her hand and then he began to talk.

"Hey, Indi, how's it going? Is that okay by the way? Me calling you Indi? Sometimes you used to call me Si, but I never used a nickname for you, did I? Don't know what made me call you Indi just now. It kind of just came to me. You ever watch Indiana Jones as a kid? One of my favorite movie series. Indiana Jones, awesome guy, right? Anyway, he had Indi as a nickname. Thought it was kind of cool. Do you like it? I like Lily by the way. Didn't get the chance to tell you that the other night. But it suits you—just as much as India does. India-Lily, beautiful name."

Simon paused to self-consciously wipe his cheeks; he hadn't realized that tears had started to fall.

Later that night, a doctor came to give him a rundown on India's condition. She had been hit by an infection that any healthy person would have easily fought off, but because her body was weakened by cancer, it had completely knocked her out. She was being pumped with antibiotics that should bring her around, but the doctor warned that long term, the prognosis wasn't good. Simon resolutely ignored this part of the doctor's speech. This doctor didn't know India, didn't know how strong she was. When she woke up, Simon was going to work everything out. He would convince her to start treatment again. They would fight the cancer together. This time she would win.

When India opened her eyes she had to blink several times—the lights up above were so bright. Slowly she became aware of the feel of tubes, so many tubes—coming out of her nose, pinned to the back of her hand, constricting her breath. She had to think hard to figure out where she was, to remember what had happened last. It came back in pieces. Standing out in the rain. Seeing Simon. Kissing Simon. And then . . . what? Was that a dream? Surely it must have been, because it was impossible that he could have found her. But then she realized that there was a hand in hers, and she squeezed it hard, almost in fright. Who was that? Where was she?

And then Simon's face was above her.

"It's okay, India. You're in the hospital, you got sick . . . but you're going to get better. I'm here for you, okay?"

India tried to respond, but her throat was dry and she couldn't form the words. Two or three people had come rushing into the room then, doctors and nurses, and as they gathered around her, Simon pulled back and she couldn't see his face any more. From there things seemed to happen in flashes as she kept drifting in and out of consciousness.

She wasn't sure how much time passed when she finally woke again, but sunlight was streaming in through the window. Gingerly she rolled her head sideways and she saw Simon sitting in a chair by her bed, arms folded, head lolling to the side as he slept. She tried her voice again, and this time it came out in a dry croak. She coughed to clear her throat and spoke again.

"Simon?" she said.

His eyelids flickered as he woke up, then he sat forward eagerly. "Hey," he said. "You're awake again. That's good."

"What happened?" she croaked.

"You're in the hospital . . ." Simon began.

"No," she interrupted. "Before. How'd you find me?"

"Oh." Simon smiled. "It was Hannah," he said.

India listened as Simon explained everything to her, and then he moved on, began to talk about how when she was better from this infection, they were going to get her started on treatment again, how they would fight the cancer together, how he was going to be right by her side, and as he spoke, India began to shake her head and eventually, when she saw his eyes were focused on his hands and he wasn't watching her, she pushed herself to speak again.

"No," she said quietly.

". . . and there's always clinical trials, things like that we could try." He hadn't heard her.

"NO," she said, louder this time.

Simon looked up at her. "What do you mean?" he asked.

"It's too late for all of that," she said firmly. "I'm sorry, Simon. I'm dying."

"But," he tried desperately, "how do you know? How do you know if you don't try?" and he was crying now as he reached out to grasp her hand.

"I saw a doctor a few days ago, when I first got back to Western Australia. I've got a few weeks, maybe a month."

"But . . . but you don't even seem that sick—I mean, you've been traveling around the world. A person who's only got weeks to live wouldn't be able to do that. They must have it wrong."

"They're not wrong, Simon. I just hide it well. I've been increasing my painkillers more and more over the last few weeks. And I've been becoming weaker; I just don't like to show it. But I'm not going to spend the small amount of time I have left racing around trying to find a cure that doesn't exist. I'm going to spend it living." She waited a moment, needing a deep breath to continue speaking, and then she spoke again. "I understand if you don't want to stay with me . . . if it's too hard."

But instead of responding, Simon climbed onto the bed next to her and held her tight. India didn't cry often. Now though, the tears were streaming down her cheeks. *It's not fair*, she thought, *I would have married this guy if I'd had the chance.*

It was difficult over the next few days. Once India was able to leave the hospital, he couldn't stop asking her questions. How was she feeling? Was she okay? Did she need a sweater? A hot drink? What did she want to do? Where should he take her?

"Do you want to travel more? Are there things that you still want to see?" Simon asked one afternoon, as they sat out on her veranda, watching Gingin Brook rushing past.

"I've done enough traveling," she replied. "But I would like to spend some time by the beach. Maybe we could take a few days to head out to Rottnest Island?"

"Whatever you want," Simon replied quickly.

"Don't do that," India said quietly.

"What do you mean?"

"You have to stop treating me like that. You have to stop giving me anything I want. You have to stop looking at me with those puppy dog eyes, like you'd do anything for me. If you want to spend these last few weeks with me, then you're going to have to snap out of it. I want to experience a real relationship. Let's have fights! Let's make up. Let's have normal, mediocre days and days where I get to make a cup of tea for *you*, for God's sake."

Simon nodded. "You want a whole relationship in the space of a few weeks?" He turned to look at her. "Careful what you wish for, hon." Then he stood up and headed inside.

"Where are you going?" India called after him.

"You'll see," he yelled back.

Inside, Simon hesitated by the phone. He had an idea, but he needed some help to make it happen. Before he could bring himself to make the call though, he had to take a minute to gather himself. Ever since that day at the hospital, when India had finally been able to convince him that this really was it, that he wasn't going to be able to save her, he had at least four or five moments like this each day. Moments where he wanted to punch a wall. Moments where he wanted to scream and cry all at once. Why couldn't he have met her sooner? Why couldn't she have beaten the cancer with that first treatment? And sometimes, still, there was that edge of resentment. Why wouldn't she try again? For him? He knew that seemed selfish—but he couldn't bloody help it. He was finally with the girl of his dreams and there was a time limit to their relationship, as though a ticking clock was hanging above them each night as they slept.

He waited until the need to smash his fist through the wall

had dissipated and then he picked up the phone and dialed his stepsister's number. When she picked up he spoke quietly into the phone. "Hannah, I need a favor."

India was finding Simon to be annoyingly secretive. It was late afternoon and they were on board the ferry on their way over to Rottnest Island. A cold wind was giving her goose bumps all over her arms and legs. Lately he kept creeping away to make phone calls or ducking out on "errands"—honestly, who actually *ran* errands? What sort of errands?

"What's going on with you?" she asked him for what must have been the fifteenth time.

He shrugged. "No idea what you mean."

"Bullshit." She stood still for a moment, staring at him as though trying to wear him down, and then she swung around. "Oh forget it, there's a couple over there who are fighting. I'm going to go and fix them," she announced.

"Hang on, put a sweater on first," Simon instructed her. India responded by poking out her tongue at him, but then she relented and pulled her hooded top on, just to please him, before striding over to the couple to introduce herself.

When they arrived at the island and found their villa, Simon vanished—off to "sort something out"—leaving India on her own in the room, feeling irritable. Being independent for so long meant it was hard for her to get used to this whole partnership thing, and she wondered if it had been a good idea to decide to spend every waking minute of her last few weeks in this world with a guy that she had, in truth, only known for about five minutes. But then she remembered how good it felt to fall asleep each night with his body curled protectively around hers, how nice it was to kiss a man who sent fireworks shooting through her veins each time his lips touched hers—and she thought, *Yeah, I'm doing the right thing.*

There was a knock on the door and India wandered over to answer it. When she opened it, though, there was no one there, just a note on the floor. She picked it up and unfolded it, reading its contents as she walked back over to the bed.

Get changed and come meet me by the lagoon. Wear that green dress, you know, the one with all the sparkly bits. All right—I know you're going to wear whatever you want to wear, but if you happen to want to wear the green one, that would be great. Oh and don't forget a jacket; it's cold.
See you soon.
x

India smiled. *Damn straight I'll wear whatever I want,* she thought. He had her intrigued, though, and after checking through her clothes, she conceded that the green dress was the best choice if they were going to be doing something special. She ran her fingers through her short hair, spiking it up, put on her favorite hoop earrings, grabbed a silvery shawl for her shoulders and headed out, hoping she would be able to easily find her way to the lagoon.

The sun was setting as she followed the wooden boardwalk through the bush and around to the lagoon. As she came closer she could see a small white tent set up, surrounded by flaming torches. A man was standing out the front, strumming away on a ukulele. As she reached the entrance to the tent, Simon stepped out to meet her. He was wearing an open-necked suit with a dark green shirt. He caught her eye for just a second, and then he dropped to his knee in front of her.

India was caught off guard and almost reached a hand out to help him, thinking he'd tripped. But then she saw the box in his hand. As she watched, he lifted the lid and looked nervously up at her.

"India-Lily," he said, and she wanted to cry at the formality in his voice. "Will you marry me?"

"But . . . how?" she began. "Simon, there's no time."

"Pretend there was a way," he replied. "Would you?"

India felt a tear slip down her cheek. "Yes."

"Good," he said, standing up and slipping the ring on her finger. "Because we're going to do it now . . . if you want, that is?" And he pulled her into the tent. She laughed when she saw Hannah with her family, a small group of people she assumed must be Simon's sisters and his parents, plus a few of her old friends from Gingin. At the front of the tent, an offciant stood waiting for them.

He whispered in her ear as they walked toward the front of the tent, "I know I've sprung this on you, but . . . are you happy?"

She nodded quickly. She honestly couldn't remember having been happier.

The ceremony was short and sweet. For the vows, they each spoke from the heart, made jokes about the short time they'd known one another. At first India had expected Simon to avoid talking about the fact that their marriage was going to be so short-lived. But he didn't, and India appreciated him for it. He looked into her eyes and held her hands and his voice was filled with con-viction as he spoke. "I know that our time together is short, but for me, our marriage will never be over. For as long as I live, I will carry you with me, India. Your energy, your fire, everything that is you—that massive spark of life that is India-Lily, will always be safe, in here," and he took her hand and pressed it gently to his chest.

And then the officiant let out a sob and everyone laughed. Through gushing tears the officiant told them to kiss and Simon actually spun her around and dipped her for the kiss, just like in one of those old black-and-white romance movies and everyone whooped and cheered.

Afterward they ate dinner at a restaurant overlooking the beach and Simon admitted to India that even though they'd had an officiant for the wedding ceremony, it wasn't actually entirely legal as he hadn't been able to get the paperwork through in time. But India didn't care. She wasn't interested in some certificate that told her she was married; all she needed was the memory of those words and the image of his face as he'd said them to her.

"So," said India, as she moved around the table to sit next

to Hannah. "This is your beautiful family, huh?" They looked across at Liam, who had Gracie curled up in his lap and one arm stretched out to absentmindedly rock Ethan in his stroller.

"Yep. That's them."

"You're lucky, Hannah," said India, and Hannah reached out an arm to pull her friend into a hug.

"I know," she replied.

There was gentle jazz music being played throughout the restaurant, and after dinner, Simon pulled India to her feet. "Dance with me," he said.

India grinned. "Only if you can get Hannah and Liam up as well."

Carol was quick to offer to take over rocking Ethan's stroller and she whispered to India on the way past, "I'm sure I saw him stirring a minute ago, might have to pick him up for a cuddle."

The four of them danced together between the tables, and India didn't care that other diners were watching them with interest. She was having too much fun to be embarrassed. But after a few minutes she felt breathless and had to sit back down again.

The rest of the night was spent eating white chocolate mud cake for dessert, and getting to know Simon's sisters. India sat around the end of the table with Amy, Riley and Hannah, listening to Riley enthusiastically retelling her side of the story about finding India's letter. She enjoyed watching Hannah with her stepsisters, seeing how much she had changed since those first days in London.

They were back in their room by midnight. Most nights

India felt like Cinderella, unable to stay out past twelve for fear of transforming—only in her case it was fear of collapsing in a heap if she didn't get into bed by a reasonable hour. Their bed was luxuriously soft and India sank into it as soon as they made it through the door without bothering to take off her dress.

"You need anything?" Simon checked, leaning worriedly over her.

"Just you," she responded, and she pulled him to her, laughing as he buried his face into her neck, kissing her ravenously.

When they made love it was slow and soft and the most intense experience of India's entire life. The way they held eye contact as Simon gently rocked above her sent shivers of delight through her body, and when they climaxed it was together—as though they were one.

Afterward, they both lay flat on their backs, breathing hard. "That. Was . . ." Simon stopped, lost for words.

"Incredible?" India suggested. "Amazing, inspired, mind-blowing?"

"All of the above," he replied.

They lay still in the darkness, listening to the sounds of the ocean, and eventually India spoke. "Simon," she said, her voice small.

"Yeah?"

"I don't want to fall asleep. Because if I fall asleep then tonight will be over and once tonight is over, I'm just one day closer to— to—" and then she dissolved into tears and Simon rolled over and held her tight as she cried into him.

"Oh God, I wish I could take this away for you. I wish I could take all of it away and make it better and make it okay," he said.

"I'm sorry," she said. "I don't mean to ruin tonight . . . I just . . . I can't seem to stop crying."

"Don't even think of apologizing."

They stayed awake for as long as they could. But as the first rays of light crept over the horizon and into their room, India finally drifted off. Simon stayed awake for much longer though, his arms wrapped around her body, his fingers lightly stroking her skin. He was trying to impress every part of this moment into his memory.

India was supposed to be in bed. They were back in the house in Gingin and over the last few days her condition had been rapidly deteriorating. Her limbs were becoming weaker and weaker and she found it so strange that she couldn't just leap out of bed and start doing jumping jacks if she so wished. That she couldn't skip or run. That she could barely walk to the bathroom. At times she found herself becoming very confused as well. Once she sat up in bed and called out for her grandmother and she was so sure it was her voice that she had heard coming down the hallway toward her. But then Simon appeared and as she looked at him it was as though the entire world rushed forward five years as she realized that she wasn't in bed with a bad cold waiting for a bowl of her grandmother's minestrone soup, but that her grandmother was gone, and that soon she would be gone too. And then she burst into tears because surely it wasn't fair that five years could vanish like that, with a click of her fingers.

Right now, though, it was one of those times when she was being stubborn. She was sick of being in bed. She was tired of staying indoors. She needed some fresh air. She crept out onto the veranda with a blanket pulled tight around her, knowing full well that Simon would probably yell at her for getting out of bed and walking so far on her own.

But it was so hard not to say, "But, Simon, once upon a time I could have crossed that distance in a few strides. Once upon a time, I could have danced across it." She wanted to shake him, wanted to ask, "Don't you see? This isn't me. I'm not weak, I'm strong. I travel the world, I fix people, I talk to strangers, I make new friends and then I move on." She didn't want the world to keep moving around her while she had to stay still. It didn't feel right.

As she tried to step down the stairs to walk out onto the grass she nearly stumbled, and that's when Simon appeared in front of her. His eyes opened wide and his brow creased and it looked as though he was about to turn into a thunderstorm. So India had purposely made herself appear frail and weak so that instead his brow smoothed and he became a warm sunset as he pulled her into his arms and whispered, "You are in so much trouble right now." But he hugged her gently and his arms told her that they were glad to see her anyway.

"Take me closer to the river please," she said. And without a word, he scooped her up and carried her across the grass.

"You should have told me you wanted to come out," he said as he carried her. "I would have brought you the whole way. And are you warm enough like this?" But she ignored him until they were right at the river's edge, and then they sat down together and she rested her head on his shoulder.

One of the nurses who had been coming out to check on her each day had told her that when the time came, she would know. India was beginning to think she was right. There was a strange feeling creeping over her. As though her entire being was gathering together, as though she were preparing for a new journey, and she wondered if she should tell Simon, if she should warn him that this was it. That it was their final good-bye. But then she thought, *Well what if I get it wrong and this isn't the end and I hang around for a few more days and then it's all awkward between us*—and she snorted with laughter at the thought.

"What?" said Simon. "What's so funny?"

"Nothing," she replied. "Just a private joke. Don't ask, you won't like it—it's morbid."

"Oh great," he replied, shaking his head at her.

"What should we do tomorrow?" he asked then. "I could take you out somewhere if you like? The nurse said it was okay, as long as you have plenty of painkillers and we take a wheelchair. We could have lunch somewhere nice. Or . . . we could head down to the city, see a museum if you want? Or the theater? Want me to check what shows are on at the moment?"

Should I tell him? India wondered. *Or should I let him believe that I still have a tomorrow?*

She took in a breath with difficulty and then responded, "A show sounds nice, let's do that." And then she took one last look at the river and closed her eyes. She fell asleep against Simon's shoulder and she dreamed of trips to the theater and to the museum. She dreamed of lunches in cafés and she dreamed of concerts and holidays by the beach and of a future with her husband. And in her dreams, he didn't need to carry her, and he didn't need to push her in a wheelchair. In her dreams she could walk. She could run and dance. In her dreams, she could grow old and the only time that Simon carried her was when he was doing it for a laugh. And in her dreams they had two children, boys with blond curly hair, and later, grandchildren, small plump grandchildren who sat on her lap and played with her necklace and called her Gran.

When Simon finally understood that this time India wasn't going to wake up, he pulled her onto his lap, buried his face in her hair, and he cried. And if it weren't for the nurse who finally arrived for India's evening checkup and gently pried his hands away, he might never have let her go.

PART SIX

New York
in the Fall

CHAPTER 17

H annah was running, feet pounding, breathing even. She felt good. The rushing wind was cool on her sweat-soaked skin. She was on her own at the moment, but she could see another runner up ahead. Excellent, she could see them slowing. She was going to overtake. And she didn't feel tired . . . yet.

She gave the other runner a nod as she passed him and then picked up the pace a little so that she could increase the distance between them. A couple of minutes later, a twinge in her knee forced her to take it a little easier again. She slowed to a comfortable jog and started thinking back over the last few months so that she could take her mind off her knee. There were still approximately ten kilometers to go, so there was plenty of time for reminiscing.

First her thoughts turned to India. It still amazed her how a person who she had known for such a short period of time had had such an impact on her. And not only that, how someone with such a huge, vibrant personality could actually be gone. Frequently Hannah had to remind herself that India really was gone, that she wasn't off traveling in some remote location. That Hannah wasn't going to get a random postcard from her. That she would never see her again.

The funeral had been beautiful and horrendous all at once. India had left behind strict instructions for the ceremony, so the music, the flowers, the photographs in the slide show, everything had been carefully selected by India herself, and each element was simply breathtaking. From the hauntingly beautiful songs that brought the entire congregation to a sobbing mess, to the crazy photos of India posing in fancy dress or falling from a canoe into a lake in God only knew which city, that had everyone laughing despite themselves.

The hardest part, though, was watching Simon. Hannah's little stepbrother, who had once felt like a stranger to her, but thanks to India, had been slowly becoming more and more a part of Hannah's life. Never had Hannah seen a person look more heartbroken. It was almost as if it wouldn't have mattered if he'd known for his entire life that this day was coming—he still would have had this sort of surprised look on his face, as though he didn't actually think it would really happen. As though right up until the moment she died, he had still been expecting some sort of miracle. Hannah had tried to keep her distance, to allow Amy and Riley to be the ones to comfort their brother. But Simon had taken her off guard by appearing by her side as they were exiting the church and taking her hand in his.

"All these other people," he'd whispered in her ear, "they don't know her like us, do they?"

"No," she'd replied quietly.

"And they'll never get to," he said, his voice cracking on the last word, his face crumpling. And then he'd pulled his hand out of hers and turned away. One of his mates was patting him on the back then, and so Hannah had turned to Liam, feeling awkward and unsure of what to do next.

Later the group had moved out into the cemetery, where India was to be buried. India's choice to be placed in the ground had surprised Hannah at first. If she'd been taking a guess, she would have thought that India would want to be cremated, and perhaps released into the ocean's waves—but when Simon had explained India's reasoning, it made sense. She wanted to feel as though she would forever be connected with the earth, he said. She wanted to think of her body as a part of nature, wanted to be responsible for the growth of new life—flowers, plants, trees—and imagine her essence traveling through the earth, tunneling into the core, spreading to each corner of the planet. She wanted to always be there, grounded in this world.

When they had been leaving the cemetery, Hannah had noticed a middle-aged man, standing by a tree, watching the service from a distance, and she had wondered briefly if he might have been someone. *Could he be India's long-lost father? Finally come to lay eyes on his daughter?* But surely that was ridiculous, wasn't it? How would he even know? And why wouldn't he actually join the funeral if that were the case? But there had been something—something about the way he held himself—that had felt oddly familiar to Hannah, and she'd had to wriggle her shoulders as they walked back to the rental car, in order to make the goose bumps that had traveled down her arms disappear. She would never know if that man had just been some stranger, perhaps visiting a parent's grave and stopping to watch the service, or if he'd actually been India's father—but then again, she supposed it didn't really matter. If it was him, he'd shown up much too late.

Hannah began to speed up a bit and her thoughts turned to how much her life had changed in such a short space of time. They had moved to Melbourne in September, about a month after the funeral. It had been a spur of the moment decision. They were just about to put down a deposit on an apartment in Leichhardt when Liam's partner had suggested that it was time to expand. She could tell he was nervous when he came to tell her about the idea.

"Han, can we talk?"

Hannah had felt a familiar spark of fear. Ever since she had returned home, despite Liam's continued assurance that he had forgiven her, she still thought each conversation that began with a serious note was going to end in Liam telling her he wanted a divorce.

"Sure, what's up?" She had become quite good at hiding her fear, though.

"Don't worry, it's nothing bad—just an ... opportunity, but we're going to make the decision together, okay?" The way he squeezed her arm and smiled reassuringly told Hannah that she wasn't quite so good at hiding her fear as she had first thought.

"I'm thinking about starting up a new branch—in Melbourne." He'd paused, giving her a moment to take it in, before rushing on, "But I don't have to do it. And I mean that, okay? If we stay in Sydney, I'll still have plenty of good opportunities. So don't think that we have to do this—because I know that moving interstate is a big bloody decision. Especially when we finally found a place we actually liked in Leichhardt."

Hannah had dropped her eyes down to Liam's feet. She was thinking. In fact, her mind was *racing*. A new start. Maybe she could make new friends. They could have Sunday night dinners with Liam's parents. She could find a new job, finally go back to work. They could pick a place close to the city, maybe on the river. A new childcare center for the kids, where the staff would be friendly and wouldn't judge her and wouldn't know that she had run away and left her children for close to two months. She could feel the adrenaline building up, as though she had been injected with a dose of pure-form dopamine. This was *exciting*.

She looked up at Liam. "That place in Leichhardt had *nowhere* near enough sunlight."

From that moment things had moved extremely fast. There were trips to Melbourne to look for houses; Liam's business could afford to foot the bill for a serviced apartment initially, but they'd need to find their own place as soon as possible. There was packing and putting their own house on the market. There were several lunches with Hannah's dad and her stepmother. Apparently Carol was just a bit devastated that the stepdaughter she had been about to begin a relationship with was now moving interstate. Hannah had to promise to fly up and visit regularly.

There had almost been a catastrophe when Hannah had realized that moving interstate would mean having to find a new psychologist. She was practically hyperventilating at the thought of starting all over with someone new, of having to explain to this complete stranger that she had abandoned her children and waiting to see if they would judge her all over again. And they had just begun to delve into Hannah's mother's suicide; Hannah was feeling on the verge of a breakthrough. Luckily, Liam had come up with the solution. She could keep seeing Elizabeth—on Skype. Elizabeth was thrilled with the idea; she said it was a window into the future for her business.

When they had finally made the move to Melbourne, things really started to change. Hannah found a job with the legal aid office and booked the children into childcare three days a week. They found a house in St. Kilda that was in walking distance of cafés, restaurants and parks and a short drive to the city for both of their workplaces.

But the big turning point for Hannah was when Ethan said his first word, and she was there to hear it. It wasn't "mummy," it was "ball"—but Hannah had squealed with delight and Ethan's face had broken out in the hugest smile and finally Hannah stopped being afraid that he hated her. She also realized that he had actually stopped screaming every time she held him for some time now and she finally started to relax with her son.

Now as Hannah rounded a corner and spotted another couple of runners up ahead, she smiled as she thought about all of the moments that she *hadn't* missed out on. Ethan's first steps. Gracie's first hip-hop concert (she was not interested in learning ballet, thank you very much). And she thought about the one thing that Elizabeth had been trying to convince her to say, out loud, ever since she had started seeing her.

She took a deep breath—which was difficult because she was currently quite out of breath—and she said, quietly but firmly to herself, "You are a good mother." As soon as the words left her lips she felt a burst of energy and she picked up the pace and overtook the next few runners. She continued to practice her self-talk as she ran. "Yes, I did something terrible. No, I will never forget about it. But I can forgive myself. Because I was not well and now I'm getting help and I am being a *good* mum to my children." She hesitated then, looked behind her to see how close the last group of runners that she had passed were, then squinted up ahead to see if she was about to catch up to anyone. When she was certain she was alone, she drew in another huge breath and yelled out into the wind, "I deserve my family!" She sprinted for the next kilometer.

•

Simon was beginning to think he would never find them. There must have been thousands and thousands of people here. A small celebration had broken out over to his right. A runner was bent forward, hands resting on her knees, taking ragged breaths of air while her friends danced excitedly around her, patting her on the back. Behind him someone burst into tears and he turned to see an older woman clasp her face, withered hands on papery thin skin. He followed her eye-line and saw an older man finishing the race. Stepping back, he allowed her to rush past him and embrace her husband.

"Told you I could do it," Simon heard the man whisper into his wife's graying curls.

Simon smiled. The finishing line of the New York marathon was definitely a nice place to do some people-watching.

"Simon!"

He swung around at the sound of his name and his face split into a smile as he saw Liam striding toward him, carrying Ethan comfortably on his hip, his other arm attached to Gracie's hand.

"Good to see you, mate, wasn't sure you would make it." Liam looked relieved as he handed Ethan straight across to his step-uncle.

"Been here for ages, just couldn't find you guys," Simon responded, shifting Ethan around so he was sitting comfortably in his arms.

"Expecting her to finish any minute now . . . I think. Been a nightmare, though, trying to hang on to Gracie. She keeps wanting to wander away; terrified I'm going to lose her."

Simon smiled down at Gracie. "All right, you, I've got my eyes on you now, k?" And he motioned with two fingers, pointing first at his own eyes and then down at Gracie's. Gracie giggled in response. Simon looked back up at Liam. "You got the camera ready then? I'll make sure Grace doesn't go anywhere."

"How are you going anyway?" Liam asked as he lifted the camera that was slung around his neck and started fiddling with the settings.

"Yeah, not bad, thanks, mate."

Liam stopped playing with the camera and looked up to scrutinize Simon's face. "Really?" he asked. "We hadn't heard from you in a little while. Thought maybe you've been . . . you know, struggling, with everything . . ."

Simon shrugged. "I'm getting by," he replied. He looked like he was going to add something else then, but his face changed and he reached out a hand to whack Liam on the shoulder. "Hey! I think that's her, coming over the hill, isn't it?"

Liam squinted into the distance and then began frantically scrabbling with the camera. "Yep—that's Han. Agh, lens cap!" And he hurried to pull the cover off the camera before hoisting it up to his face and clicking as fast as he could.

Hannah was feeling something strange. It was an icy tingling that was starting in her gut and spreading out, along her arms, down her legs. It was taking the ache in her back and encasing it in a cool jelly. It was circling the twinge in her knee, winding its way around and around until the joints felt like rubber. It shot up her neck and sent sparks flying from her face.

She could see the finish line up ahead.

It was euphoria.

For a split second she felt as though she could turn around and do another lap, another entire forty-two kilometers. In fact, she could sprint it! But another idea was tugging at her, and that idea was slowly becoming much more appealing. What she would actually quite like to do was let her legs fold up underneath her and collapse, preferably into a cold swimming pool, with someone there to hold her head above the water so she didn't sink under the surface and drown. Oh, and maybe someone else there to rub her feet—that would be nice too. A thought crossed her mind. She was remembering the rubbish she used to post on Facebook, the lies she used to tell the world when she was pretending everything was okay when it wasn't. And she was thinking about what she could write on Facebook right now. Maybe something like, *Fuck you, postpartum depression, you're no match for a girl that can run a marathon.* Yep, that was perfect; it was about time she told the truth. She would have to remember to log on later today.

Focus, Hannah! You're almost there!

As she crossed the finish line, two things happened.

First, she heard a voice, a high-pitched voice, rising above the noise of the crowd, yelling out, "Go Mummy! Go Mummy!"

Second, she saw a face, behind Liam and Simon. A face she hadn't expected to see at all—because, well, it was impossible for her to be there. But as quickly as Hannah spotted the face, it vanished once again, and Hannah was left to wonder if it was simply her imagination playing tricks on her.

And that feeling of euphoria absolutely exploded from within as she finally stopped running.

Afterward they found a café. It had couches outside on the sidewalk with bright orange and red cushions. Liam watched his wife in awe as she ferociously devoured two plates of food. "So apparently marathons make you really hungry," she said with her mouth full. "Huh, who knew?"

Gracie sat playing with sugar packets, her forehead creased with concentration as she tried to build a castle with them, and Simon entertained Ethan, bouncing him up and down on his knees and watching him gurgle with delight. Simon looked happy enough, but after a while, Hannah noticed his gaze wandering and she leaned across to ask him how he was really doing.

"I'm okay," he said firmly.

"Honestly?" she persisted.

He paused and then he shrugged. "Honestly, I think about her every single day. I miss her like crazy. But I'm getting there."

They stayed there late into the afternoon, until eventually Ethan fell asleep on Simon's lap and the staff began to give them enough significant looks to indicate that they had been there for far too long. When they finally stood up, Hannah discovered her legs had turned to jelly, and they all laughed as she walked unsteadily away from the table, with Liam supporting her around the waist. When her legs had returned to normal, she held hands with Liam on one side and Gracie on the other. Simon walked a few steps ahead, still holding a sleeping Ethan, and Hannah wondered whether she should tell Simon what she had seen as she had finished the race, if she should say, *She's still with you, Simon.* Because when she had spotted India's face in that crowd, she had been just behind Simon's shoulder, and her arm had been casually looped around his waist, and she had been smiling—that comfortable, effortless smile that you wore when you were arm in arm with the person you loved. But then again, perhaps it was all in her imagination.

EPILOGUE

~~~~~~~~~

"Excuse me? *Excuse* me? Hello?"

Hannah swung around and saw a petite, attractive girl with round blue eyes staring at her, looking slightly annoyed.

"Oh sorry, were you talking to me?" she asked in surprise. She was at Sydney airport, waiting in the queue to check their baggage. They'd just spent the weekend with Jack and Carol; Liam was waiting for her in the food court, giving the children their lunch.

"Yes, actually," said the girl crossly. "Here, can you take this letter for me? It's for a girl called Jess, she lives in New Zealand, works at the Gloria Jean's on Park Street in Wellington." The girl held the letter out and tapped her foot impatiently.

"But I'm not going to New Zealand, I'm flying to Melbourne."

The girl huffed irritably. "That's not the point. You're supposed to pass it on to someone else on your travels. It'll get there eventually. Don't you *know* how this works? It's all over the Internet; this is how everyone sends their love letters now. It was started by some Indian girl with cancer or something. This one is from a guy called Ryan in the States."

"How romantic," said Hannah, not quite sure what else to say as she took the letter.

"You think? Personally, I think it's getting a bit passé. Maybe it was romantic, like, three months ago when it first started, but, you know, whatever."

Hannah couldn't help but smile as she was called forward to check her bags.

India would have absolutely loved this.

ACKNOWLEDGMENTS

A gigantic thank you to Steve Menasse, Diane Moriarty and Jaci Moriarty for reading my earliest drafts and giving me so much incredible feedback and encouragement. I'm also grateful to Liane Moriarty for listening to the original idea for this story and providing advice and support.

Thank you to Sally Findlay for being my Elizabeth, to Kelly Murray for letting me borrow your Facebook status and to Min Lyman, Brooke MacDonald and Kerry Lockwood for helping me out with my medical research.

Pippa Masson at Curtis Brown is the best agent a writer could wish for and Beverley Cousins, Patrick Mangan and Annabel Adair at Random House all worked very hard to make this book complete.

Thank you to Carrie Feron and the team at William Morrow for bringing *Paper Chains* to a brand-new audience in the United States!

To all of my family and friends, thank you for your continued support, especially to Steve, Maddie and Piper for being amazing.

To any readers and book bloggers who have contacted me via email, Facebook and Twitter—you don't know how much that means to me: hearing your kind feedback makes me infinitely happy.

ABOUT THE AUTHOR

Nicola Moriarty is a Sydney-based novelist and mum to two small (but remarkably strong-willed) daughters. In between various career changes, becoming a mum, and completing her Bachelor of Arts, she began to write. Now she can't seem to stop. Her previous works include the novel *The Fifth Letter*, which was published in several countries and optioned by Universal Cable Productions for film and television.

More from
NICOLA MORIARTY

PAPER CHAINS

From the acclaimed author of *The Fifth Letter* comes this touching story of secrets, friendship, family, and forgiveness—and the serendipitous twists of fate that shape our lives.

THOSE OTHER WOMEN

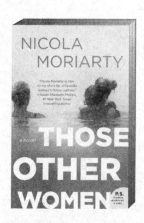

Nicola Moriarty weaves another stunning domestic drama in this story of working women whose Facebook group, designed to forge connection and solidarity among childless women in the workplace, quickly descends into something much more sinister.

THE FIFTH LETTER

Nicola Moriarty made her US debut with this stunning new women's fiction novel in which four women get together for their annual vacation... but what begins as a relaxing trip to the beach turns shocking when decades-old secrets are revealed, long-held grudges surface and a hate-filled anonymous letter shakes the very foundation of their life-long friendship.

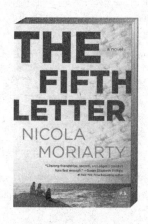